FIRE KNIFE DANCING

FIRE KNIFE DANCING

BY JOHN ENRIGHT

THOMAS & MERCER

The characters and events portrayed in this book are fictitious.
Any similarity to real persons, living or dead, is coincidental and
not intended by the author.

Published by Thomas & Mercer
PO Box 400818
Las Vegas, NV 89140

ISBN-13: 9781612185019
ISBN-10: 1612185010
Library of Congress Control Number: 2012923476

This book is dedicated to the memory of my island brothers

Tau Hunkin and Joe Kennedy.

CHAPTER 1

—— ○ ——

FOR MANY YEARS IT WAS THE ONLY HOUSE OUT THERE, A house of elegant exile. The road to it was little more than a track cut through the jungle over black lava ribs and down red mud hollows. The poles along the road carried power and phone lines to that house alone. The house crouched on a black and barren cliff above the reefless sea. Even in calm weather, the sea could dispatch rogue breakers into the cliff face with enough strength to raise a plume of spray twenty feet high. In storms the mist was so thick that the house seemed submerged in an aerated sea.

But it was a strong house, built to be in just that place. Its sturdy rolled eaves suggested a wrestler's slouched shoulders, always on the defensive. It hugged the contour of the land it held. No one else had ever thought to build there, at the margin of two inhospitalities—the choked jungle on a landscape of fractured volcanism behind and the kinetic and potential violence of the world's largest ocean knocking at the front door. The jungle's verge was guarded by thickets of sword-edged pandanus. The sea's sole amenity here was its vista.

Detective Sergeant Apelu Soifua had been inside the house only once, maybe ten years before, for a lavish party on a

1

sea-peaceful starry night. The hosts had hired a van to ferry their guests over the road in and out so that no one had to endanger their vehicles. Besides, there was nowhere to park there. The party had been for some visiting entertainers. He remembered a large, lantern-lit patio overlooking the starlit black-and-white coastline—the black ever stationary, the white always in motion. It had been a good party. Servants kept glasses full. There was too much to eat. The entertainers entertained. He had been glad for the ride back out. He couldn't have driven it.

But what Apelu remembered most about the house was the interior—the foot-friendly Persian carpets, the warm glow of polished hardwood, walls hung with Polynesian folk art and show biz memorabilia, rafters, recessed lighting, and always the sound of the surf exploding below them. At the end of a spacious, people-filled living room was a bar like one lifted from some sixties nightclub. Apelu liked to drink just a little too much at parties like that so that he could savor the illusion that he belonged there in those surroundings, owned it all, at least for an hour or two.

The house's isolation, though, was probably its most notable feature among the local populace. Thousands of years of island experience had inbred in Samoans the assurance that safety feeds on numbers, on human proximity, on being as close to the social center as possible. Everyone knew that marginal places like the one the house occupied were *aitua*—haunted, dangerous, and only for entities with powers that exceeded theirs.

Entertainment people really are a class apart. They lack a common fear. What seems like shallowness is really just a focus elsewhere. Entertainers see themselves through a following lens of imagined observation. They are best at routines they've run through before and are seldom surprising in any original way. Real artists are different. They may be employed as entertainers by chance, but rarely, and then only secondarily—the way caged animals don't think of themselves as spectacles of anything.

The owners of the house, the hosts of that long-ago party, had lived their lives as professional entertainers in Polynesian dance troupes in Hawaii and California, even in the movies. They were retired old pros, with hidden-camera smiles and perfect body language. Even in their sixties they were still entertainers in a show of being themselves that had slowly replaced their real lives, the way minerals mimic trees in a petrified forest.

Apelu had been an entertainer himself for a while. Soon after his father had moved the family from Samoa to San Francisco when Apelu was fourteen, a distant auntie in LA learned that back in Samoa Apelu had been trained as, and had performed as, a fire knife dancer. She ran Polynesian dance shows in LA, Las Vegas, and Palm Springs nightclubs. She could always use a new, young, Samoan fire knife dancer. His family needed the money since they were trying to build a place for themselves in the Mission District. She flew up from LA to check him out.

If it hadn't been for his mother, Apelu's formal education probably would have ended there. His father quickly signed a contract for him. Apelu couldn't recall exactly how he felt about it. His fear of starting at Mission High School with next to no English was probably on a par with his dread of being removed from his family. But as a boy, a *tama*, he really had no say in the matter. His distant auntie, Sia, was a gigantic woman—close to six feet tall and well over three hundred pounds—who was always dressed as if she were about to introduce the next act. *Imperious* was not a word Apelu would learn for many years, but she became its definition when he learned it.

Auntie Sia had Apelu off packing his meager clothes and possessions when his mother finally weighed in. They were staying with some cousins, the whole family sharing one bedroom. Only Apelu's sister was with him in the room as he searched for his clothes. They both were crying. Everything about their lives was falling apart. What could they ever know or trust again? How would they know what to do, who they were outside the family, without one another?

Normally Apelu's mother was soft-spoken, the peacemaker in the family. Her strength came from soothing. But as Apelu and his sister stopped to listen, they could hear their mother's voice downstairs in the kitchen slowly rise in volume. In fiery Samoan she denounced their father, then turned her full rage on Auntie Sia. The tidal wave of her emotions was unanswerable. Auntie Sia quickly left the house, and his father was evicted soon after. Apelu and his sister had sat in silence, in shock, staring at each other. Then their mother had come into the room, holding the pieces of the torn-up contract. She was weeping. They went to comfort her.

In the end, a compromise was worked out. Apelu worked part-time for Auntie Sia when his mother allowed it—summers, school breaks, occasional weekends if there was a gig in Reno or Lake Tahoe. His father was let back into the house. Apelu's oldest sister ended up dancing full-time in one of Auntie Sia's reviews. It was during those years that Apelu first met and fire knife danced for Ezra and Leilani—the owners of the grand house—though they claimed not to remember him from those days.

It was not the first complaint that the department had received about Ezra Strand discharging a firearm at hikers and boaters along the cliffs near his house in Piapiatele. Sometimes a patrol car was sent out, but usually someone in the commissioner's office gave Ezra a call and told him to cool it. But this time he'd made the mistake of blasting away with his shotgun over the heads of a pair of *National Geographic* photographers. Some errant, low-diving buckshot had hit their equipment. The commissioner had gotten a call from their DC attorney.

Apelu was on duty and underemployed—by his captain's estimation—so he was sent out to Piapiatele to bring in the weapon and ask for particulars. Apelu hadn't seen Ezra in a while. On a small island like Tutuila you normally saw most of the people you knew just by shopping and going to the post office. There were only two main roads, and island pastimes included identifying people by their vehicles and catching the eye of oncoming drivers. Days later, acquaintances would tell you who was in your truck with you when you whizzed by or where they saw your truck on Tuesday afternoon when your wife had it. Other people's whereabouts were part of the shifting unconscious social map everyone kept inside their heads. Apelu had once started receiving curious condolence calls at work after their old truck had broken down in front of a casket shop, and Sina, his wife, who was driving it at the time, had just left it there.

But on the ride out to Piapiatele, Apelu realized—checking his mental maps—that Ezra had pretty much disappeared. He still saw Leilani around—always looking petite and great for a now old lady. She always gave him a kiss on his cheek and would hold his hand in that backward way women have when they want to hint you're special. But he couldn't remember the last time he'd seen Ezra. Apelu had heard that Ezra had gone pretty much to ground, and was hiding in the house. The warning shots at hikers were part of that. Apelu wondered how much booze had to do with it. Ezra had once been fairly famous for his transgressions in that arena.

There were a few more houses on the road out to Ezra and Leilani's house now, and the road—just an unpaved driveway, really—had been improved, smoothed out a bit at least, until he got to the last stretch. Apelu stopped the squad car well short of the chain that blocked the road at the edge of Ezra's land and studied the ruts and boulders in front of him. The chain was wrapped around two coconut trees on opposite sides of the road. Well, he would have to get out and walk from there anyway, he thought, might as well spare the squad car this last stretch. So he got out of the car and started walking toward the chain and the house beyond.

They were the two biggest fucking dogs he had ever seen. Mastiffs or something. Apelu was only halfway to the chain when they exploded toward him from somewhere near the house. Besides being large, they were loud, they liked showing off their teeth, and they were coming straight for him at motorcycle speed. Apelu retreated to the squad car, just beating them there. Adrenaline rush. He hit the emergency lights and the siren, put the squad car in gear, and slowly bounced and scraped the big Crown Royal up to the chain. The dogs went berserk. Apelu noticed they foamed at the mouth, and when they attacked his tires it was the first time he had ever considered the possibility that a dog might actually damage a steel-belted radial.

Apelu sat there for a while with the lights and the siren on because he was beginning to enjoy the dogs' frenzy. They were good-looking animals, actually, with wide shoulders, square skulls, and no necks to speak of. One was coal black and the other was lion-colored—beautiful short-haired coats. Well fed, well cared for. He turned off the siren but left the flashers on. The dogs calmed down. They looked a little worn out. Apelu used his PA speaker to broadcast a message in Samoan to Ezra.

"Chief, Ezra, Mr. Strand, I'm just here to check on you and have a few words. Come out and call off your dogs."

It was getting hot in the squad car because Apelu had rolled up the windows—now with dog slobber drying on them—to keep the beasts out. He rolled the two front windows partway down, but the dogs were ignoring him now, using their excess saliva for a nice lick-down. Apelu turned off the flashers and waited. After a while he clicked the mike back on and asked, "Chief?" A few more minutes went by and then Ezra appeared, walking slowly over the rise that hid the front of the house from the driveway. He was dressed in a long-sleeve white shirt and a pair of khaki shorts. He was carrying a shotgun cradled under his arm, muzzle down—a hunter's carry.

"Put down the shotgun, Chief," Apelu said through the mike. "I'm not armed."

"Good!" Ezra yelled back, and then he raised and leveled his shotgun and pulled the trigger. The blast took out the squad car's windshield, but Apelu was on the floor before that. The dogs again exploded into action, attacking the car.

Without sitting up fully, Apelu turned on the ignition and put the squad car into reverse. He sat up far enough to try to back out the car through the route he used to come in, figuring Ezra wouldn't fire at the car with the dogs all over it. But when Apelu took a look back in Ezra's direction, he was walking back toward the house. He had evidently called the dogs, for they were running after him.

In his sixteen years of police work—six years on the SFPD and ten years here in American Samoa's Department of Public Safety—Apelu had never before been fired on. He was probably lucky that it was Ezra who had done it, and that he hadn't seemed all that interested in finishing the job. Apelu backed the squad car up until he could pull into a driveway and call for support.

Apelu's wife, Sina, belonged to a cult that worshipped a dog. Well, sort of. Nominally they were Catholics, but several years before, a young female dog had been discovered in their village of Leone. The dog was fortunate enough to be born with the image of the Madonna and child clearly emblazoned in black and white on its side. A year previously, a large leaf bearing the same (or nearly the same) image had been found in the same neighborhood. Together, these two events led to a belief that Leone might be the Blessed Virgin's next touch-down spot, like Lourdes or Fatima or that other place.

Apelu had seen the bitch, examined it actually—to his wife's disgust. The image was real. It wasn't painted on or anything. Apelu had pointed out, however, that it could just as well be the outline of a cumulus cloud.

"Then worship the clouds," Sina had said disdainfully.

The dog had gotten a lot bigger, being pampered and overfed, and the image had gotten distorted as it grew. But still every year on some Feast of the Virgin, it was paraded through the village in the back of a pickup truck in a candlelight procession, along with the now laminated leaf. A walking chorus sang hymns. Young bare-chested men with shotguns escorted the appointed and adorned pickup truck. Apelu wondered what they would do if the bitch ever got knocked up, but he kept that to himself. Sina marched in that parade. He did diss the dog, though, saying something about how every year it looked more like the Buddha.

Sina would say he'd gotten shot at for dissing her holy dog and then tormenting Ezra's two. He knew the way she chose to understand things. She wouldn't think that Ezra had anything to do with it because she had no connection to Ezra; somehow it always had to do with her. Otherwise there was no point in trying to make any sense out of it, was there?

Another, more likely explanation—at least to the part of Apelu's brain that was colonized by police work—was that Ezra was involved in some sort of criminal activity inside the house. Well, that would soon be over. Apelu could think of at least five crimes Ezra could be charged with just for taking a shot at the squad car. Whatever was going on inside the house wouldn't be a secret for long. Apelu checked his mental maps for Leilani. It had been several weeks since he had seen her. Was it that simple? Some sort of domestic craziness? Leilani hurt or held captive or something? That shit happened here just like everywhere else.

Or was Ezra making some sort of last stand, some final statement to a life that already had a pretty full plate of dramatic events—of which Ezra himself had been both the author and the leading man? There was the drunken death threat leveled at the head of state in his native, neighboring country of independent Western Samoa, which had made him permanently unwelcome there. There was the string of Samoan swear words he had inserted into his dialogue while playing a native in a *Tales of the South Seas* TV episode—no one important had discovered it until after the broadcast. He once threw a punch at Ronald Reagan in an LA bar when Reagan was head of the Screen Actors Guild. He hid from the IRS here on Tutuila then got caught while trying to sneak back onto the mainland. There was the should-have-been-dead skull fracture from the beating he received from an irate husband. Put together, all the Ezra stories were like a fond, folk scrapbook of warrants and mug shots and newspaper clippings. When such collections of negative legends gained enough bulk, they earned one the grudging respect of the community at large. All of the cumulative transgressions were forgiven in light of the larger genius—a portrait of a person being consistently and so self-destructively himself. But he'd gotten rich at it too, rich enough to retire to this fancy keep.

It took almost half an hour for another squad car to get there, and they had been told to wait for reinforcements. Apelu sat waiting outside his squad car, sitting in the shade of a breadfruit tree, leaning against its trunk. The inside of his squad car was filled with cubes and grains and slivers of pulverized windshield. Several projectiles of shattered glass had been stopped by his scalp. He'd gotten them out, but his hair was too thick for him to stop the bleeding, so rivulets of dried blood marked his neck, forehead, cheek, and back. He wasn't aware how much. He had no water to wash them off, and the nicks didn't really hurt. He noticed the rusty hot water leaking out of holes in the squad car's radiator, and pellet holes in the headlights and rooftop flasher lights. Big spread, he thought.

If he sat without moving, the birds returned to the bush around him—honeyeaters, bulbuls, even a kingfisher came to watch him from its perch on the telephone wire above the road. A drab flightless rail scooted out into the open, saw him, and made a sharp turn back into bushy seclusion. The only things to listen to were birdsong and the distant boom of the surf. He smoked a cigarette. It was funny how often lyrics from old rock-and-roll songs came to him at odd times like this, like errant messages he couldn't interpret.

This time it was an old Simon and Garfunkel song that had nothing to do with what was going on. The chords of the song ran through his head, simple chords. He played them on an air guitar even after he'd forgotten the rest of the lyrics. It sure was quiet out here in the middle of the day.

After the first squad car pulled up, quite an entourage of emergency vehicles began to arrive, including an ambulance, backed up one behind another on the two-rut road. The EMS guys cleaned the blood off Apelu, including some spots on his back and shoulders he hadn't been aware of. His shirt was ruined. As a detective sergeant, Apelu dressed in street clothes, and the shirt he had put on that morning was one of his favorites—a blue-and-white cotton/polyester mix with the skyline of Manhattan on it. It had been a birthday present from Sina. She would be pissed that he had trashed it. It was supposed to be one of his "good" shirts, not a work shirt. She had even said something about that when he'd left the house that morning. Once more he would have to put up with her being right.

When Apelu climbed out of the ambulance, he was surprised to see the commissioner's black Chrysler SUV with its midnight-tinted windows pull up at the back of the line of vehicles. Both the commissioner and the assistant commissioner emerged from it. Then he saw the guns. Firearms were not part of an American Samoan policeman's standard equipment. They were supposed to prevail without them, and besides, none of the officers were trained to use such weapons. But from the back of the commissioner's SUV the assistant commissioner issued three assault rifles and twice as many handguns. It would seem that the commissioner—or maybe even the governor—had decided that Ezra taking a potshot at Apelu's squad car was a serious enough event that red-alert precautions were in order. The officers with the weapons were loading and checking them. Everyone was grim. Except for the metal-on-metal clicks of the weapons the day was almost as quiet as before, but without birdsong.

Everyone had been issued Kevlar vests as well, black with LHPD in large yellow letters on the back. LHPD stood for Laguna Honda Police Department. The vests were recycled and had never before been used by anyone in this department. Some of the officers needed assistance donning and adjusting them. All this for Ezra? Maybe there was something Apelu didn't know about.

Apelu walked over to the commissioner, who was talking with Apelu's captain, the commander of the CID, which was the police department's Criminal Investigation Division. The captain was looking down, still fumbling with the buckles on his bulletproof vest. He was sweating. Apelu stopped a respectful distance away, so that he couldn't be accused of listening in. Apelu realized that—in his now red, white, and blue shirt—he sort of stood out among all the dark-blue uniformed officers in their black vests.

The commissioner saw him. "Sergeant Soifua, should you be walking around?"

"I'm okay, Commissioner. Sorry about the car."

"What exactly happened here, Soifua?"

"Well, after the complaint, the captain here sent me out to bring in the weapon and get Ezra's side of the story. I drove up to that chain that he's got across the road and PA'd for him to come and talk. He came out with his shotgun and shot the squad car. Then he walked back to his house." Apelu knew that the commissioner liked things kept short and to the point. "That's about it. Oh, and he's got a couple of really good-looking guard dogs. Is there something I don't know here, sir? I mean, it's only Ezra. Has anybody tried to call him on the phone and just ask him to come out without his gun?"

The commissioner looked at the captain, who shrugged and shook his head and looked around.

"Why don't you try that, sir?" Apelu said to the commissioner. "It's bad shit, but it's only Ezra, and who knows where Leilani is at."

Apelu knew that the commissioner had a soft spot for Leilani, who always came and danced for free at his benefits and fundraisers. The commissioner called his secretary on his cell phone to find Ezra and Leilani's phone number. The commissioner called the number and looked down the road in the direction of the house he was calling. A surprised look came on his face.

"*Talofa*, Ezra." The commissioner spoke in Samoan. "Ezra, this is Commissioner Papali`i. How are you? Ezra, I'm just down the road from your place. I was wondering if I could have a word with you. It has to do with some gunfire around your house." Pause. "Oh, I see." Pause. "Well, Ezra, how about I come up to the house in a bit, and we can talk about it? And, by the way, Ezra, how is Leilani, that sweet girl of yours?" Longer pause. "*Oka, oka*! You don't say? Well, you know how women are sometimes, especially the pretty ones. Say, Ezra, I'll be up to see you in a couple of minutes."

Apelu gestured with his hands to the commissioner, who covered the mouthpiece of the cell phone and looked at Apelu.

"Tell him no gun, no dogs," Apelu said. He hated to think of those animals getting shot up for nothing.

"Oh, and Ezra, please—*fa`amolemole*—just come out yourself. No guns, no dogs. Just a talk. Thank you, Ezra. *Fa`afetai tele lave. Fa.*"

The commissioner stood there in silence a few seconds after clicking off. "Ezra says it wasn't him that did the shooting." He looked at Apelu.

"It was either him or his twin, Commissioner," Apelu said.

"He also said Leilani wasn't there, that she was off in Apia spending his money."

The assistant commissioner was holding out a Kevlar vest for the commissioner. The commissioner tried to put it on, slowly and with assistance from the assistant commissioner, who was a small man, maybe half the commissioner's mass; it was a sort of Laurel and Hardy routine. It didn't work. The commissioner was of a much greater girth than anyone who would have ever been allowed to work for the Laguna Honda Police Department.

"Screw it," he said, tossing the vest aside. "Let's go."

The commissioner's car was the last in line, so he got in the front squad car, which crawled down the road toward Ezra's. The armed officers tried to spread out in a line on either side of the road but couldn't because the pandanus was so dense. They regrouped in the ruts behind the squad car. Apelu walked with them, the only one unarmed and unarmored. When they got to the spot where Apelu had stopped earlier, they stopped too, and the armed officers fanned out along the low lava stone wall that marked what Ezra deemed to be his property line. The assistant commissioner got out of the squad car with a bullhorn and approached the chain. No dogs. Good, thought Apelu. He had walked up to stand beside the rear window of the driver's side, where the commissioner was seated. The assistant commissioner stopped at the chain and called out through the bullhorn in very polite high-chiefly Samoan. He asked Ezra to come out and have a *fono*—a meeting—with his high chief, the commissioner.

Ezra's gray head crested the rise between the house and the chain. Along the line of the wall Apelu could hear weapons being cocked. Ezra was wearing a dark-green-and-blue aloha shirt and a pair of black slacks. He was not carrying the shotgun. His hands were empty. As he approached, he waved to the commissioner in the squad car. The commissioner got out of the squad car and went to meet him, stepping over the chain. They shook hands and then stood and chatted for a while. Then the commissioner invited Ezra to come with him. After they had passed over the chain, the assistant commissioner apologetically and quickly patted Ezra down. The commissioner walked Ezra back to the SUV at the back of the line of vehicles, and they drove away.

CHAPTER 2

───────── ○ ─────────

E ZRA STRAND DOES NOT SOUND LIKE A SAMOAN NAME EXCEPT to Samoans. The last name had been in the islands for as long as the white man had been—five or six generations. And his first name was biblical—one of the prophets, wasn't it? A book in the Old Testament. It wasn't uncommon for Samoans to have biblical names. Apelu's name, in fact, was the Samoanized version of Abel.

The first Strand had been a missionary. One of his sons had married a Samoan and opened a store on Beach Road in Apia on the neighboring island of Upolu. That was back when Beach Road was about the only road there and there weren't any roads at all on any of the other islands. It became a pretty big clan as the family tree grew. Intermarriages with other *afakasi*, or half-caste, families kept most of them a shade or two lighter than full-blooded Samoans. They enjoyed the advantages of their small, merchant class in a mainly subsistence society—advantages like New Zealand educations and a taste for imported luxuries. Ezra's father had run an interisland shipping line and built a mansion at Vailima near where Robert Louis Stevenson had lived in the hills above Apia.

Leilani was also *afakasi*, but of a much more mysterious blend. She claimed to be Samoan. Her name was Samoan, and she spoke the language well. But unlike most Samoans, she never bragged about nor even mentioned her forebears. She seemed uninterested in her lineage. She had been born in Hawaii, and her slim figure and fine facial bones testified to an ancestral ethnic mix that included Portuguese, Japanese, and Polynesian. One didn't learn much about Leilani from Leilani. There were children somewhere off-island, grandchildren. If Ezra's life was public scrapbook material, Leilani's was a locked and hidden diary. She had danced professionally all her life, since she was a little girl. It was what she knew of life. That and Ezra. Apelu realized that if he went through the list of the people he liked, a shared trait among them was that they spoke little of themselves. Leilani led the list in that respect.

After Ezra drove away with the commissioner, a discussion ensued between the assistant commissioner and the CID captain about whether or not they should continue on to the house and secure the shotgun as evidence. The assistant commissioner wanted a search warrant. The captain didn't agree. He argued it was a crime scene—attempted murder as he gestured toward Apelu—and that they should be allowed to proceed, seize the weapon involved, and secure the crime scene. Those two liked arguing about things like that, pretending that they were lawyers. In the end there was a compromise. The assistant commissioner called downtown on his cell phone to request a search warrant to be issued, and the captain, with the few CID guys, went on to the house, just to find the shotgun and wait on the warrant for a proper search.

Yeah, right.

The assistant commissioner had taken back all the weapons and vests after Ezra had been driven away, but Apelu asked the assistant commissioner to reissue one of the handguns to him. He was thinking about the dogs. Apelu reminded the assistant commissioner, who was a prissy, officious sort, that he was one of the few officers in the department with clearance to use a weapon due to his SFPD training. The assistant commissioner gave him a gun, a big automatic that Apelu loaded and strapped on. It felt very strange wearing a gun again, something he'd done every workday for so many years back in San Francisco. He had forgotten how heavy it was. He hoped he didn't have to use it.

As they approached the house, the dogs started barking, deep barrel-chested barks, but they sounded more like questions rather than the life-threatening barks of before. The barking was scary enough, though, to make everyone stop in their tracks. Apelu unholstered the gun and clicked off the safety. The sound was coming from the back of the house. Apelu walked slowly toward the sound while the captain and the other officers waited. The dogs were in a roofed and fenced kennel. They barked louder when they saw him, but it was more like they were happy to see him than angry. No foam.

Apelu thumbed the safety back on and holstered the gun. "Yo, puppies, howzit?" he said and made the kissing sound that always calmed down his dogs. The black one, a male, continued to stand and bark, but the lion-colored one, a female, sat down and started licking her privates. They weren't wild or unmanageable monsters. They were well-trained and reasonable animals, which meant that they had been ordered to attack Apelu earlier. He called out an all-clear to the others, whose arrival set off a more excited bout of barking.

"They're secure," the captain said. "Let's leave them alone." And they all went around to the front of the house.

"Those were dogs?" one of the officers asked. "I didn't know they made models that big."

The front door and the kitchen door were locked, but on the patio Apelu found one of the sliding glass doors wide open. Inside, the house was not as he remembered it. A plywood wall had been constructed diagonally across the long living room.

Some native *tapas* and prints had been pinned to the wall, but it was unpainted, unfinished. It gave what was left of the room an under-construction feel. At the front, angled end of the wall was a single door. The room had a deserted sense and smell. A pot of past-fragrant potpourri sat on a lonely coffee table. A piece of lace was draped over a stuffed chair by the cliffside windows.

The wall took a turn at Apelu's left, into a narrow passageway back along the patio windows that led to the kitchen and the bathroom. Midway along the passageway wall was a locked door. The wall didn't ascend all the way to the peak-beamed ceilings, but was about ten feet high. The back of the house had an even older smell of mold and things left unmoved for a long time, a hint of sick sweetness—a male geriatric smell.

They searched the kitchen and its storerooms first for the shotgun. In a back hallway they found cases and cases of two-liter bottles of cranberry juice. One storeroom was filled with unopened tins of *sao* crackers and cardboard boxes of canned peaches. A freezer in the breezeway was packed with frozen T-bone steaks. But no shotgun. Two of the officers were about to break down the door in the plywood wall when the captain motioned them aside, pulled a small ring of elbowed wires from his pocket, and promptly picked the lock. Apelu couldn't remember the last time he had been surprised by anything the captain had done.

Beyond the plywood wall, the old-man smell was stronger. The newly walled room had been ceilinged as well. The room was windowless and dark. Its air was heavy and still. The captain found a light switch that turned on a fluorescent overhead fixture. The room was like an odd-shaped bunker with two original doors in the farthest wall. The room was a warehouse of unopened boxes and shrink-wrapped goods of all kinds.

To what extent does what we own, what we end up embedding ourselves within, define us? Apelu wondered. He drove a ten-year-old pickup truck, had a job as a cop, a wife and four kids under fifteen. He lived on family land in a house that his father had built and that he had added onto. Apelu owned three pairs of shoes and had a ridge-top plantation of bananas, coconut, and taro to care for. He rarely got to choose what was playing on their one TV set. He still had two guitars, one strung with steel strings. But was that him? A lot of him seemed to escape through that rough net of his few possessions. He would still be himself without his shoes, without his old guitars, his job. It was memory, not things, that held his self together—memories from the past and obligations to the future. Those things defined him, not his possessions, poor as they were. Would it be different if he were rich?

At the San Francisco Police Academy, Apelu had been taught the Rules of Evidence, how lawyers could make or break a case on the most pointless details of how or when something had been seen or heard. It didn't matter if what had been seen or heard was obviously accurate. If all the rules hadn't been followed, the evidence was inadmissible. The mere fact that there were rules made a game out of the whole thing. If the ref didn't see you step out of bounds, you got to keep the ball. In any event, most of Apelu's fellow CID officers hadn't had much training in the finer points of such rules, so it was not a shared concern when they entered Ezra's inner sanctums. Curiosity was the driving force. They weren't looking for just the weapon any longer; they were just looking. And the weapon, their excuse for being there, wasn't there.

Apelu suggested to the captain that they should withdraw and wait for the search warrant. By now the other officers had discovered that one of the other doors led to a bedroom with walls papered with old *Playboy* centerfolds. The captain agreed and pulled everyone back to the patio. Then, to keep the men busy, he set them to searching the grounds and the cliff for the shotgun. "Need that weapon," he said to them.

They didn't find it. Word that the search warrant had been issued arrived an hour or so later, and they went through the rest of the house. No shotgun, no shotgun shells. There was an illegal handgun—all handguns were illegal in the territory—a twenty-two caliber, but no bullets for that either. On the floor beside the bed in Ezra's bedroom Apelu found the white shirt and khaki shorts Ezra had been wearing earlier. As Apelu suspected, the door that opened from the sunny front of the living room led to Leilani's bedroom, which from the look and the feel of it had not been occupied recently. But it was neat, with no signs of anything unusual.

In a corner of Ezra's bunker-like room they found a pair of dancers' fire knives. Light, polished, and nicely balanced, they looked as if they had never been used. Apelu took them out onto the patio and hesitantly started turning and twirling them. He tried a little three-turn toss and caught them cleanly coming down. It had been a dozen years at least since he'd performed, but the muscle memory was still there. As he played with the knives, feeling muscles that he hadn't heard from in a while, he had to laugh to himself. Of course Samoans would dance with knives. Of course they would set them on fire and toss and twist them around their bodies. They liked dancing with long, sharp, flaming personal weapons so well, liked the self-image so well—the warrior for whom danger was just a welcome playmate—that they had made it a traditional cultural feature of their dance performances. After all, these were people, his people, who fashioned cricket bats like war clubs and had made a contact sport out of shark catching. While everywhere else in the Pacific the natives caught sharks the sensible way: with a pole, line, and hook. In Samoa, the style was to attract the shark to your canoe—maybe by splashing your hand around in the water—then slip a hangman's noose around its snout up to the dorsal fin, jerk it shut, and yank the shark's head out of the water to beat its brains in with a club that might pass as a cricket bat. Great fun. Try it sometime while balancing in a slender outrigger canoe about the same size as the shark. Fire knife dancing was a natural up-on-the-beach progression from that, as natural as the thrills of rugby or football. You had a weapon in your hand, for one thing. Apelu executed a few slow leg passes and another, higher toss, but he misjudged it on the catch, and the knife hit the patio with a clatter and skittered away on the flagstones.

"You had it there for a minute." It was a woman's voice, speaking English. She was standing on a patch of sea-spray-browned lawn below the patio, looking up at him.

"I was distracted by all the applause," Apelu said, going to retrieve the dropped knife. "Who are you?"

"My name is Asia. I live down the cliffs that way," she said, nodding her head over her shoulder. "I was wondering what was going on over here."

Apelu looked west down the cliffs in the direction she had nodded. He didn't know there were any houses down that way for at least a mile, until you got to the edge of the village of Vaitogi. He couldn't see any houses.

Asia was very Scandinavian-looking—tall, broad-shouldered, blonde, with weathered outdoor skin, and a half smile. From the ground up, she was wearing sturdy leather sandals, a short brightly patterned piece of lavalava material wrapped around her waist, and a faded blue work shirt with the sleeves cut off. She was neither young nor old. The sea breeze kept her long hair off her face.

"My name is Apelu," he said. "I'm a police officer. We are here conducting a search of the house."

"I thought I heard a siren earlier," she said. She had very pale blue eyes.

"And a gunshot?" Apelu asked.

"No, no gunshots. The surf makes those sounds sometimes, though, in the blow holes. Is Mr. Strand all right?"

"Oh yes. Ezra's fine. The commissioner took him downtown for a visit, some questions."

"I've been worrying about Mr. Strand recently. He's become so removed, so gruff, almost unfriendly."

"You see him often?" Apelu put the knives down on a table and walked over to the edge of the patio, sat down on its edge.

"No."

"Oh."

"When his wife was here, sometimes I'd visit." Asia folded her arms across her chest, cocked her head to one side, and studied him. "That's blood all over your shirt, isn't it? Maybe you shouldn't play with those knives."

"They're not self-inflicted wounds," Apelu said and smiled.

She smiled back. "Is it a new style I'm not aware of?"

"Police chic," he said, "badge of public service and all that. So, how long has Mrs. Strand been gone?"

"A couple of weeks at least."

"Do you know where?"

"No," she answered matter-of-factly. "Well, Apelu, nice meeting you." Asia stepped over and held her right hand up to Apelu, who shook it. It was a strong hand. "Good luck with your search, for whatever it is you're looking for, and keep up the knife dance practice. I think you may have the knack. *Tofa*."

"*Tofa*," Apelu said to her back as she turned and walked away. "By the way, Asia, do you have a last name?" he called out after her.

"Yes," she said, "several." She waved the back of her hand at him as she stepped down off the lawn onto the rocks.

Apelu picked up the fire knives from the patio table and put them back where he had found them in the corner of Ezra's bunker. The captain set two men to cataloging anything of interest that was discovered in the house. The other men, including Apelu, he dismissed, telling Apelu to take the rest of the day off.

Apelu had learned it by rote.

"By god, you will do it the way I teach you, or I'll cut off all your little pricks and feed them to my dog," Seutia would yell at them from his wheelchair, trying to get close enough to whack them with the bamboo switch he brought to classes. They would all take one whack, then dance away from his reach. "Back, back, from the start, you little worthless pieces of shit." The two wooden drum *pate* players would again initiate their double-time syncopation, and Apelu, Tavita, Junior, and whoever else was there would start the fire knife routine from the top. Seutia knew—it was how he had been taught and performed—that if you had the opening down and knew how you were going to end it, the middle part would take care of itself. For each dance, the beginning set up whatever you would invent later. It was like a philosophy of life for which dancing was only a metaphor.

Seutia was right. He was a good teacher. Apelu had cried for hours when they buried him, missed his wisdom and his whacks. Apelu had been only ten then, but now, more than a quarter of a century later, Seutia was still a regular in his dreams. He was scolding him, telling him to keep his back straight, how to open his body to the audience, how to be a servant both to them and to the dance itself, how to make it all about the dance, not about himself, and how to take care of his fire knives.

"Remember, you are nothing," he would tell them. "Everyone's eyes are only on your flames, make them sing."

Part of Apelu's current routine was writing crime reports. He enjoyed doing them and he liked to write them when everything was still fresh in his head. So he didn't take the rest of the day off; it was still early in the afternoon. He got a ride home in one of the squad cars and while the driver waited—snoozed, actually—he showered, shampooed, and changed his clothes. He put his ruined shirt in a plastic bag and buried it in the garbage, woke the driver, and they drove back downtown to headquarters.

As he was writing up his report, it struck Apelu that if the shotgun was still anywhere on Ezra's premises it was probably in the kennel, the one place they hadn't searched. He didn't put that in his report, though, because it would just make them look stupid. It would be easy enough to check the next day—if anyone wanted to walk into that cage with those dogs—hungry dogs, by then. He also didn't mention the captain's proficiency with lock-picking tools, or even the fact that they had entered that room before the search warrant had arrived. Crime reports were meant to be helpful constructive tools, not potentially damaging confessions.

Ezra had been booked on charges of reckless endangerment and unlawful discharge of a firearm, and would be spending at least the night in jail. He still claimed it wasn't him who did the shooting. Apelu carefully block-printed out his report and turned it in to the captain, who again told him to go home. He did, or at least he headed that way in his pickup—west along the coast road—when he left town. But his mind kept returning to those dogs and how hungry they must be getting as the day slid toward sundown. There would be no one there to feed them, to make sure they had enough water. So, at Futiga he turned back on the golf course road, and took the turn onto the road out to Piapiatele. His old Ranger pickup truck with the big plantation tires was more suited to that road than the made-for-freeways police cruiser. On his tape deck he was playing an old slack-key Hawaiian rock-and-roll tape by Moondance. At the last bush store he stopped and bought himself a large, cold bottle of Steinlager. Maybe after taking care of the dogs he would sit on the cliffs and watch the sun set. It had been a fairly nonroutine day; he could use some downtime.

The sun was still a ways above the horizon when Apelu pulled up to Ezra's chain and turned off the engine. He took his cold bottle of Steinlager with him and walked toward the back of the house. No barking greeted him. In the now nearly horizontal brassy sunlight he could see that the kennel was empty. His first impulse was to freeze and look around himself. He followed that impulse, switching his grip on the Steinlager bottle to make it a club. The thought of those dogs out there foraging for dinner was a bit unnerving. But he was all alone, and when he walked up to the cage he saw that the gate had been relatched. Animals don't tend to be so tidy when they manage a jail break.

Apelu went into the kennel. At least he could search for the shotgun without having to figure out what to do about the dogs. He had hoped that their routine would be to get fed around this time of day, and that he could find their food, or some food—maybe those T-bone steaks—and feed them so that they would have reason to trust him enough to share their kennel with him while he searched it. No need now. There was a strong doggie smell, not unpleasant, but the kennel was quite clean. He searched it. No shotgun, though on a shelf under the eaves of the house he found a partly empty box of shotgun shells. He latched the gate behind himself when he left, leaving the box of shells where he had found it.

Apelu found a good seat on the cliff top above the surf. It was a natural cup in the rock filled with coarse sand that faced more west than south. People had probably been coming to sit here for thousands of years, he thought, a perfect spot. He opened his bottle of Steinlager with a church key on his key chain. The first swig of beer relaxed him. Below him the big waves built up white heads to slam against the cliff face. Farther out as they rose in height, the slanting acetylene sun turned them momentarily transparent turquoise before they broke. That was the waves' routine—beauty and the burst. He looked west along the high, broken coastline, where the scene was repeated in cove after foamy cove with rhythmic hypnotic regularity, no two explosions the same. It was comforting—nothing human-made in sight, no lights besides the sun setting into the sea. He watched for the famous green flash as the sun vanished, its light now living only in the clouds, but was again denied it. Far off in the distance he heard a deep-chested dog's howl, then another join it a half octave higher in harmony, making, along with the waves' tympani, some sort of nature chorus. By the time he finished his Steinlager only the highest clouds still held the light, and he stumbled in the dark on the way back to his truck.

CHAPTER 3

———— o ————

I N REALITY, AMERICAN SAMOA'S IDENTITY CRISIS SHOULD HAVE been much more pronounced than it seemed. A chain of six tiny islands with a total land area of seventy-six square miles, for more than a hundred years now it had been a "possession" of the United States of America, five thousand open ocean miles away. It was the only piece of US territory in the southern hemisphere. The relationship never had made any sense. It was just one of those uncorrected accidents of history, the result of a minor tactical move in nineteenth-century gunboat diplomacy that had remained so far removed from the great powers' attention and so unimportant as to never get set back right again.

For fifty years the place had been run by the US Navy as if it were a ship with an unfortunate cargo of natives. Then the distant territory's administration had been ironically transferred to the Department of the Interior, the folks who already oversaw the rest of America's reservations. Traditionally, the governorship had been bestowed upon naval commanders who couldn't be trusted with a real, sinkable ship and, later, to hack redneck politicians who had been voted out of office back in Arkansas or East Texas. The result was eighty years of short-term, appointed, white male governors of varying degrees of racist assurance and administrative acumen; they were rarely stellar. Only in the last generation had American Samoans been enfranchised to elect their own governor and legislature, though the Secretary of the Interior still held veto power over everything. Technically, the islands were "an unincorporated and unorganized" territory of the greater USA. Apelu had never been sure exactly what that meant, but it did sort of explain—or at least sum up—a lot of his feelings about his home and its governance. He had been born here on Tutuila, the main island, and for all but ten years of his adolescence and young adulthood he had lived here. He had no plans to go anywhere else.

But America's backhanded adoption of the islands had led to a strange set of circumstances when it came to allegiances. It was like a child whose father is *palangi*—Caucasian—and whose mother is Samoan. The father is benevolent, speaks English, and pays the bills, but he is seldom home and doesn't understand basic stuff about how everything fits together. The mother speaks Samoan and makes each day work. She is always there and knows all the gossip and why everything happens or doesn't happen. Whom do you love more? Your father or your mother?

Apelu was a good enough example, even though he wasn't *afakasi* but full-blooded Samoan. At work—a *palangi* job being a cop—he wore *palangi* clothes; at home Samoan, a simple lavalava and no shirt. At formal affairs these styles clashed together, and current custom dictated a tailored gabardine skirt and suit jacket with a wide colorful tie. Although the vast majority of his conversations took place in Samoan, most of his reading and writing was done in English. His plantation supplied much of what his family ate, but for lunch he had *palangi* fast food. Sina could use old home remedies to fix most of what his kids came down with, but the hospital was always there as a scary alternative. And from there the divide went deeper into the order of things on the list of what's really important, into what you would fight for, whom you would choose to forgive, what children mean, what a chief is—things that *palangis* would never understand.

Of course there was the other side—the fact that the standard of living here was considerably higher than in any other islands in the region, from New Zealand to Hawaii. Thanks to the US dollar, US aid, Pago Pago had become a sort of border town—a town on the relatively richer side of the border. A frontier town surrounded by ocean. The lure of America drew the strivers and climbers from places as close as Western Samoa and Tonga, and as far away as Korea and the Philippines. That was a big reason why the population of the territory had increased threefold in Apelu's short lifetime, nudging up toward sixty thousand people now.

Ezra's bunker had become a warehouse of commercial treasure, but, as in the kitchen, volume not diversity was the guiding principle. Ezra seemed to deal only in case lots. The list that the CID guys had drawn up of what was in there was fascinating in a way that was new to Apelu. Crazed consumption, but something else too—a disconnect. Among other hoarded items there were cases of Rothmans cigarettes, but neither Ezra nor Leilani smoked; there were no ashtrays in the house. Cases of tampons, though Leilani was decades past menopause. Cases of disposable diapers and motor oil, but no babies and no vehicles. Cases of both blank and recorded CDs—none were opened and there was not a single CD player in the place. The recorded CDs were packaged commercially in shrink-wrapped lots of twenty, each lot a single album by a different group or performer, all island sounds.

The morning after Ezra's arrest the captain had given Apelu the search warrant list to see what he could make of it. Ezra seemed an unlikely suspect for a smuggler, but that would be the most likely explanation for such a cache. The cigarettes especially spoke to that. Rothmans were a New Zealand brand made in Western Samoa. Without all the import and territorial taxes, they were much more profitable when smuggled in. Apelu wasn't sure about the other items on the list. Maybe there was a big enough difference in the prices of tampons and Pampers and motor oil between the two Samoas to make their untaxed transfer profitable. Apelu didn't know. Or maybe they were just stolen goods. In order to find that out they would need more identifying numbers than the officers had written down, box lot numbers and such.

Apelu pointed that fact out to the captain, and shortly thereafter he was on his way back out to Ezra's place to take a second look. As Apelu was leaving headquarters the assistant commissioner stopped him and asked him to wait up a minute. There was someone here from the attorney general's office to go with him. Apelu gave the assistant commissioner an incredulous look and said "What?" Normally the AG's office would not be involved until a crime report was submitted to them with a recommendation for prosecution.

"Just wait," the assistant commissioner said. "And cooperate."

"Yes, sir," Apelu said and shrugged. More irregular bullshit.

The young man was small, compact, but very well put together, with the solid, muscle-rounded shoulders and light gait of an athlete, as brown as Apelu but slender, not a Samoan. He introduced himself as Matthew Sparks. "But everyone calls me Mati," he said with a distinct Kiwi accent. He had a youthful smile. He was carrying a camera bag. "Pleased to meet you, Apelu. I've heard about you."

All the way to Piapiatele, as Apelu played road solitaire with the potholes, Mati talked, but Apelu didn't listen very closely. Mati talked about himself. It was as if he had some nervous need to confirm his existence by reciting his past. What Apelu registered of the recitation was that Mati had been born in Niue—one of those really small and isolated islands somewhere to the south—but had grown up in a Polynesian ghetto in Auckland. Through a cousin in California he had parlayed his natural ability in soccer into a scholarship at USC, where he had majored in criminology. The job at the attorney general's office as an investigator seemed like a natural choice—back in the islands, his field. He was single and lived alone in an apartment. The only thing wrong with the story was that Mati was older than he initially appeared. And, though his manner and speech were lively, his eyes somehow never got fully involved in the fun. His glance would patrol and then focus, like someone on a conning tower, focusing on a house or a person by the road, almost as if he were taking photographs with his eyes. He would take long looks up every dirt side road as he kept talking, turning his head and leaning back as they passed.

They were an hour or so into their work at Ezra's—luckily, Mati shut up when he worked—when Apelu heard the dogs. It sounded like they were barking a greeting to the house. The sound got louder, and Apelu walked out to the patio. Coming across the lava field, a straining leash in either hand, was Asia. She was leaning back as she walked, pulled forward by the dogs' enthusiasm. They were still a ways off. Apelu waved and the dogs barked louder. Asia jerked them in, and they calmed down a bit. Just as they were coming up onto the lawn Mati came out onto the patio and stood beside Apelu. The dogs went off again. Mati bolted for the sliding glass door into the house with a "What the fuck!" and swiftly slid the door closed behind him.

"Nick, Nora," Asia called out to the dogs, pulling them in. Then, "Hello, Apelu. Still searching?"

"Still searching, Asia. What are you doing?"

"Being dragged around by these dogs," she said and laughed. The black dog had gotten up to Apelu's legs and was sniffing him.

"So, this is Nick, I gather," Apelu said as held out the back of his hand for the dog to smell.

"That's Nick," she said.

Nick licked Apelu's hand, wrist, and forearm with one swipe of his big tongue and became uninterested, looking instead toward the glass door from behind which Mati was watching them.

"And this is Nora," Asia said, patting the blonde dog's side. "Those are my names for them. They have Samoan names but I can't remember them. They seem to like Nick and Nora. I was just taking them out for a walk but they wanted to come home. Is Mr. Strand back?"

"No, he's not, I'm afraid. Still in custody." Apelu scratched Nick behind his ears and he promptly rolled over to have his huge chest scratched. "You came and got them yesterday?"

"They were sounding awful lonesome, and they hadn't been fed, so they came home with me."

"Well, they look happy enough now."

"They're sweethearts," Asia said. "But at my place I have to keep them tied up. They'll be happier here in their kennel where at least they can walk around."

"But without your company," Apelu said, and then he suddenly realized that since the start of their conversation they had both been speaking Samoan. He looked at Asia.

"*Ioe,*" she said, yes. Then in English, "I'll just put them back in their kennel and let you get back to your work. What are you searching for?"

"Reasons," Apelu said, "just reasons."

On the way back to headquarters, on the coast road approaching town, coming into the bay, Apelu pulled off onto a gravel turn out at one of the points that stuck out into the sea and turned off the engine. Mati had been silent most of the way back. "What?" he said now, looking back at the passing traffic.

"*Matu'u sina,*" Apelu said. "Heavy omen. We'll wait here awhile." He pulled a pack of Marlboro Light 100s out of his pocket and lit one. He offered one to Mati, who refused with a wave of his hand.

"What's that you said—*matu'u* something?" Mati asked.

"A white reef heron. What's the English word for it? Oh yeah, an albino reef heron, all white. Real ones are always slate gray. It's been following us. Look." Apelu indicated with his eyes where Mati's eyes should look, and there, about a foot above the breaking waves, a good-sized, wide-winged, crook-necked, snow-white bird cruised past them then turned back and alighted upon a wet black boulder just off their point. It didn't look right at them. But then that was part of the story why the reef heron had become Apelu's clan's totem bird—that it didn't have to be looking at you to see what you were doing. *Matu'u* was a part of their extended family that lived in the nonhuman animate world. "We'll wait, see what happens."

Mati looked from Apelu to the bird then back to Apelu. "Okay," he said. "Whatever you say." Then silence as Apelu smoked and watched. "Those things aren't good for you, you know."

"So I've heard," Apelu said. In Apelu's clan whenever you saw a *matu'u* you acknowledged it, paid attention to it. He had heard of the white one—there were stories about it—but he had never before met it. He must pay very close attention. A wave broke on the rock where the white one was standing, but it didn't rise up in the air as most birds would. It let the surf froth wash around its feet and legs and remained unmoved. It turned its yellow dagger beak so that it was pointed directly at Apelu, and then it turned back to profile, paused a second, and then with a snake-like motion of its neck took off. Apelu flicked the butt of his cigarette out his window, started up the squad car, and pulled back onto the road, following the *matu'u sina*, which soon turned out to sea and vanished between wave tops.

The break came on the Rothmans. The case lot numbers Apelu had copied down from Ezra's hoard immediately preceded the case lot numbers on smuggled cases that Customs had intercepted a few months earlier. Customs had checked with authorities in

Western Samoa and had found out that those cases had been reported stolen. So that solved that quandary—they were both stolen and smuggled. And that put the rest of the items in Ezra's stash in the suspicious column as well.

Tracking down the paperwork had taken a couple of days, by which time Ezra had had his initial court appearance on the weapons charges, and bail had been set at five thousand dollars. But Ezra had refused to pay the bail and was still in the correctional facility. Apelu arranged to interview him there. Ezra had also refused to hire a lawyer, so the court had appointed an assistant public defender to represent him. She was late. When Ezra was brought into the interview room he was wearing a faded cotton lavalava and an equally old short-sleeve shirt with buttons missing. He was barefoot. He refused to speak English. This was a problem because the assistant public defender, a mousy, unpleasant young woman only a year or two out of law school, was *palangi* and didn't speak Samoan. She refused Apelu's offer to act as translator because of his "bias." Same for any of the guards. The warden was finally sent for, and he agreed to translate, and she accepted, under protest.

Ezra's name was no longer Ezra. He insisted upon being addressed by his long Samoan name, a title that had been conferred upon him decades before in Western Samoa. It was a title Apelu was unfamiliar with. The assistant public defender had trouble with the name change, but Ezra wouldn't answer to anything else. Apelu had to spell it out for her. It was fourteen or fifteen letters long, depending on whether you counted a glottal stop as a letter.

Ezra denied that he lived at Piapiatele. His address was the village outside of Apia where his title originated. He knew nothing about the contents of the house. Why should he? He didn't live there. When asked about the whereabouts of his wife, Leilani, he claimed that his wife had died years before and that her name wasn't Leilani but Dorothea. Of course, he knew nothing about any shotgun. Both Apelu and the warden accorded Ezra the respect due to an older titled man. His lawyer was dumbfounded and incredulous until she realized she might have a diminished-capacity defense being handed to her and promptly drew a close to the interview.

After Ezra and his lawyer—whom Ezra had wholly ignored—had left, Apelu and the warden were left alone.

The warden chuckled. "Who would have thought old man Strand could pull off such a genuine Apia chief performance?" he said.

"Pretty convincing," Apelu said.

"I'll have him moved over to cellblock C with the more permanent inmates. He'll get more privileges and respect over there, and it looks like he may be with us for a while."

"That's good," Apelu said. "I'll stop by now and then to see if he needs anything. He doesn't seem to have any family here."

"Crazy Ezra," the warden said and shook his head.

On his way back to headquarters Apelu thought about crazy people. There were a few true local sociopaths locked up permanently at the correctional facility. Then there was the crazy cleaning lady, who spent her days feverishly weeding and picking up trash from selected areas in the neighborhood of the governor's house, talking incessantly to herself. Apelu had noticed that recently she had adopted a stretch of beach by a stream mouth near the yacht club, which was clear not only of debris and broken glass, but also of all stones. She had assembled a small, makeshift lean-to for herself there beneath a fau tree. There was the crazed slow-motion jogger in secondhand boots that didn't fit, layers of dirt-dingy clothes, sunglasses, a hat you wouldn't want to touch, and, recently, a white cardboard cup clenched between his teeth covering his nose. Every day he performed a high-stepping pantomime of slow-mo running up and down the sidewalks of downtown. There were the crazy walkers—all men.

Two were shoeless, shirtless Samoans dressed only in soiled lav-alavas—one who wandered, immersed in an endless unfriendly dialogue with no one, and one who strode in silence, encased in inner fierceness, as if he was in a battle he could never quite catch up to. There was even a crazy *palangi* walker, a slight young man with sandy hair, always in sandals, shorts, and a clean T-shirt, who could be seen at almost any time of day walking the coast roads. No one seemed to know him. His gaze never wavered from six feet in front of his next step. He always wore an almost-empty schoolboy's backpack. If he talked to himself, all of the voices were kept inside his head.

None of these people were dangerous. They passed ignored, unbothered, and uncommented upon. They were part of the landscape. When one of them vanished, they were missed, and people would mention their disappearance as if a favorite tree had come down. Stuka was gone—their harmless, gaunt, giant town drunk. And the old white-haired, white-bearded, brain-busted Vietnam vet, whom the kids had called Captain Whacko because he would spend hours at a time just standing up to his beard in the waters off the yacht club beach. He had died a lonely death. People used to wait to see if, when he emerged, he would have any clothes on or not. Sweet, birth-addled Sarge, who, dressed in a metal-enhanced Boy Scout uniform, would open the door for, greet, and salute every patron going into and out of the bank, had been given almost a chief's funeral when he died. Everyone missed his cheerful salutes. All of these crazies were, or had been, just themselves, played out in full in the public sphere. They were left alone, admired almost for their dedication to being them-selves. No one tried to change them, medicate them, or put them away somewhere. No one tried to "feel their pain" because such a leap of imagination seemed presumptuous and wholly unneces-sary. They were who they were.

Back in the SFPD, the deranged—or whatever you were cur-rently supposed to call them—had made up a significant portion of Apelu's clientele. The city was a magnet for them. They were not only strange; they were strangers, unlike here where they were more like family—maybe not his, but somebody's family. Like Ezra—the scion of a famous family, but, just as important, Leilani's husband. Family was everything here in Samoa. Family came first, then village. You, as a person, came somewhere down the list.

CHAPTER 4

———— o ————

S INA DIDN'T LIKE IT. TOUGH. APELU WAS PACKING AND SINA was in the kitchen, going *musu*. *Musu* is Samoan for that state of mind and that demeanor that says, "If you want what is best for everybody, you'd better leave me alone." It was a sort of silent hostility. There wasn't any one word in English for it; it was part description, part warning, part excuse. Everyone got to go *musu* sometimes. It was always best to leave them alone. Apelu had borrowed a many-zippered athletic bag from Sanele, his oldest son, because he had no luggage. He also didn't have that much to pack. But he would only be gone a night or two. A squad car was waiting.

The assistant commissioner had decided that it would be a good idea for Apelu to go to Apia and follow up in person any further connections between what had been found in Ezra's house and what the Western Samoan authorities had on similar stolen or smuggled goods. The Apia cops didn't want to do all that checking, and, besides, it would be a good opportunity for Apelu to find out how they worked over there, what they might know that the department here didn't. It had taken a couple of days, but the assistant commissioner had persuaded the

37

commissioner and the CID captain that it was a good idea and a bona fide use of travel funds and manpower. The assistant commissioner, however, wasn't the one who had to convince Sina. Apelu knew better than to get close to her for a good-bye hug or kiss. As he was leaving, he stopped at the door to the kitchen and told her that he would call her from his hotel room in Apia and give her the number.

"Don't bother," was all she said in a voice that could have been a telephone recording.

What does she think I am doing? Apelu wondered as he left. Running off to Apia on the department's dollar for a one-night floozy fling? From Sina's farewell comment, Apelu figured this would be a class-orange *musu*, one grade below the rarely reached top level when the red magma of hostility boiled hot enough to crack through the catatonic shield, and furniture, windows, and appliances would get broken in the eruption. But a class-orange *musu* could go on for three days. Apelu thought about extending his stay in Apia until it blew over. Sina would be okay then—quiet, a little chagrined, and vaguely apologetic for showing so much emotion. After seventeen years of marriage, Apelu thought he knew the pattern well enough.

In recent years, though, Sina seemed to be more often and more deeply irritated with him. Sometimes it seemed like he could do nothing right. Their marriage had changed with the move back to Samoa. In San Francisco they had been a happy enough American couple isolated in their own little world inside the big city, but back in Samoa, they had drawn apart into their separate social worlds. Apelu had his work and his sphere of male friends. Sina had her job at the shipping company, her church, and her various women's *komitis*. Apelu knew she had a thing for the new young pastor. Now Sina was more a working mother and church lady than a wife. And, of course, there were the kids, four of them now, not just the one boy they had back in San Francisco. Sanele was fifteen now, entering that dense-as-it-gets phase. Now there were also his two little chubby angels—Sarah was ten and Isabel was eight—and three-year-old Toby. Tobias was the unplanned child and Sina's special pet.

Apelu didn't know what he could do differently, how he could change things for the better. In San Francisco they used to go out dancing. It had been years since they had done that. Now Sina had her bingo games three nights a week. From the gossip she brought home, it would seem that a primary conversation topic with her women friends was complaints about husbands.

Sex had become infrequent and routine for them, filling more a physical than an emotional need. In spite of the distance that had grown between them, Apelu still cared for his wife. But where once it had seemed that they shared the same brain, now he often found himself watching her, wondering what she was thinking, and wondering who she was. He had never been unfaithful to her, though he sometimes wondered if that might only be because secret liaisons seldom stayed secret for long here in Samoa.

Although his male acquaintances rarely spoke of their wives, it seemed much the same for all of them. Their brides had become the mothers of their children, and lust had given way to the tug-of-war of living together. Walking on air had become walking on eggshells. And for both husbands and wives, the comfort zones in their lives had become the company of their same-sex peers.

At the airport while checking in, Apelu was displeased but not surprised that Mati was checking in too. As they waited for their plane—an old twin-prop twenty-passenger DeHavilland Twin Otter that made the half-hour trips between the neighboring islands—Mati chatted about his previous travel adventures, nothing that rose too far above the mundane. Apelu only pretended to listen, thinking about Sina and about how he had wanted to make it right before he left. But he knew from many years of various degrees of trying how impossible that was when she went this way, that his trying would only have made things worse and threatened her somehow, like attacking something when it was only an egg before it had had a chance to grow its essential defenses. Fight or flight, he thought, as he strapped himself into his seat across the narrow aisle from Mati, who looked nervous and had stopped talking. It turned out that Mati had never flown in a small plane before. The copilot's rushed and rote instructions over the crackling PA system about seat belts, smoking, and flotation devices were unintelligible, even though they could see him reading them into his tiny microphone a mere ten feet away. Within a minute or two they were airborne, banking west.

Apelu remembered his first small-plane flight, out of some little private-plane airport east of Oakland, headed for Lake Tahoe. He had been sixteen. Auntie Sia had needed him to fill in for a gone-missing fire knife dancer in a special New Year's Eve show she had booked at a casino there. Apelu was on Christmas break so his mom had given the okay. It had been freezing cold inside that plane, a single-prop six-seater. Aside from himself and the pilot, there were only two other passengers, two very skinny chorus girls who spent the whole trip huddled together under a blanket in the back. The pilot let Apelu sit in the copilot's seat, showed him how to put on the earphones and mike and how they worked. The plane was old, and from the beginning, the pilot was worried about ice building up on the wings. They flew low, beneath the cloud cover, following the Sacramento River Valley through the Coastal Range then across the gray Central Valley, while rain streamed off the windshield. When they hit the foothills of the Sierras, the pilot stuck to the valleys, just below the icy ceiling, until all Apelu could see out his window were walls of tall pine trees, their tops hidden in mist. Apelu remembered the pilot's almost constant litany of swear words as the plane banked and dove, banked and rose again, searching for gaps between ridgelines and the clouds' steel-colored floor above them. It was like being a bird. Apelu had never felt so full, so alive. He could have swooped there forever. He stepped out of the plane onto the snow-frozen tarmac at Tahoe a different person from the boy who had boarded the plane. And, as though to confirm that transformation, that trip to Tahoe was the first time that Apelu had gotten laid.

It was one of his sister's dancer friends. That night, during the finale of the show, he had burned his hands trying to put his torch knives out. The rags he had been given to smother the flames must have been used to wipe up spilled kerosene when the knife head's fabric had been soaked. Apelu had run outside to plunge his hands into the snow to chill them. The girl—she was just a girl, only a year or two older than he was—had followed him out, concerned. They had ended up fucking in a snow drift beyond the edge of the parking lot's lights, her on top while his back melted a hole into the snow. Apelu loved flying in small planes.

In Apia, Apelu and Mati took a taxi from the airport to an inexpensive hotel Apelu knew on the edge of the waterfront. Mati had never been to Apia before. Over the years Apelu had been in and out of Apia many times—on family business or on quick getaway vacations with Sina, whose mother's family was from there—but never on department work. Apelu liked Apia. It was relatively cosmopolitan compared to Pago Pago. There was a real downtown centered on Beach Road surrounded by leafy urban neighborhoods sprawling up into the hills behind the town. There were tourist hotels and nightclubs with live bands. There were restaurants and bars and cheap taxis. Apia was a capital, as opposed to Pago's frontier town. It was also third-world inexpensive. The exchange rate between the Western Samoan *tala* and the US dollar was almost three to one.

It was late in the afternoon when they checked in. The rooms at this hotel were big, if simply furnished, and meant for traveling families. Each room had at least three double beds but little else. Apelu and Mati took a room together, so that Apelu could pocket much of his per diem that could've been used toward a more expensive single room. Mati said he was exhausted, chose a bed in a corner as his, and went to sleep. Apelu got a call through to his house and left his Apia phone number with one of his daughters, having her write it down then read it back to him. Sina was out. His daughter wasn't sure where.

Sarah and Isabel always played a game on the phone with him; they spoke only in English and tried to sound like the same TV cartoon character, so that Apelu couldn't be sure which daughter he was talking to. That was the point of the game. It always kept him on the line longer as he tried to determine—by one trick or another—if it was Sarah or Isabel he was speaking with. Those girls were always together. They weren't twins—Sarah was two years older—but they might as well have been. They lived a part of their lives in a separate world of their own making. S-and-I-ville, Sina and Apelu called it. "Where are the girls?" "In the back, in S-and-I-ville." One trick Apelu had learned was to get them to laugh. Isabel giggled; Sarah snorted. But then they had learned to get on the phone together. He could imagine them in the kitchen, their little heads pressed in on either side of the receiver, taking turns talking in their shared cartoon voice. They always called him Popo, which they couldn't say in their disguised voice. This time he tricked them by asking what they wanted him to bring back for them from Apia.

"Candy!" said one, dropping the silly accent.

"A dress!" said the other.

"Okay, Sarah, I'll bring you some candy, and, Izzy, I'll bring you a dress. Be nice to your mama, and I'll be back in a day or two." Then Apelu did his version of their cartoon voice to tell them he loved them because they were so silly, and they insisted that he was the silly one.

Apelu took a shower, shaved, and changed. Mati was snoring when he left. Over the ocean the sky was still bright with the end of sunset. There was a stiff on-shore breeze. He walked.

The ten-thousand-crowd noise of mynah birds in the tall twisting plane trees over Beach Road was suitably raucous as the early evening traffic of taxis and sedans raced by. At least they drove on the right side of the road, Apelu thought, thanks to the Germans. A hundred years before, when Eastern Samoa had ended up in America's Yankee watch pocket, Western Samoa—and the other four inhabited islands in the archipelago—had been tucked under Deutschland's paternal eagle's wing. Germany was one of those imperial powers that had recognized—unlike the USA— that being a good colonialist was primarily a matter of enhanced bureaucratic suffocation. Even their copra plantations stretched out in perfect straight lines of coconut trees in every direction as far as the eye could see. Then, at the start of the First World War, New Zealand troops, backed by the British Navy, had seized the place without a shot being fired. For the next almost fifty years, the Kiwis ruled here in a manner that would have made the Nazis proud, including a nasty dash of racism they had learned while trying to annihilate the native Maori back in New Zealand during the preceding century. It wasn't until 1962 that the western islands finally won independence to become one of the poorest countries in the world. New Zealanders still dissed the place by habitually mispronouncing the name of its capital, placing the emphasis on the first, rather than the second, vowel in Apia.

Apelu wasn't sure where he was headed; he was just out with a clean shirt on and some money in his pocket. He wouldn't mind hearing some music, but it was still early. A century before, Apia had earned a reputation as a sailor's South Seas port. Beach Road had been famous for its sins, saloons, and financial monkey business. Pirates like Bully Hayes had called it home. It had never quite lost that illicit tingle, in spite of all the Christian churches now fronting on the harbor. There was still that sense of being in a place where the potent interface between western wealth and jungle poverty always simmered near the surface, where dirt-poor side streets emptied onto fluorescent glass and burnished metal avenues, and where things officially forbidden had only to be casually asked for. Once, in the middle of the day, only a block or two off Beach Road, Apelu had been surrounded by two gangs in a bloody conflict—a gang of town dogs and a gang of town pigs. They had swirled and snapped and screamed around his legs until he was spattered with their blood. Taxis honked at them to get through. The dogs lost, the pigs won.

Apelu stopped for a beer at an old open-air saloon downtown across the road from the harbor. It was a place he remembered well, and it hadn't changed. A draft Vailima—the local beer—was cold and cheap. The other patrons were all locals—it wasn't a touristy place—clerks and office workers having an after-work beer and some laughs. The tables were sticky and carved with initials. The overused dart boards were chewed up. Regulars reigned at the pool tables. There was a Tom Jones song playing, the only thing in English to be heard. It soon gave way to one by Joe Cocker, but no one seemed to notice, and the noise level remained the same.

Apelu sipped his beer and felt the rare peacefulness of ano-nymity. Being nobody was an opportunity that an islander at home was seldom offered. Someone always knew who you were or knew your family or pieces of stories about you—what *palangis* called gossip but really wasn't. Within the enclosed and entangled world of island society no one was given the freedom of being a stranger. Even in the bush there were no secrets. There was an old proverb about that—*Ua lauliloa e pili ma se*, which roughly means, "It is known by every lizard and stick insect." Secrets weren't things that no one knew; they were things that no one needed to talk about. You were defined by how your story was woven into the larger writhing, evolving narrative of who everyone was, like a strand of *lau `ie* plaited into a fine mat, appearing and vanishing, but held in place by the other strands around you as surely as you enmeshed them. It was not a world given to self-definition. Not even the crazies were allowed to be outcasts.

Within the first ten minutes, Apelu had exchanged greetings and pleasantries with five different people he had never met before. By the time he ordered his second Vailima, he was in a discussion with a young man about junk food. The chap was ordering a round of drinks for his table and was disappointed that there was no more *oka,* raw fish in coconut cream, to order. He had to take a couple of bags of fried breadfruit chips instead and complained that they never filled him up. He paid for Apelu's beer along with the rest and invited him over to his table out by the sidewalk.

There were four other people at the table—two women and two men. Apelu introduced himself and almost immediately forgot all their names. They were all well-dressed young professionals. Apelu's arrival—there was an extra chair—barely interrupted the flow of their conversation. One of the women, part-Chinese with an array of gold bracelets on her slender arms, was making a point about something to one of the men. She wore stylish gold-rimmed glasses and at regular intervals of around twenty seconds she would push the glasses back up the diminutive bridge of her nose with the index finger of her left hand—no wedding ring, no engagement ring. There was something unintentionally pugnacious about the gesture that appealed to Apelu. The end of her presentation—the point of which Apelu had missed—was greeted with unanimous laughter, including the laughing concession of the man she had been addressing, who held his hands up in front of him in surrender. Everyone took a drink. The other woman gave a little you-go-girl punch to the shoulder of the part-Chinese woman, whose eyes were now on Apelu.

"So, Apelu...right? Apelu, over from Pago on a visit?" she said, pushing her glasses back up her nose.

"Yes, that's right. How did you know?"

"The Reeboks, the haircut, the fact that you're Samoan and we have never seen you before. What brings you?"

"Oh, business," Apelu said.

"What kind of business? If I might ask," she said as she moved empty bottles aside on the table to make room for another round of drinks arriving.

"Police business," Apelu said. That response was guaranteed to drive a conversation off the road, but what the hell, thought Apelu, he didn't feel like lying about it, and he had nothing to hide. There was a silence around the table as if everyone was busy examining their consciences or adjusting their self-editing machines.

"Well, we're in the same industry," she said. "I'm a lawyer, with the Department of Justice. What are you working on?"

"Smuggling."

The other people at the table were getting ready to leave, rushing their drinks, looking at wristwatches.

"Lisa, you coming?" the man she had been haranguing asked, standing up.

"Yes, I'm with you," she said, getting her briefcase and purse, looking around her, then standing up. The others were leaving. "Party to go to," she said. She stopped and fumbled a few seconds in her briefcase before producing a business card and handing it to Apelu. "Give me a call," she said, "about smuggling." The others had waved down two taxis, and they all left. Her card, with the seal of the Western Samoa Department of Justice on it, said her name was Lisa Ah Chong.

Apelu sat alone at the table and sipped his beer. Most of the last round of drinks had been only partly drunk. The table was covered with empty and half-empty bottles and glasses. For some reason it was the custom here for the waiters and waitresses to leave all the empties on the table, as if to announce how much this group of people could afford to drink. He knew no one would come and clear the table until he had left. He sat there and listened to the music—Willie Nelson and Waylon Jennings now—and thought that the people on the sidewalk passing by and looking in must think he was very rich and very drunk.

Apelu ate dinner alone that night at a small, out-of-the-way Indian restaurant he was glad to find was still there. On his way back to his hotel there was a new bar called the VIP Lounge at an old bar's location out toward the darkened end of Beach Road. He stopped for a nightcap. It was a karaoke place now, but no one was singing along. On a big TV screen a Japanese woman was walking through a park looking wistful, as below her on the screen the English lyrics of "Will You Still Love Me Tomorrow?" were turning word by word from yellow to white. But the music was turned down so low that the conversational drone of the bar patrons drowned it out. Apelu sat at the bar and ordered a brandy straight. All they had was Christian Brothers, so he asked for a glass of ice to pour it over. Another karaoke video started on the TV set behind the bar, but Apelu turned his back on it to look out through the wide veranda at the street. At this end of Beach Road, outside the business district, there was little traffic that time of night, just an occasional taxi racing by. He could smell the ocean across the road.

Seated like that, Apelu was the first person in the bar to see her as she appeared out of the dark of the road and crossed the veranda into the light. She was tall and dark-skinned, with thick black Samoan hair. She was wearing a simple black sort of evening dress, but she was barefoot and walked like a woman not aware she was wearing an evening dress. She walked—at her own pace, neither hurried nor concerned—as if she were coming into a village from the bush or out of some historic photograph of how Samoan women had once looked. She was quite striking. She walked up to the bar a few stools down from Apelu and without sitting ordered a rum and Coke. No one else in the bar seemed to take any special notice of her. When her drink came, she too turned her back to the bar. She remained standing. Apelu didn't see her pay for her drink.

"It is a beautiful evening," she said in Samoan.

Apelu knew she was talking to him. "Yes, it is," he said.

She looked at him, then came over to stand a barstool away from his. "I've never seen you here before."

"It's been a while since I've been here," Apelu said.

"You're not much of a drinker, are you?" she said, glancing at his now drained glass of ice cubes.

"Just one before bedtime," Apelu said, feeling quickly foolish and slightly intimidated.

"You were a fire knife dancer once, weren't you?" she said, still looking at him.

"Yes, a long time ago. How did you know?"

"I could tell from the scars on your hands and arms. My brother was a fire knife dancer and had the same scars."

Apelu forced a smile and resisted the impulse to look at his hands. "A long time ago," was all he could manage.

"It is a young man's occupation," she said.

"And you? Are you also an entertainer?" Apelu asked, looking her full in the face for the first time, a young face that for a moment turned very old with anger, then went young again and smiled.

"Oh no, not me. I've never been an entertainer. What do you do now that you are no longer a dancer?"

Earlier it had been easy to tell the truth about his occupation—I'm a cop—but this time Apelu wasn't sure he wanted the conversation to end so abruptly. "Import export," he said.

She turned around to face the bar, leaned on it, and gently put down her now empty glass. "You son of a pig," she said. "You washed-up carrion of a useless fish, you offspring of incest." Her Samoan words were precise and biting, but not loud. "You insult me and incense me with your lies." This was now loud enough so that other patrons were turning to watch. "People like you, you many-faced people, are not worthy." Her voice was now loud enough to quell conversation throughout the bar. There was enough silence now that Apelu could hear the karaoke machine playing "Pretty Woman." "Fuck you and fuck everyone like you. You're a fucking cop!" And she turned and left, disappeared across the veranda and into the dark of the road.

"I guess you pissed her off, buddy," the bartender said. "Nice work."

Then the first rock hit the sheet metal roof of the bar, then another, then one smashed into in an empty table on the veranda, then more hit the roof. They could hear her screaming Samoan obscenities from the dark beach side of the road. Apelu looked at the bartender.

"Like I said, you pissed her off, copper," the bartender said.

"Aren't you going to call the police?" Apelu asked.

"She'll be gone long before they could get here," he said.

The barrage of stones and swear words lasted another minute or two, then abruptly halted.

"Uli was angry tonight," the bartender said to the room as a whole. Some of the regulars nodded their agreement. Couples began to get up and leave. Apelu followed them out. His temples pounded all the way back to his hotel.

CHAPTER 5

——————— o ———————

POLICEMEN IN APIA WORE TAILORED, GRAYISH-BLUE POLYES-ter uniforms—a lavalava, a jacket, and a very British Colonial-looking topi-like helmet, all the same color. It gave them a very conservative, keepers-of-the-peace look—more like museum or palace guards, though, than like the quasi-military American model. Members of the force—in full, hot uniform plus white gloves, with their helmet straps fastened firmly beneath their chins, and shiny sterling whistles clasped firmly in their teeth—directed downtown traffic from low-rise podiums in the center of the hubbub at the major intersections along Beach Road. Maestros of vehicular confusion amid blue clouds of not-fully-combusted leaded gas exhaust from trucks and buses and taxis, they orchestrated the daily chaos with heroic élan. Apelu was glad that duty was not part of his job description.

Mati and Apelu were in a taxi caught in the morning rush-hour congestion. They were headed for police headquarters. Apelu had decided, but hadn't told Mati, that after they got set up with the records they needed to check, he was going to slip away. There were a few items on his to-do list that he would rather do alone. Besides, Apelu was no good with numbers. Too much concentrating on numbers made him physically dizzy. Apelu liked to think it was just a physical malady like motion sickness, but he knew that its roots had to be psychological. He didn't want to go there. He'd leave Mati checking the numbers.

That wasn't that hard to do as it turned out. Mati was happy to do all the lot and stock number searching alone, preferred it actually. At police headquarters Mati turned on his boyish charm, and within an hour Apelu was able to leave without anyone especially noticing or minding. Mati was set up at a desk, and people were bringing him ledgers and files.

Apelu caught a taxi to the small village outside Apia where, years before, Ezra had been given his title. There were still some Strands listed in the telephone directory with that village as their address. He had the taxi driver drop him off at the gas station-store-lumber yard that was the major business in the village. He went into the store and bought a soda and a manapua, sweetened pork inside a rice flower bun. There was a bench out front, and he sat there to eat it. It didn't take Apelu long to find out where the Strand place was and get directions. He walked there because it wasn't far. Apelu had been told to look for a white *palangi*-style house, set back from the road.

He was standing in front of such a house now, but it was more than just a *palangi*-style house. It was an old, once-white, Victorian *palangi*-style house. It had curlicues and fretwork along its eaves and a slightly sway-floored porch with latticework railings. A grass track ran from a break in a wall of hibiscus along the road to the house's front steps. The yard of randomly spaced, isolated fruit trees and flowering bushes was well tended. Orchids grew from the half husks of old coconuts stuck in low tree notches. As he walked toward the house, Apelu could see a small, open-walled Samoan *fale* off to one side. As he came to the front steps he stopped and called out a traditional Samoan greeting.

The Samoan voice that answered seemed to come from the house itself, rather than from an occupant of the house. The voice was strong, pleasant, feminine, elderly, and surprised. "Is that someone calling? Now, who could that be? They know they are welcome here. Whoever you are, I am honored. Come in, come in."

A young girl of maybe seven or eight came running through the house to hold the screen door open for him. The inside of the house was the opposite of the outside of the house. The outside had been *palangi* rococo, but the inside was Samoan simple—woven pandanus mats on the floor, no furniture aside from a few venerable old trunks, all the windows open to the air and the light, and nothing on the walls. There was a smell of old wood and flowers. The young girl smiled, skipped down the hall to a doorway on her right, and gestured Apelu there. Seated cross-legged in the middle of the floor was an old woman. She was washing her hands in a porcelain pot of water beside her. The water was charcoal colored. In front of her on the mat was a piece of *siapo*—fine bark cloth—onto which she had been painting an intricate geometric design using pandanus seed brushes. Beside her knee there was a half-coconut-shell bowl with her ink in it. If it was the same as what Apelu's grandmother used to use, the ink was made from water, tree bark squeezings, and candlenut ashes. Her long white hair was held back by a plastic tortoiseshell comb.

"Sit, sit," she said. She dried her hands on a tea towel and pushed the bowl and towel aside. The young girl came and took them away. "What a pleasure to have a handsome young man come to visit me. How shall I call you?"

"Apelu," he said. "Apelu Soifua."

She was wearing a sun-faded blue-and-white cotton muumuu. Her face was a study of wrinkles. There was a sprig of flowering *moso'oi* behind one ear. She had beautiful dentures. "Such a wonderful name, Apelu Soifua!"

She pulled a pack of Rothmans and a cigarette lighter out of her muumuu pocket, took one, offered one to Apelu, then allowed Apelu to light their cigarettes. The young girl appeared with an old tuna can ashtray. Apelu admired the old woman's handiwork. The girl came with two opened drinking nuts cradled in chipped tin mugs, then returned with a plate of sugary store-bought biscuits. They talked as the girl sat watching them from the doorway.

The woman's name was Apolima Ti`ifau Strand. She was old enough to forget her exact number of years. This had been her husband's parents' house before it had been hers. She had been a widow for almost thirty years now. Lotteries supplied her only sense of the future. She wanted nothing to do with organized religion. The young girl was "just some scamp" that she "put up with." The young girl smiled at the compliment of being mentioned at all.

Apelu asked about Ezra. When was the last time she had seen him?

The old lady smiled at the cigarette between her ink-stained crooked fingers. "Ezra," she said and shook her head. "Is Ezra in trouble again?"

Apelu didn't answer.

"The last time I saw Ezra was at a funeral over on Tutuila," she said. "He was on crutches. That would have been Auntie Luisa's funeral, at least ten years ago, maybe longer. What's he done now?"

"He shot up a police car," Apelu said.

"Mercy. Over there?"

"That's right. At his home in Piapiatele."

"Too many ghosts out there," the old lady said. She was losing interest. She motioned for the girl to come and take the biscuits away. They had gone untouched and flies were now buzzing around them. "Why ask me about Ezra?" she asked.

"I was wondering about his visits here, his business dealings, if you knew of any of his friends or business associates he had here." Apelu now offered the old lady one of his cigarettes, which she turned down.

"I wouldn't know anything about any of that," she said. "Ezra and our side of the family were never close. Especially after he married that woman."

"Dorothea?" Apelu asked.

"No, not Dorothea, whoever that is. That little oriental whore."

"Leilani?"

"Yes, her."

They were interrupted by the sound of a van pulling into the yard and its door slamming shut.

"That would be Siaosi," she said.

The young girl jumped up and ran to the back of the house.

It was barely ten in the morning, but Siaosi was already seriously drunk. He stumbled through the screen door and down the hall, stopping and steadying himself with a hand on the doorjamb of the room they were sitting in.

"Mama," he started, "I need—" Then he saw Apelu seated there and stopped and stared, trying to focus, wavering a bit. The odor of alcohol filled the room. He was not an attractive example of the human race. He was big but not tall. His face was puffy and scarred by old boils. He was balding, which was rare among Samoans. Below his lavalava his calves and feet were diabetes-blue and swollen. "Wha?" he said.

"What is it, Siaosi? Can't you see I have a visitor?" the old lady said matter-of-factly.

Siaosi had managed to focus in on Apelu's pack of Marlboro Light 100s and his cigarette lighter on the mat beside the ashtray. With considerably more grace than Apelu would have anticipated possible, Siaosi sat himself down and reached for the pack of cigarettes. "A visitor, huh?" he said, lighting one. "What sort of visitor? American smokes, heh?" Siaosi's red eyes looked at Apelu. His look carried no meaning.

"Apelu here just stopped by to inquire about your Uncle Ezra. Now if you could leave us alone, that would be nice," the old lady said. Apelu noticed that as she spoke she was busy moving pieces of *siapo* and ink bowl and mugs behind her, away from her son, the way one would move things out of a toddler's harm's way.

"Uncle Ezra? Fuck Uncle Ezra!" Siaosi said. "Who the hell are you to come here and ask about that piece of dirt?" He was enjoying his cigarette. "This is my house, my land. You have no right to come here and mention that crap's name."

"Siaosi, behave yourself now," the old lady snapped.

"No. Who the hell does this guy think he is to come into my house and say shit like that? I ought to punch his teeth in for even saying that name here. What are you, some sort of pimp or pervert, you faggot?" His Marlboro Light 100 was only half finished but Siaosi stubbed it out clumsily, knocking over the tuna can of ashes and butts. "Fuck you. Get the fuck out of my house before I hurt you."

Siaosi was trying to get to his feet, but Apelu was standing before he got anywhere close. "Don't get up. I'm leaving," Apelu said, picking up his cigarettes. Siaosi was still trying to get up onto one knee. With a firm hand on one of his shoulders, Apelu forced him back down onto the mat. "I said stay there. Don't move." Apelu gave him a shove and Siaosi rolled drunkenly onto his side with a groan, then had trouble getting back upright.

"Thank you for your hospitality, Apolima," Apelu said, bending down to take her hand and touch his cheek to hers.

"You are welcome, Apelu. Come back again," she said, squeezing his hand.

Siaosi had gotten himself upright enough to punch Apelu in the side. "And you can tell that still-born miscarriage of a boss of yours Schneider to go fuck himself too. Uncle Ezra and Billy Schneider, fucking shark bait. Right, Mama?"

"Shut up, Siaosi. You are worse than your father. Good-bye now, Apelu."

Walking back to the gas station, Apelu rubbed his ribs where Siaosi had punched him. It had been a good shot. He stopped and pulled a small pad and a pen from his pocket and wrote down the name Billy Schneider the way he had heard it. He had no idea who Billy Schneider might be or what his connection to Ezra might be or why Siaosi would assume he was Apelu's boss. Just the ranting of a brain-damaged drunk? And why would Apolima call sweet Leilani a whore when she had been married to Ezra for, like, forever? This was all history, deep family history of earlier battles and bad blood that would go back years and probably had nothing to do with what Apelu had hoped to learn about Ezra's suspected smuggling operation.

Back at the store he bought a bag of rice, a can of Crown corned beef, and a ridiculously expensive can of salted peanuts and asked for them to be delivered to Apolima Strand. Apelu figured that with those good fake choppers she might enjoy the peanuts. He waited on the bench in the shade for a taxi headed back to town, and soon enough one came. His side ached. He went to light a cigarette and realized that Siaosi had taken his lighter.

At Strand's General Merchandise Store near the central market downtown Apelu found two more of Ezra's distant relatives. They were both considerably less interested in the object of Apelu's inquiries than Siaosi had been. One expressed surprise that Ezra was still alive. They knew nothing, but at least they were polite about it. He bought a new cigarette lighter there.

Apelu checked in on Mati at headquarters to see if he wanted to get some lunch, but Mati was already eating with his new friends—Styrofoam take-out plates of barbecue chicken with taro and bananas in coconut cream, a six-pack of orange soda pop. Apelu asked Mati if he needed help with the number checking, but Mati insisted he had plenty of help and that everything was under control. Apelu went back to the hotel and had a light lunch in the bistro downstairs.

Sina was on his mind, so back in the room he called his home number. Nobody answered. The muscles around his ribs where Siaosi had nailed him were cramping up. He hoped he didn't have a cracked rib. He took a long hot shower. That helped. Then, sitting on his bed with just a towel wrapped around his waist, he dialed the number on Lisa Ah Chong's business card.

The first Chinese—all men—had been brought to the island basically as indentured slaves back in the early colonial days. If they had not been claimed outright as property by some planter or business, they might as well have been. A handful of the really hardened ones hung on, got a little business going, found Samoan families with enough extra daughters so that they could have one, then worked themselves to death creating a commercial niche for their half-caste kids to get their toe into and raise themselves up. The Samoans didn't especially mind. Those kids and their kids and their kids' kids were Samoans now, with just slightly different eyes and family names that were at least simpler to say than the other new German, English, and European family names. The surnames of those few original Chinese merchant families could now be seen on business signs throughout the town. They had been efficiently absorbed, not marginalized. There was no Chinatown.

Lisa was in but was busy until four. Could he stop by then? Sure. Apelu put on a lavalava and a T-shirt and went down to the small bar in the bistro to get a double shot of Korbel for his ribs, drank it back in his room, then took a nap.

The period of German occupation before the First World War had not left much of an architectural imprint upon Apia. Wood is not the medium for leaving monuments in the tropics, and wood had been all there was to build with. There was one remaining notable exception—the old courthouse on Beach Road at the corner of `Ifi`ifi Street. It had been the German colonial administration building and had somehow survived the termites, rot, neglect, and hurricanes. A rambling, two-story, filigreed, steep-gabled, veranda-jutting, and crumbling reminder of an eclipsed idea, it stood surrounded now by cement curbs and parking slots, looking lonesome for an era of horse traffic. Its cubicle warren of shabby offices now housed not only the High Court but also the Department of Justice and various other government agencies.

The corner of `Ifi`ifi Street and Beach Road was a landmark in Samoan history. It was at this intersection in 1929 that the Samoan independence leader Tupua Tamasese and fifty-eight of his supporters, while leading a peaceful protest march, had been shot and machine-gunned by the occupying New Zealand police force. Paramount Chief Tamasese had died a slow and painful death from his wounds, to the end urging his people to avoid further bloodshed and continue their nonviolent campaign for independence. Apelu knew all about Tamasese because Apelu's mother, the peacekeeper, had been related to his family, and Tamasese had been her hero. Tamasese's Gandhiesque pacifism was part of Apelu's genetic identity.

Apelu, dressed now in slacks and an aloha shirt, stood on the curb at the corner of `Ifi`ifi and looked up the street at the old police headquarters building. The second-floor veranda where the machine gun had been mounted was still there, the line of fire still unimpeded. It was raining a light misty rain, and the roads were full with end-of-work traffic. Whenever he came to Apia, he always stopped here and studied the seven-decades-old crime scene. It always made him think of his mother, dead now for more than a dozen years, and her telling and retelling the story of that day, Black Saturday.

None of the office doors inside the courthouse were marked and, it being after office hours, the building was virtually deserted. Apelu knocked on a dozen gray doors before finally getting an interior answer. Lisa let him into her small, cramped office filled with piles of journals, books, and files. The screen of a laptop computer cast a bluish light behind her desk.

"Good security measure," Apelu said.

"What's that?" Lisa asked, moving behind her desk to close what she had been working at on the computer.

"Not having numbers or names on any of the doors. It would take a hit man far too long to find his victim."

Lisa laughed. It was a good laugh, sharp and quick. "Oh good," she said, "our detective has the mind of a hit man. The fact is that nobody enters this building except under dire necessity, so they just have to find their own way. Quite Kafka."

"I guess," Apelu said, still standing by the door. "I've never understood what people meant when they said that."

"Said what?" Lisa said, looking up at him with a slight smile.

"Kafka, Kafkaesque, whatever," Apelu said. "I know it means more than weird, but I'm not sure in which direction."

"Think nightmare," she said, "one of those frustrating nightmares."

"Okay. Like where the corridors keep changing and clerks are always losing your papers?"

"Right, and nobody knows who you are." She shut down her machine. "Let's talk here, if you don't mind. Please sit down. Hand me that." She had motioned him to a chair where her briefcase was sitting. "Thanks. I guess first off I should ask you for some identification, so that I'm sure whom I'm talking to. A policeman, not a hit man."

Apelu pulled out of his pants pocket the case with his badge and ID and handed it to her. She copied down his name and badge number and handed the case back to Apelu.

"You said you were here in Apia on a smuggling case investigation. I didn't think it usual for you people to expand your investigations here." She said it just like a lawyer.

"It's not—usual, that is—but this is a case that involves checking a lot of numbers in your police department's records. As a courtesy, your department let our department come over to do the boring work."

"You don't strike me as a man of numbers, Detective." She was still lawyering.

"Well, we don't have many of those, so I had to make do, and I've got someone to help."

"A team of investigators?" She raised an eyebrow as she pushed her glasses back up her little nose. "Might I ask from whom you received permission to conduct an investigation here, outside your jurisdiction?" Now she sounded more like a prosecutor than just a plain lawyer.

"I just pull the assignments, ma'am, I don't make the arrangements. I believe it was set up between my commissioner and your Public Safety Department." Now Apelu felt like he was a witness, a hostile witness.

"Exactly what kind of smuggling are you investigating?"

"Retail goods, cigarettes and the like. We have reason to believe that some items we apprehended may not only have been smuggled out of here but were also stolen goods. Hence the cooperation." Apelu noticed that he was sitting up in his chair as he would in a court witness stand—back straight, both feet on the floor, elbows all the way back on the arms of the chair, hands clasped in front of him.

"Any luck?"

"I don't know, ma'am. We just started today, and I haven't checked in with my cohort yet."

"Apelu...may I call you Apelu? Apelu, would you please stop calling me ma'am? Call me Lisa."

"Well, you are coming on sort of hard-nosed for us to be on a first-name basis."

"Was I?"

"Yes."

"I just wanted to get...I only wished to establish in my mind your...qualifications, your official position, so that I could judge whether I could...confide in you or not." Lisa was standing now, and Apelu could tell that she wanted to pace, but there was no room to pace. When she stood up, Apelu relaxed a little in his chair.

"Actually, Apelu, when we met last night so fortuitously, it crossed my mind to enlist you for some assistance. I hope I haven't foreclosed on that opportunity by being too hard-nosed."

"I like the way you talk," he said. "What's the favor?"

"I'm afraid it involves more checking of records," she said.

"Not numbers, I hope."

"No, not numbers." She sat back down at her desk and picked up a legal-size file folder. "This also has to do with smuggling of sorts, but we're not talking cigarettes, we're talking young women."

There were eight names on the list that Lisa showed Apelu, all women's names, all between eighteen and twenty-one years old. All of them had departed Western Samoa for American Samoa months before on thirty-day visitor's permits. None of them had returned.

"It started from a single inquiry from a concerned parent," Lisa said. "Immigration ran a check to see if the girl had returned and just hadn't gone back to her village, but they could find no record of her returning."

"How did they do that?" Apelu asked.

"You know those entry forms you have to fill in whenever you come here? Well, every day someone over at Immigration types up a list of that day's entrants. Or at least they're supposed to. They went through those lists for the months she'd been missing."

"That sounds like a lot of checking."

"Those Immigration guys don't have much to do. Most of the time they're just sitting around waiting for the next flight. Anyway, when nothing turned up, the mother of the girl came to see me to see what she could do about finding her daughter, which is not much really. But I got curious and ran an ad in the *Observer* asking other people or families with similar concerns about overstayers in American Samoa to contact the Department of Justice. Not many people came forward, but that didn't surprise us. It is a bit like turning in a member of your family. They are technically breaking American Samoa law by overstaying. But these additional seven young women stood out because they fit the same profile as the first girl."

"Which is?"

"Sex, age, recruited as short-term domestic help, gone missing."

"You had them checked against Immigration's returnee's lists?"

"Yes, and their names weren't there." Lisa took the list back from Apelu and put it back in the file folder.

"And you want me to…?" Apelu asked.

"Do a little checking for me. Your Immigration people have been no help at all. They say there are so many Western Samoan overstayers that they can't be concerned about just a handful. We know that for every thirty-day visitor's permit issued there has to be an American Samoan sponsor, but we don't have those sponsors' names and your guys won't release them to us. I want to know what happened to these women." Lisa didn't sound like a lawyer anymore. This had become personal.

The immigration problems between the two Samoas, like so many other problems, went back to policies put in place during colonial days. From the very beginning the governors of German Samoa and the governors of American Samoa had tried to limit movement between the two parts of the once-contiguous-now-divided archipelago. Those efforts and all subsequent efforts to establish an artificial, political, people-proof border had never fully succeeded because the Samoans themselves never embraced the idea. There was but one language, one culture, one social order across all the islands. New barriers weren't going to change that. There were always ways around *palangi* regulations, especially when it was Samoans who were supposed to enforce them. For Samoans family came first, and abstract government rules were so far down the list as to be practically meaningless. There were even more *palangi* rules and regs now. Like anything artificial they inspired little respect. All they did was create another underworld, like smuggling, where such exchanges still occurred but under a cloak of deceit that was not so much cynical as realistic, not so much evil as necessary. Not that deceit, the need for deceit, was a good thing. It wasn't. It rewarded people who shouldn't be rewarded. It left deep shadows where eight young women could disappear.

Apelu took Ms. Ah Chong's list of missing persons and said he would look into it as soon as he got back. She still seemed uncertain about trusting him, but she thanked him. He found his own way out.

CHAPTER 6

―――――― o ――――――

FOR SOME REASON IT ALWAYS SEEMED HOTTER IN APIA THAN anywhere else in the islands. More buildings and cement perhaps, or maybe it was the traffic exhaust that filmed on your sweat. There wasn't a breeze, and the earlier light rain steamed off the still-hot pavement. Apelu took a taxi back to the hotel. It was too early to eat, and he could use another shower.

Mati was waiting for him at a sidewalk table outside the hotel's bistro, drinking Vailimas with two women Apelu recognized from police headquarters. Mati was dressed in swim trunks and a short-sleeved shirt, flip-flops on his feet. Beside him on a chair was one of their hotel room's towels.

"There you are," Mati said, standing up. "We were just about to leave without you. Bloody hot. We're going for a swim. Want to come along?" Because Apelu had been introduced to the women already that morning, he was not introduced again. They said hello, and he said hello back but didn't come close to giving them names.

"No, I don't think so, Mati. Thanks. Just a shower and a lie-down for me. Where are you going?"

"I don't know, some beach out near Agnes's house," Mati said, picking up his towel. "Well, we're off then."

Apelu shook hands with the women and said "*Tofa*," and they were gone, taking the taxi that he had pulled up in.

Back in the room, after taking a shower and stretching his cramped-up ribs under the hot water, Apelu discovered that someone had gone through his things. It wasn't anything obvious, but when he unzipped his unlocked bag for clean clothes something was amiss, not as he had left it. He wasn't sure what at first. Nothing seemed missing. He checked for his passport, ticket, and American cash that he had stashed at the bottom of the bag, and they were still there, but now the bills were tucked into the back of the passport. He was sure he hadn't done that. He searched for the ring of keys that he had just tossed in there—not needing them while not at home—and couldn't find them. Then he saw them on the carpet beside where his bag had been.

Well, it wasn't a thief or his passport and cash would be gone, Apelu figured. So that left Mati. Somehow that was an easy leap to make, and getting payback seemed not only fair play but a necessary chess move. Mati's luggage was locked, but Apelu picked the cheap latch easily with the file point of his fingernail clippers. Mati had brought more clothes than Apelu had, including a very nice pair of expensive Italian loafers. From a side net pouch Apelu pulled out Mati's passport and return ticket and a large stash of cash, then put it all back just as he had found it. He felt through the clothes without unpacking them—nothing. As he was putting the fancy Italian loafers back in place, Apelu noticed that one shoe seemed slightly lighter than the other. From the toe of the heavier shoe he pulled out a nicely tooled black leather case. Inside it was a small gold badge and a picture ID: Matthew Sparks, Special Agent, Federal Bureau of Investigation. Apelu made sure that everything was put back just as he had found it, the latch relocked. So, Mati was someone else altogether.

The question of whether or not the FBI's jurisdiction extended to American Samoa had never been reasonably resolved. It was one of those quandaries left over from the colonial muddle the US had made of the place. The territory's "unincorporated and unorganized" status basically meant that though it may be a possession of the United States, it was not a part of the United States. Citizens of American Samoa were not US citizens, but US nationals, whatever that meant aside from the fact that they could not vote for the president. The president technically "owned" the territory because the US Congress had never ratified a proper treaty incorporating it into the US system. American Samoans had their own separate constitution that differed in several significant ways from the US Constitution. They even had their own separate immigration system and immigration laws. The place was outside the borders of any federal court district. The relationship was quite confused, which was the way the Samoans liked it.

In any event, in the past the FBI had pretty much treated American Samoa as they would a foreign country. They knew their federal warrants could not be legally served there, and there really wasn't much of anything going down worthy of their investigation. Apelu could remember only two instances since he had been on the force when the feds had snatched someone out of the territory and whisked them back to Honolulu, to US soil, to be formally charged—just as they occasionally kidnapped dope dealers out of Mexico or Colombia. Both of those cases had involved non-Samoan federal fugitives, most-wanted types. Both of those times the federal agents had enlisted the assistance of the local police in the take-down. But otherwise there had been no FBI presence in American Samoa. Or at least Apelu had never heard about it. And he would have heard. At least part of the reason for the FBI's past efforts to cooperate had to be the fact that they knew they weren't welcome in American Samoa, and that they were on shaky legal ground in an almost foreign land.

Apelu sat by himself at one of the bistro's outside tables and listened. It was sundown and still no breeze. Beside the hotel was a vacant stretch of land filled with the bunch grasses, thistles, weed trees, and low shrubs that were always the first to reclaim once-cleared land. That time of day it was rich with birdsong. The bird chorus here was different than that of back home. Even though only fifty miles of open ocean separated the most proximate points of this island and his island, there were a few different species of birds here, and the mix of songs and calls was like another avian language. They had the *Miti* here, for instance, the Polynesian Triller, which was totally absent from Tutuila. Its insistent chatter and trilling runs seemed to intimidate the other birds and altered their songs.

Then a mynah bird fight broke out. A half dozen of them swooped down onto a grassy hummock near the center of the empty lot. One of them, for whatever mynah bird reason, was on the outs with the rest. In appearance there was no difference among any of the birds—black head, dark stocky body, and those distinctive flashes of white on the spread tail and wings. One of the group kept picking a fight with the bird on the outs—a lot of jumping and squawking with wings flapping. Whenever the outsider was getting the worst of it, the other birds would duck in for a screech and a quick peck. Then they would all stop and for a minute or two act like an all-friends family of identical birds on a peaceful lawn. Apelu figured that these breaks were a genetically dictated pause for a mutual predator check. Then they would start in all over again on the outsider. Apelu had to watch closely to see if it was the same bird that always got picked on. Because they were so identical, the birds could get confused in the melee. But it was always the same bird, he was sure. What had it done? Where had it arrived from to make it the enemy? Apelu wondered. Of course Mati would want to keep his true job a secret—and Apelu would let him keep it that way—but what was the job that called for him to be there at all? Why had he flown into their flock?

That night, Apelu again had dinner as a party of one. When he returned from dinner, Mati had come and gone, judging from his wet swim trunks in the shower and the discarded short-sleeve shirt on his bed. Apelu wondered if he was wearing his fancy loafers, then took several of the pain pills he had packed and went to bed. He had trouble getting comfortable. Maybe Siaosi had cracked a rib, after all. Apelu awoke when Mati returned late, smelling of beer, cigarette smoke, and poor perfume. But Apelu didn't let on that he had awakened, and he went quickly back to the dream he was having of being on stage and singing a song whose words he had to make up as he went along. It was a country-and-western song.

In the morning Mati said he was close to being done with his checking, that he had a few calls to make to some wholesalers and importers, but that he ought to have it wrapped up by the end of the day. He still didn't need any help with it. He asked how Apelu's investigations were going, and Apelu said fine, that he too should be done today. They agreed to fly back late that afternoon, if they could get a flight. Mati said he would look into the reservations, as he would be at a desk with a phone all day. The two most upscale hotels in Apia were Aggie Grey's and the Tusitala. They anchored the opposite ends of Beach Road's run through the town area. That morning, Apelu visited both of them.

The Tusitala was only a short walk back toward town from their hotel, so Apelu walked there and had breakfast in their swank poolside restaurant, reading the morning paper, starting with all the crime and trial stories. The paper, the *Observer,* was quite different from his hometown *News.* It was more professional and cosmopolitan, with more regional and international coverage. It was also a bit more risqué. In an article about a manslaughter trial, a defense witness, identified as a transvestite bartender, was quoted as testifying that the manslaughter victim—later whacked and stomped to death by the defendant, the bar's bouncer—had drunkenly ordered four beers, refused to pay for them, then "stood up on the bar, unzipped, and told me to suck his dick." That was language that would never appear in the *News*. It didn't say whether she had complied with this order or not.

After breakfast Apelu stopped at the front desk and inquired if his old friend Leilani Strand was registered there. She was not. In the lobby gift shop he bought a bottle of pain pills and a bottle of water to wash a bunch down. He caught a taxi to Aggie Grey's, asked the same question, and got the same answer. But as he turned to leave a manager-type man called him back.

"Who was it you were asking for, sir?" the man asked.

"Leilani Strand, an old dear friend," Apelu said. "I heard she was in Apia and thought she might be staying here."

"I thought that was the name I overheard. Mrs. Strand was staying with us, but she checked out a few days ago. However, she did leave a telephone number where she could be reached. She was expecting you to stop by."

"She was expecting me?" Apelu asked.

"Well, she said a young man might stop by inquiring after her. I assume that would be you." The man had stopped searching for the number and looked up at Apelu.

"Yes, that would be me. She's a clever old gal," Apelu said.

"That she is, sir, that she is. Here we are." He handed Apelu a sheet of hotel notepaper. On it in a very nice hand was written Leilani and a six-digit local telephone number.

"Thank you," Apelu said. "May I?" gesturing toward the lobby phone.

"Of course."

The taxi driver knew the place. It was one of the larger estates in a plush enclave in the foothills above the town. Apelu had been invited to lunch.

"That's the place," the driver said as they cruised past a stop sign at a well-shaded intersection. All Apelu could see was a high stone wall running in both directions from the opposite corner. "A corner of it, anyway." About a quarter of a mile farther down the road there was a break in the wall with a gate that the driver got out to open then shut behind them. The driveway was two smooth ribbons of cement with grass growing between them. It curved along the edge of a wood, around a large sloping lawn, then rose through a high hedge of hibiscus. When it appeared, the house was a bit of a surprise—low, ranch-style, very Southern Californian, hidden behind banks of more hibiscus and beneath overarching mimosa trees. Off to one side was a long garage.

This was the house of the daughter of one of the highest-ranking families in the islands. Her father had been one of the founders of the new state after independence. Her name was one of those twenty-letter chiefly extravaganzas, but everyone called her Gigi. Apelu had spoken to her when he called from the hotel, not giving his name but just identifying himself as a friend asking for Leilani.

"Oh yes, Leilani's friend. She's been waiting for you to call. You must come up for lunch. Leilani is out just now, but she'll be back shortly. Do come up. I'm afraid I have an engagement else-where, but Leilani would love to see you." And she gave him the directions that turned out to be unnecessary.

At the time he didn't know with whom he was speaking. It wasn't until he started to give the taxi driver the directions, and he said, "Oh, the Ali`ivao place," that he started to put it together.

The house girl who came out to meet the taxi was Fijian and quite beautiful. Apelu stood outside the passenger-side door of the taxi, fumbling with the foreign bills and coins trying to pay the driver and give him a proper tip. As always, the accounting flustered him, and her quizzical smile as she watched him didn't help. Her teeth were very white, her dark lips were very full. He felt underdressed and out of place. The taxi driver handed him a slip of paper with his phone number on it, so that he could call him later when he needed a ride back down to town, any time. The Fijian girl showed him to a chair on the patio beside a glass table and brought him an iced tea in a tall glass. The words of the Rolling Stones' song "Brown Sugar" started repeating themselves in his head along with the chord progressions. She disappeared back into the shadows of the house, still smiling.

From where he was sitting Apelu could see the ocean's horizon beyond the trees. It was empty. It was very blue. It sparkled. He listened to the song inside his head, Jagger's voice, Wyman's solid bass line. He bobbed his head to the music and smiled at himself for being so obvious.

"Willie, so good of you to come." It was Leilani's soft, lilting voice coming from behind him. Apelu turned, distracted from his fantasy but still smiling.

"Oh, I'm sorry. It's not Willie at all, is it? Is that you, Apelu?" Leilani had stopped short, and her diminutive left hand with numerous rings covered her delicate collarbones. "Oh my, Apelu. What are you doing here in Apia?"

Apelu immediately stood and went over to her, put his hands on her shoulders, and bent down to press his right cheek against hers. "*Talofa*, Auntie Leilani. How are you? I didn't mean to surprise you like that, but I was over here on business and wanted just to say hello. We miss you in Pago."

"I wish I could say the same about Tutuila, but it's much lovelier here, don't you think?" Leilani had recomposed herself. The Fijian beauty had reappeared with an iced tea for Leilani. Leilani and Apelu sat at the round glass table.

"This is a fine spot," Apelu said.

"How are Sina and the children?" Leilani asked, patting him once on his forearm. The conversation turned that way for a while. Then Apelu asked if she had heard anything from Ezra recently.

"Why no, I haven't, Apelu, not in some time."

"Did you know that Ezra was in jail?" Apelu asked.

"Oh." Leilani spread her diminutive hands out on the table and stared at them. Apelu wondered whether she was seeing the gold there or the skin beneath the gold. "No, Apelu, I didn't know." More staring at her hands, which she now allowed to touch. Her hands were like strangers, thumbs delicately feeling each other out, hesitant fingertips caressing rings on the opposite hand. "I hadn't heard. Poor Ezra. Perhaps he's better off there. I'm sure the other prisoners will treat him well. He's such a legend."

"He seems content," Apelu said.

"He doesn't eat much," Leilani said, "but, oh my, he must get his cranberry juice. There's no telling what might happen if Ezra doesn't get his cranberry juice. Would you look into that for me, Apelu? Make sure Ezra gets all the cranberry juice he wants. They wouldn't have that at the jail, would they?"

"No, ma'am, but I'll make sure he has a steady supply."

"He can get quite...angry without it, you know."

"No, I didn't know, ma'am."

"Oh yes. A doctor once prescribed it for his mood swings. Ezra swears by it."

"And T-bone steaks?" Apelu asked, fishing.

"Oh no, Ezra can't have any of that. No red meat. Doctor's orders. Don't get him anything like that, Apelu."

The Fijian girl returned with their lunch—large papaya halves filled with a lightly curried seafood salad, thick chips of deep-fried breadfruit, more iced tea. They ate in silence. Leilani had a healthy appetite for a bona fide little old lady, and she ate like one of Apelu's growing daughters—bowed over her food, intent on how each bite was assembled and delivered. Her eyes never left the skirmish field of her plate until she was done, pushed her plate away, dabbed her lips with a victory napkin, and took a polite sip of tea.

"So, who is this Willie whose wonderful lunch I have just consumed?" Apelu asked, also pushing his plate away, at which signal the Fijian girl came and removed them. She leaned close to Apelu when she did so, brushing his shoulder with her breast, giving him her scent for just a moment.

"Oh, just the son of an old friend, who was supposed to be in town and was supposed to come up and say hello. He'll show up one of these days. Young people. But it is such a delight and a surprise to have you here, Apelu. Young Willie and I can have lunch another day."

"Willie Schneider?" Apelu asked, still fishing.

"Why yes. Do you know him? Fine young man."

"No, I haven't met him, but I've heard of him. Import/export business isn't it? What he's in?"

"Oh, I wouldn't know, Apelu. Young people these days are involved with so many different things. Who knows? Not like the old days. My father was never anything but a fisherman, and all I've ever done was dance."

"Maybe people were better at what they did when they only did one thing," Apelu said, watching the unchanging horizon.

"Well, have you ever been anything but a policeman?" Leilani motioned something to the Fijian girl in the shadows of the house.

"Okay, right. But I don't think of myself as a cop the way you think of yourself as a dancer or the way your father thought of himself as a fisherman. It's just an occupation I accidentally fell into. It's a job, a nine-to-fiver, a paycheck I can't afford to give up. And actually I once was a fire knife dancer when I was young, remember?"

The Fijian girl reappeared with a tray bearing a one-liter bottle of Vailima and two frosted glasses. Apelu glanced at her once then looked away. She was much too attractive, and her soft smile seemed to both mock him and invite him at the same time. He stared at the horizon as she poured their beers and he didn't turn back to the table until she had left.

"So, do you still think of yourself as that, a fire knife dancer?" Leilani asked, taking a sip of lager.

"No, that's gone, like being a high school football player. Now I'm just a farmer who can't support his family from farming, who has a day job for the government, which happens to be in the police department."

There was the sound of a car approaching, then a British racing green Land Rover drove slowly past them all the way to the garage. Apelu had never met Gigi and was rather looking forward to it, when a man of about his own age emerged alone from the driver's-side seat. He was tall with black hair and dark skin, but you could tell from his facial bones that he had *palangi* blood in him. He didn't seem to have seen them sitting there in the shadow of the patio. He opened one of the garage doors, then garaged the Rover. He came out of the garage carrying several plastic shopping bags, put them down, pulled his key chain out of his pocket, and clicked it. The Rover answered with a lock-up beep. He closed the garage door, picked up his bags, and headed for the back of the house. He was conservatively dressed in gray slacks and a blue polo shirt. He was trim enough to look good in it.

Leilani called out to him, "Werner. Oh, Werner."

The man turned and saw them. "Auntie Lani. I'll be right there." Then he went into the house through a back door.

"Do you know Werner, Gigi's husband?" Leilani asked.

"No, I don't. We've never met," Apelu said.

"He makes her so happy. She's a different woman since they've been together." Leilani refilled their beer glasses, finishing the bottle. "You'll like him. He's not at all stuffy."

Werner opened the patio's sliding screen door with his elbow. In one hand he held a fresh liter of beer, in the other his own frosted glass. He closed the screen door with his heel behind him.

"Auntie, we're going to take the rest of the day off." Werner spoke in English, an English that in its youth had been marinated in the open, half-Cockney accents of Auckland boarding schools. "Life is too bloody short, and the beer is cold. Hello," he said to Apelu, putting down the bottle and glass on the tray, "I'm Werner Gottlieb." And he stretched his right hand across the table.

Apelu had stood as Werner approached and leaned forward to shake the extended hand. The Germans had left behind few genetic souvenirs of their colonial decades here, the Gottlieb clan being one of the rare exceptions, notable for the fact that after four generations of intermarriage, few of them had sunk very much below their originator's elevated social class. A large commercial building on Beach Road bore the family name. A recent Miss South Pacific had been a Gottlieb. Apelu remembered her photograph, could see the family resemblance in Werner. Apelu introduced himself, and they sat down.

"Apelu came to tell me that Ezra is in jail," Leilani said calmly.

"Bloody hell. You don't say?" Werner was pouring himself a beer. "What's the old coot been up to now?"

"A couple of weapons charges. He's been taking potshots at visitors," Apelu said.

"Serves them right for wanting to visit him." Werner seemed unsympathetic. Leilani said nothing. "So, Apelu, you over from Pago? Business?"

"Apelu is with the police department," Leilani said.

"Then you must be here on holiday. We don't allow any crime here."

"Actually, I'm here investigating a possible smuggling case," Apelu said. "Leilani, do you have any idea why Ezra would have all those cases of motor oil, perfume, cigarettes, music CDs, and all stored at your house?"

"Why, I have no idea what you are talking about, Apelu. All those cases of what?"

"Cases of stuff he obviously didn't need."

"In the house at Piapiatele?" Leilani asked, tilting her head to look at him.

"That's right."

"Well, I'm clueless," she said. "Except that Ezra had gotten the idea at one point of opening some sort of retail store, but Ezra gets all sorts of crazy ideas he never follows up on. I figured that was one of them."

"Maybe that explains it," Apelu said and took a sip of beer.

"You think that old Ezra was into smuggling?" Werner sounded incredulous. He raised both eyebrows as he looked at Apelu. "That would involve other people trusting him, and frankly—sorry, Auntie—no one in their right mind would trust old Ez."

"You're probably right. It does seem incredible," Apelu agreed.

A phone rang in the house and was answered. The Fijian girl came to the screen door and said, "Mr. G, it's for you." Werner excused himself and went into the house, taking his beer. In his absence there was silence. It was as if the possibility for polite conversation had been canceled somehow.

When Werner returned he asked Apelu if he needed a ride into town. He had to go back. Something had come up. Apelu accepted, but first he had to use the loo. Werner walked him into the house and pointed the way.

As he washed his hands, Apelu could hear their voices, so when he opened the door to leave, he did so slowly. Through the partly opened door he could see an angle of the kitchen down the hall where the voices were coming from. He saw the Fijian girl walking away, then Werner following her, grabbing her by the elbow and turning her around.

"What if I don't just do that?" she said to his face.

"I'm telling you leave it alone, leave it to me," Werner said.

She looked at him defiantly. He put a hand on her waist that slipped familiarly down onto her buttock.

"Let me take care of it," Werner said softly.

Apelu gently reclosed the door, counted to four, then reopened it loudly, waited for another two count, then emerged. Werner was standing in the kitchen doorway. The girl was gone.

"Ready?" Werner asked.

CHAPTER 7

———— o ————

B Y SUNDOWN APELU WAS HOME. THE TRANSITION HAD BEEN uneventful. Werner had said next to nothing on the speedy trip back to town. He had dropped Apelu at police headquarters, where he reconnected with Mati, who had them booked on the three o'clock plane back to Tutuila. A taxi to the hotel to check out and get their things, another taxi to Fagali`i in time to catch their flight, then another taxi to his house. Mati hadn't had much to say either, thankfully.

At home, the kids were glad to see him and Apelu felt like a shit because he hadn't remembered to bring them anything from Apia. He hadn't gotten a present for Sina either, but that didn't matter so much because she was still acting chilly. But in bed that night she moved close to him and curled along his back and in that way she had reached over his hip to touch him and make him hard, wrapping her fingers around him as if his cock were a giant bolt she was trying to unscrew from his groin, stopping to reach down and roll his balls in her palm, then returning to his shaft, coaxing him out of his foreskin, squeezing and turning him. In automatic and welcome response Apelu rolled onto his side to embrace her, return her attentions, when a sword of flame flashed from his rib cage up to his shoulder and his neck. An involuntary gasp of pain escaped his open mouth and he rolled farther over onto his side, pushing Sina away, searching for a position that would give him respite.

"What?" Sina said.

"Ah ahh ah, jezus," he said and twisted his torso about trying to make it right again. His cock went limp in her hand.

"What is wrong with you?" Sina asked, letting go of him.

He was in too much pain to explain. All he could think about was the pain. "Ah, fuck," he said and rolled away from her, seeking comfort. The moment of reconciliation was broken. Sina went instantly *musu* again, She didn't want to hear any explanations. Apelu was in too much torment to offer one. He was thinking about whether or not he should make a trip to the emergency room. As Apelu hugged his side and rolled away, Sina slipped from the bed and then the room. Too late Apelu called out her name to try to explain, but she was gone.

Apelu awoke late after a difficult night to an empty house. School day, everyone gone. His side was vaguely better, a constant ache but no shooting pains until he sat up to get out of bed. In the bathroom medicine chest he found a bottle of Extra Strength Tylenol and took three. He decided against trying to shower. Getting dressed took a while. Sina had taken the pickup truck, so he walked up to the road to catch a jitney bus to town and work. He was late.

The captain followed Apelu to his desk. "Nice vacation?" he asked.

"Productive, I think." Apelu sat down and pulled a report form and a pen out of his desk drawer.

"Don't get too comfortable. The commissioner wants to see you."

"Know why?"

"Didn't say."

"When?"

"Better get up there now."

Apelu didn't really know the commissioner. He was new to the job and new to the department. The previous commissioner had left under a bit of a political cloud a year or so before, and this one had been brought in out of left field. His previous position had been as director of the Department of Parks and Recreation. He seemed like an okay guy, but he wasn't a cop; he was a politician.

The commissioner's office took up about a third of the second floor of headquarters. Its reception area was twice the size of CID's squad room. The commissioner was there, sitting on the edge of his secretary's desk with a cup of coffee, joking around with his office staff. He was finishing a story about a shark, a squid, and a fisherman with elephantiasis of the testicles. The punch line wasn't that funny, but everyone laughed, the commissioner most of all.

"Sergeant Soifua," he said, "come into my office."

Apelu followed him into his vast inner office and closed the door behind them.

"Soifua, when I agreed to send you over to Apia I didn't know that I would have hell to pay for it." The commissioner's Samoan, like his jokes, was crude. "What in the name of a pig's cunt were you doing over there?"

"Just the smuggling investigation I was okayed for," Apelu said.

"Well, it's out of my hands now. The attorney general wants to see you and he's asked for an internal investigation."

"Into what?" The shooting pains had returned to Apelu's side.

"I guess we'll find out sooner than later, but for now you're suspended, leave with full pay, until this gets sorted out. Any questions?"

"Plenty."

The commissioner had stood and turned to end the conversation, but Apelu refused to stand up.

"You are dismissed, Sergeant. Get your sorry ass out of my office."

From the commissioner's office Apelu went to the assistant commissioner's office, but he wasn't in. Then he went to his captain's office.

The captain was just hanging up the phone. "The commissioner says you're on suspension and that you should go see the AG and see if you can get this straightened out."

"You don't know what this is about?" Apelu's anger was rising. If this had anything to do with Mati, he would break his sneaking back, FBI or not.

"Something to do with your Apia vacation is all I can figure. But get over to the AG's and see what he's got to say. I guess you don't have to report to work until I hear different."

"Well, this sucks," Apelu said, feeling suddenly helpless, and a twang of pain shot up his side. He cringed and bent over.

"What's wrong with you?" The captain seemed almost concerned.

"Nothing," Apelu said. "Nothing."

The attorney general wasn't in either. Apelu made his secretary write down that he had come to see him and the time.

"When will he be back?" Apelu wanted to know.

"He's in court. I can't say." The AG's secretary was short, round, and professionally unfriendly.

Apelu walked to the shipping agent's office where Sina worked. He stuck his head in the door and told Sina—and the other women working there—that he needed the pickup truck but would have it back in a couple of hours. He didn't give her a chance to respond. He took the truck and drove to Shimamatsu's store and bought four large bottles of cranberry juice, and then he drove out to the prison in Tafuna and dropped the juice off with the warden, telling him it was essential that Ezra get the juice right away. Then he drove around for a while, stewing, at a loss to figure out what was going on.

Back at the AG's office, the AG was out to lunch. Apelu said that he would wait and sat down on a broken-springed couch in the reception area. On the wall he was facing was a gallery of photographs of all the attorneys general of the past twenty years, *palangi* then Samoan, ending with the current AG, all of them political appointees, none elected. Apelu knew the current AG by reputation only—one of those sons of a ranking family who had been sent off to college on the mainland and returned with a law degree and an enhanced sense of entitlement. He was one of their native son success stories—a dedicated golfer, a cautious prosecutor, a bit of a ladies man, a political comer with an eye for higher office.

When the AG came through the outer door and cut across the reception area toward his office, Apelu stood and followed him.

"Sir," the secretary said as her boss swept by her, "there is someone waiting to see you."

The AG paused long enough to ask, "Who?" and long enough for Apelu to be just off his right shoulder when he turned to look.

"Detective Sergeant Soifua," Apelu said about a hand span from his face.

The AG took a startled step backward then another to his office door. "Come in, Sergeant," he said.

The AG circled immediately behind his desk and was on the phone, summoning assistance to his office. "Have a seat, Sergeant," he said as he hung up, but neither of them sat. Apelu moved away from the door before it opened and two large Samoan men came through it.

"Sit down," the AG said again, taking his seat behind the substantial desk covered with piles of files. The two men took positions by the door, their hands folded in front of them like guards, and Apelu found a chair where he could watch them.

"Sergeant Soifua, are you aware that the United States of America has a Department of State and that the Department of State has a consulate in the independent state of Western Samoa?"

"Yes," Apelu said.

"Then are you also aware that any and all dealings, especially legal dealings, between our government and the government of Western Samoa must be managed on a diplomatic level between the US Consulate in Apia and the responsible parties in the Western Samoan government?"

"I don't know what that means to me," Apelu said.

"It means that by conducting a criminal investigation in the independent state of Western Samoa you have, without any vested authority, overstepped and transgressed treaty agreements between our two countries."

"I didn't know it meant anything like that, and I was only following orders."

"I have seen no written authorization, directions, or requests for permission for your extraordinary activities, Sergeant."

"The Western Samoa police had no problems with our investigation."

"This transcends being a police matter. You have violated tenets of international law. This is a sensitive and serious allegation. It impinges upon questions of diplomatic reciprocity and yet to be achieved agreements of jurisdiction and extradition."

"It was the assistant commissioner's idea. The commissioner and my CID captain agreed to it."

"The assistant commissioner is off-island at present and not here to supply his side of the story. And as for the commissioner and your captain, I have reason to believe that they only thought your trip was a short vacation perk for a veteran officer, not that you would become the cause of an international incident."

"An international incident?" Apelu's voice rose just as he did from his chair. One of the men took a step toward him.

"And there is also the matter of reports of your public drunkenness in Apia, your involvement in a public civic disturbance involving property damage and terroristic threatening at a drinking establishment called the VIP Lounge, and your association with a Miss Ulifanua Malolo, a known underworld figure."

"What the fuck are you talking about?" Apelu was now standing in front of the AG's desk and his voice was loud. Both of the men at the door came toward him, and the AG pushed himself in his chair backward from the desk.

"I'd advise you to get a lawyer, Sergeant, and prepare for an extended dose of litigation, the specifics of which you will be served with in due time by this office. And I would hope you will cooperate fully with your department's own internal investigation by turning over any notes and records of your activities in Apia." The AG was gripping the arms of his chair as he seemed to recite this, staring at Apelu. "You can go."

One of the men took Apelu's elbow to lead him away, but he jerked his arm loose. "What about your man Mati, Investigator Sparks? He was there with me. Wasn't his presence your office's mark of approval for our investigation?"

"Tavita?" the AG asked one of the men.

"Sparks has been on vacation the past week, sir. He said he was going off-island. He's not due back until Monday," the man who hadn't grabbed Apelu answered.

"On assignment?" the AG asked.

"No, on leave."

"And I think you had better leave, Sergeant," the AG said, "before you get yourself into more trouble than you are already in with false accusations."

The AG's goon took his elbow again and again Apelu jerked it away, but he left, peaceably, shaking his head.

Apelu didn't return the truck to Sina. She could get home without it. First he drove home and found Lisa Ah Chong's business card. The line the AG was taking sounded familiar. He was lucky and caught her in her office. He was surprised when she recognized his voice before he could introduce himself.

"Surely you don't have news for me already, Apelu?"

"I'm not sure if this is news to you or not, Lisa, but I'm in trouble over here, and it sounds suspiciously like what you were quizzing me about."

"Trouble? What kind of trouble?"

Apelu decided not to tell her about the suspension. "An investigation by the attorney general's office into what I was doing in Apia and what international laws I may have been breaking by doing so. I was just wondering if you had shared your concerns about that with anyone else."

There was a silent pause. "You mean, did I rat on you to my superiors?" Lisa sounded a little pissed.

"Something like that, yeah." Apelu tapped a cigarette out of his pack and lit it. Sina had declared the house a smoke-free zone, but he was in a rules-breaking mood.

"Listen, Apelu, I do not appreciate that suggestion. We may not have hit it off, but I'm not going to go out of my way to get you in trouble, especially seeing as I haven't been exactly kosher by enlisting your assistance. Nobody else knows about our little meeting. As far as I know, nobody else in this department even knows you were over here or what you were doing."

"How about your friends at the table that night?"

"Only one of them works here, and he's in contracts. He wouldn't have noticed if you were carrying two dead babies."

"Well, somebody got a complaint to the AG and fast."

"I can't believe anybody here would want to make a big deal over it. For one thing it would also get the people here who cooperated with you in trouble."

"So, you don't know anything about this?" Apelu stretched the cord on the kitchen wall phone to the max so that he could flick his cigarette ash into the sink.

"No, I don't, Apelu. Goddamn it." There was another silent pause, but Apelu didn't fill it. "Listen, Apelu, I'm sorry if you've got your thing in a wringer, but I had nothing to do with it." Another silence. "Apelu? You there?"

"Yeah, I'm here." Pause. "I believe you."

"Oh, thanks."

"But could you sort of snoop around, see where all this is coming from?" Apelu turned on the kitchen sink faucet to put out his cigarette.

"I'll see what I can see." Lisa didn't sound terribly enthusiastic. "Can you still look into that list of names for me? Or does this…?"

"No, no, I'll follow up on that for you." I'll have plenty of time on my hands, Apelu thought.

"So, how can I reach you if I find anything out?" Lisa asked.

"No, don't reach me. I'll reach you. I'll call you back in a few days when I find something out. Listen, Lisa, no hard feelings. I'm just trying to figure this all out. I thought maybe you had to file a report or something or that someone may have asked you about me. Just trying to figure it out, that's all."

"All right. I guess." Pause. "If you can't reach me at this number, try me at home." And Lisa gave him her home phone number. Apelu wrote it down on the back of her business card.

Then Apelu went for another ride. He hit the back roads that he seldom drove on—the dirt tracks off the ends of the asphalt, the gravel ruts that dead-ended at deserted seaside cliffs, the no-exit plantation roads where the grass got so high he had to stop and switch his wheels to four-wheel drive. He drove slowly, as if searching for something. It calmed him.

Late in the afternoon he ended up at the country club bar. There was seldom anyone in there at that time of day. The golfers in their cleats would be drinking at the open-air beer stand downstairs. The lunch crowd had left, and it would be hours before the first dinner cocktail customers would arrive. He had the bar to himself and ordered a Steinlager. In front of him, behind the bar, a plate-glass window ran the length of the counter. The view was out over the back nine holes of the golf course with its occasional tall trophy banyan trees, the island's green mountainous spine beyond, a stretch of white foam-boarded coastline jagging out toward a distant vanishing point, and the ocean.

Apelu recognized the attorney general coming in from the eighteenth green with a couple of other department-head types, but it didn't mean much to him. Apelu was thinking about the mountains, how when he was a kid he and his buddies would escape there for entire days, hunting birds with slingshots, raiding plantations for coconuts and bananas, pretending to all sorts of freedoms, and by living out their pretensions making them real, at least for that day.

Apelu remembered a story his grandmother told. It was meant to scare them, but he, his brothers, and their male cousins loved the story because it offered an alternative, an escape from the lives they knew and sometimes chaffed against. It was the story of the wild man.

The Samoans called him Malua, though that Samoan word couldn't have been his real name because he was a Solomon Islander, a Melanesian, as black as basalt—or as Apelu's grandmother had put it, as black as a hole in the ground in the middle of the night. The story was that back when blackbirders—*palangi* slavers who captured or enticed natives of one island group to be sold as plantation laborers elsewhere in the Pacific—still plied the islands, several Solomon Islanders had escaped from their captors while en route to somewhere else. The escapees ended up on the shores of Tutuila, where they took to the mountain jungles. Over the years two of them either came in from the bush or died, and only a third, Malua, was left in hiding. He survived for twenty years in splendid isolation off what his vast jungle keep offered in abundance. Here was an actual jungle boogeyman in the bush. He was used to frighten a whole generation of Samoan children into fearful social compliance. Apelu's grandmother had been one of those children, and she kept the boogeyman alive in her stories long after his capture and death.

For Apelu and his childhood mates Malua was still there in the mountains—him or someone like him, an offspring maybe. In the bush you always felt like someone was watching you. With a Malua there that someone took on form, drama, meaning. When you stopped to glance over your shoulder at a distant movement that you had felt but hadn't seen, when you all froze at the sound of a branch breaking down the hidden canyon, when you came across a track in the bush that you didn't remember being there before—their causes had an embodiment, a name, a mystery attached to them. Sometimes they would pretend to search for Malua's campsites—an excuse for exploring beyond the ridgelines and valleys they already knew. Sometimes Apelu still dreamed he was Malua, a barefoot wild man for whom the deepest bush was like a playground through which he could glide like a barracuda across a reef face or swoop like an owl from ridgeline to ridgeline. He was the ultimate outsider, lone survivor, someone needing no one but himself, secure in his solitary powers. That childhood fantasy entertained him now as he sat at the bar and watched the darkness deepen in the mountain clefts. He saw himself sitting on a thick mat of new-cut leaves on his ledge of a camp high in the back of one of those valleys, watching the light show of another day dying on the expanse of the ocean below, sipping...what? A fresh drinking coconut? Some sort of chunky, syrupy, jungle-made toddy? Apelu ordered another beer. Was part of his fantasy that he would be free of his job and its hassles, free of his bosses and social obligations, free of his marriage, free of all those things that made him feel trapped?

The reality was it was sunset, he had the truck, and Sina would need it soon to get to her bingo game. He drank up, knowing that for the time being at least Sina would not want to—nor need to—know anything about what was happening in either his real or fantasy lives.

CHAPTER 8

───────── ○ ─────────

THAT NIGHT APELU SLEPT ALONE AND VERY UNCOMFORTABLY on the sofa in the front room. He left before first light, before anyone else in the house awoke. He caught a jitney bus to town. He hadn't told Sina, who was still ignoring him, about his suspension. It was strange going into town and not having to go to work. He ate breakfast at a place near the market, then walked to the governor's office building. He was first in line at the Immigration office when it opened its doors. As it happened, he knew the clerk he drew, not well but well enough so that they both pretended that they were old friends. The guy knew that Apelu was a detective, so Apelu didn't have to show his badge or falsely claim that he was there on official business.

"We got a missing person I'm trying to track down. I'm hoping you guys can help," Apelu said.

"How so?"

"Well, it looks like she's an overstayer on a visa from Western. Her family is worried about her. We just need the name of her sponsor so I can follow up on it." Apelu pulled Lisa's folded-up list from his pocket.

"Her family doesn't know who her sponsor is?"

"Seems not." Apelu shook his head, commiserating with the clerk's incredulity. "Is there some form I have to fill out or something?"

"We normally don't give out that sort of information."

"Well, this is a police matter."

"Still." The clerk looked down then left and right. "Wait here." And he went off toward an office whose door had a sign saying Assistant Chief Immigration Officer.

Apelu waited. There were by now half a dozen people in the line behind him. At the next window over, a very fat, very loud woman was waving a fistful of papers in another clerk's face, telling him that he was an idiot, the descendent of famous idiots, and that if she didn't get her appointment with the Immigration Board she would personally make sure that no more idiots would be born in his part of the idiot family. That clerk also disappeared. The lines grew longer. The door to the assistant chief immigration officer's office opened, and a portly bureaucrat in a dress shirt and tie and dress lavalava looked out at Apelu, then the door closed again.

Five minutes later Apelu's clerk returned, carrying a cup of coffee. "Fill in this form with the information you're requesting and I'll pass it along, Apelu. That's the best I can do."

It was the wrong form, but Apelu filled it in as best he could, putting lines through items that didn't apply, adding an explanatory note at the bottom of the page. He only asked about the first girl on Lisa's list, but the clerk noticed the other names and asked about them.

"Yes, those too," Apelu said. "But let's do them one at a time, seeing as it's not normal for you to do this. If you can do it for this one, I'll come back for the others." He knew this was not a time to be pushy.

"Same request? Request for the sponsor's name?" the clerk asked.

"Yeah," Apelu said and looked at him.

"Then give me that list and I'll xerox it, attach it to the form, a blanket request. No reason for you to stand in line every time."

"Okay. That's cool. Let's do that." Apelu handed him Lisa's list, and the clerk went off to make a copy. Maybe this would be easier than he had expected it would be, after all, Apelu thought. He added another note to the bottom of the form, asking for the same information for the names on the attached list. Then he signed the form and gave it to the clerk.

"How long will this take?" Apelu asked.

"If it's approved, it wouldn't take half an hour to pull the names from the files," the clerk said. "They'll give you a call."

"No. That's all right. I'm seldom at my desk at headquarters, and they're no good at taking messages. I'll check back tomorrow. Who should I ask for?"

"Assistant Chief Pouli, I guess." The clerk handed Lisa's list back to Apelu and stapled the copy to the back of the form.

This time Apelu borrowed the pickup without telling Sina. He drove out to Piapiatele, to Ezra's place. Why should he spend his money on cranberry juice for Ezra when he had a whole room full of it?

As he pulled up to the house he could hear the dogs barking back in their kennel. As before, the doors were locked except for the sliding glass door onto the patio. The dogs were still barking. The place looked the same inside until he got to the kitchen. The hallway that had been piled with cases of cranberry juice was empty. He checked the storeroom that had been filled with tins of crackers and boxes of canned fruit—empty. He checked the freezer in the breezeway—all the T-bone steaks were gone. By the time he got to Ezra's bunker it didn't surprise him that it had also been cleaned out of its boxes of booty. The fire knives, though, were still there. Well, the fire knives aren't hot, he thought, then laughed at himself.

Apelu went to the back of the house to check on the dogs. They stopped barking when they saw him and came over to the chain-link fence to slobber on it. He could see that there was water in the tin tub that served as their water dish. The kennel was clean.

"Yo, Nick, yo, Nora," he said. "Howzit with you guys? Back home, huh?"

Nick gave three sharp barks and put a huge paw up on the inside of the gate. Nora flopped down to lick her privates.

"I guess somebody's looking after you. Are you two happy monsters or what?"

Nick gave him a deep back-of-throat rumble and two barks and banged the gate again.

"Can't right now, guy. Ain't got the key." Apelu held up the locked Yale to show the dog.

Nick barked four very precisely timed barks in the imperative voice.

"Sorry, big guy." As Apelu walked away both of the dogs started barking again.

When Apelu rounded the corner of the house Asia was standing there with a shotgun, a familiar-looking shotgun, and once again it was pointed at him. He slowly extended his hands sideways, palms out. "Animal lover, just an innocent animal lover," he said.

"Oh, it's just you," Asia said and lowered the muzzle of the gun.

"Nick and Nora look good," Apelu said, lowering his hands. "Back home."

"They're just too much to deal with out of the kennel. I hate keeping them tied up."

"Why the firepower?" Apelu asked.

"I heard them barking and thought someone was bothering them."

"And…?"

"And some strange stuff has been going on over here."

"Like people coming and going?"

"Yes, that. And I know that Ezra is still in jail because I tried to see him. So I came over here thinking Leilani was home, but it wasn't her, just some men with a truck. I left them alone. Then they came back again later last night. I could tell it was them because the truck sounded the same."

"Bum muffler?"

"Yes."

"Maybe they hit one of those boulders in the road."

"Maybe. What are you doing here? More police work?"

"No. I came to get cranberry juice to take to Ezra."

"He likes cranberry juice."

Apelu nodded toward the shotgun. "Do you think you could put down that gun? It makes me nervous."

"What?" Asia seemed surprised that she was holding a gun. "Oh yeah." And she uncocked the gun and leaned it gingerly against the wall of the house.

"Where did you get the gun?" Apelu asked, walking away from it, hoping Asia would follow him. She did.

"From Ezra, the day you picked him up." She followed Apelu around onto the patio. "After I heard the police car siren that day I came over to see what was going on, and Ezra gave me the gun and a handful of shells and said he would have to be going away for a while and would I mind guarding his house. Leilani and I had been trying to get that gun away from him for some time, so of course I took it. I didn't think I'd have to use it, but thus far I have done a bad job of guarding his house. Did they take a lot?"

"Yes, but nothing personal."

"Did they take the meat?"

"Yes."

"Those were treats for Nick and Nora."

"Sorry. Tell me about the truck."

"It wasn't new. It wasn't that big. I don't know anything about makes and models. The back had wooden sides that looked homemade. The cab was black. They had a lot of blue tarps to cover things with. It didn't have any license plates, at least not on the front. There were four men."

"They weren't police officers?" Apelu asked.

"No, I don't think so, no. No uniforms. Some of them had long hair. There was nothing official about it. No one was marking down what they loaded on the truck. I saw two of them stop and smoke what I took to be a joint the way they passed it back and forth."

"You were hiding?"

"They were scary. You know, without Ezra here anchoring down this end of the cliffs I feel vulnerable. I guess that's why." And Asia nodded back at the shotgun, now looking very benign removed from human hands. "I have to go now. It's just you. I trust you."

"Better take the shotgun," Apelu said. "No point in leaving it here for them to take on their next visit, if there is one."

"Yes, I'll take it. You'll see that Ezra gets his cranberry juice? They won't let me see him." Asia was looking straight at him, and the look of concern in her very blue eyes made her look younger, girlish.

"Got it covered," he said, and her eyes smiled.

"He likes mango *seemoy* too, if you can find any. Ezra's like a kid when it comes to mango *seemoy*."

"I'll see what I can do," he said. Then as she picked up the shotgun and turned to go, "Be careful."

"I'll do that," she said as she walked away. "You can count on it."

There was a stretch of road by the golf course that on occasion became a toad-killing field. The blacktop was spotted with flattened toads. The toads—a large species—were not native to the island. They had been brought in on purpose fifty years before to eat mosquitoes or something. Another bright *palangi* idea. Apelu had heard on the radio that there were now several million of them on the island. And they were everywhere. For some reason they liked to come here to die, get run over. Sometimes at night on this stretch of road you could hear them hopping, banging their heads against your floorboards as you drove through. Suicidal alien amphibians, maybe homesick for their native land. The thing about the toads was that even dead they were poisonous, so nothing, not even scavenging dogs and chickens, would eat them. After a while you learned to ignore them. That day Apelu had trouble ignoring them and found himself trying to drive around their pancaked corpses.

Apelu returned the pickup truck to where Sina had parked it that morning. She probably wouldn't even know it had gone missing. It wasn't lunchtime yet. He walked to headquarters to find out what he had to do for this internal investigation the commissioner wanted. No one seemed to know. The captain hadn't gotten any instructions. The commissioner wasn't in. Nobody else even seemed to know he had been suspended. The captain told him to go home, but he hung around. He had nowhere else to go.

Apelu hung around headquarters the next day too, waiting for the investigation to begin. He tried to contact Mati, but was told that he was still on vacation. He tried to reach Assistant Immigration Chief Pouli and was told he was in a meeting.

The call came in around twelve-thirty when most of the CID officers, including the captain, were at lunch. A body, a floater, had been found beneath a pier at the Marine Railway in Satala. Officer Tupuono was the only one on duty. Officer Tupuono was known for his aversion to corpses. He asked Apelu to come along.

The Ronald Reagan Marine Railway was a facility for hauling the tuna fishing boats out of the water when they needed refurbishing, scraping, and painting. It was called a railway because the ships were hauled out of the bay on floating frames winched up submerged tracks onto the dock. It was not a technologically sophisticated procedure or facility. It was located adjacent to the

SeaKing tuna-packing plant—the territory's sole major industry—on the far side of Pago Pago Bay. It was only a ten minute drive from headquarters. They got there first, well before the EMS crew.

The body was that of a woman, a young woman. She hadn't been in the water long. She wasn't bloated or badly discolored yet. She had been caught at the waist by the lowering tide at the Y-intersection of two I-beams that held up one of the ship-hauling tracks. She drooped there, facedown, her head and feet still in the oil-slicked water. Officer Tupuono took one look and headed off to interview the men who had found her. Apelu sat down at the edge of the dock above the body and lit a cigarette. His side sent out shots of pain. It wasn't his job to haul her out. That was the EMS crew's job. The corpse was wearing a stylish sequined tank top and a pair of denim shorts. Her long black hair was loose and floated up and down with the wave wash. He couldn't see if she was wearing any jewelry because her hands and neck were submerged.

"Nice butt," a voice behind him said.

Apelu looked back over his shoulder. A young Samoan male with a hard hat on was standing there.

"Recognize it?" Apelu asked.

"Can't say particularly, but it's one of the boat girls. That's the outfit."

"Boat girl? You mean a prostitute?"

"Yeah, one of the girls that do the fishermen." The young man gestured with his head toward the banks of long-liner and purse-seiner ships docked four and five deep at the cannery dock.

"You know them?" Apelu held up his pack of cigarettes, offering the guy one. He took it. Apelu handed him his cigarette to light it.

"You mean do I fuck them? No. I don't ever have to pay for it. They only fuck them Asian and Portuguese fishermen on the boats. They almost live there." He sounded disgusted. "Samoan girls too, all Western. Just whores. Nobody knows them. They don't even use their real names. Too *ma*." *Ma* means shame in Samoan, but more than just personal shame, a shame that involves the whole family, chiefs, ancestors, village, and all.

The young man walked away. Apelu sat looking at the body, whose limbs moved with the bay's gentle wash in a graceful and obscene parody of dance. Party girl, Apelu thought, or indentured sex slave? Both? More. A girl with little brothers and sisters she once took care of back in her village, whose white Sunday church dress would be found safely folded and packed away in her meager luggage, who would have sent what money she could hang onto back to her family, pretending she was a nanny or a cleaning girl somewhere. Random phrases and chords of an old Crosby, Stills, Nash, and Young song drifted into his mind with the rhythm of the waves, a song about children and what their parents shouldn't know about them.

The EMS guys arrived. They had to borrow an aluminum outboard skiff from the dock crew to get to her, and she was so wedged in that it took four of them to dislodge her. As they grappled the body into the boat Apelu could see that one side of her face was badly bruised. The EMS guys got her up onto the dock, and before they bagged her Apelu took a look. Aside from the blow to her face there were no other obvious wounds. None of her limbs seemed broken. She had on no jewelry at all, which struck Apelu as strange. Beneath her clothes she was wearing a bra and panties. Her fingernails and toenails were all intricately painted with glittered pink stars.

Apelu patted the pockets of her shorts. They all were empty except her left rear pocket, which held something flat and thin and hard. Apelu borrowed a pair of surgical gloves from an EMS guy to reach into that pocket and he pulled out a soaked Western Samoan passport. He carefully opened it to the ID page, and there smiling out at him was a younger, prettier version of the corpse's face. She had just turned twenty. She was from Vaimoso.

Her name was the same as one of the girls on Lisa's list. He slipped the passport back into her pocket.

"Soifua, what are you doing here?" It was the captain. "You're on suspension, remember?"

Apelu stood up and took off the gloves. "Officer Tupuono throws up on dead people, remember? No one else was around to come out with him."

"Well, get the hell out of here. Where is Tupuono?"

"Here, sir," a voice said from the back of the gathered crowd.

"Wrap her up and get her to the morgue," the captain told the EMS crew. "Everyone else disperse but don't leave the premises. Tupuono, get up here. Soifua, get your ass gone. Now."

Apelu slipped past the police guards now at the gate of the Marine Railway and started to walk back toward headquarters. The road ran along the water's edge. A ways down the road the old naval cemetery climbed up the embankment on the inland side of the road. Apelu stopped, then crossed the road and walked up an unmowed path between the graves. Some were raised and rimmed with cut stone. Some had gravestones, some just engraved slabs set in the weeds. Others were just piles of stones or coral slabs. Years before he had learned where Malua the Wild Man's grave was—a pile of rocks off at the very edge of the burial ground. He went there and sat on the grave for a while, watched the ambulance with the girl's body speed back toward the hospital under full lights and siren, as if its passenger was in a hurry to get somewhere. There was something wrong about all of this.

CHAPTER 9

———————— o ————————

OFF TO THE LEFT IN THE BUSH BEHIND APELU'S HOUSE WAS A church whose major investment in western religion was a high-powered sound amplification system. They managed to—and were allowed to—disturb the public peace of the village several nights a week and Saturday afternoons with their blaringly bad, over-amped, distorted version of Baptist hymns and squalling in tongues. But Sundays were the worst. It started around ten in the morning. Sina and the kids had already left for their church. Apelu, who almost never went to church—baptisms, weddings, and funerals, only because they were entirely too much trouble to skip—was home alone. Sometimes the awful excuse for music seemed louder or more off-tune or more grating than usual. This Sunday morning it seemed especially gruesome. Over the years he had complained to the village mayor and even the church's minister—who as a result had amped down his yelping, hysterical sermons—but the music never got turned down. They had one of those electric keyboards with its variety of idiot rhythm settings that could wander away from the most basic melody. There was an all-female choir under the direction of a maniacal obese contralto who, yelling at the tops of their lungs in praise of an obviously deaf or ear-plugged deity, could not hear themselves well enough to be properly embarrassed. Theirs was the self-righteous assumption that they had the God-given right to inflict this travesty of worship not only on their noncoreligionists in the village but also upon all the birds and beasts and peace of the forest. Friends living more than a mile away complained about it, but there was nothing to be done because the torture was being committed in Jesus's name.

This Sunday morning Apelu hit upon a new plan of attack. He would borrow a decibel meter from the EPA, put on his sergeant's uniform, and go over there to the bush church with a clipboard and take readings. He would take readings in his own backyard as well and keep careful records of times and sound levels. He knew that the territory had no noise abatement ordinance and that even if there were such regs he couldn't get them enforced against a church, but at least he would have evidence. That would make him feel better anyway, and maybe if he was obvious enough he could scare them down a few volume notches, maybe even bring a civil complaint. But that morning there was nothing to be done about it, so he put on the Marshall Tucker Band's *Greatest Hits* album and turned it up loud enough to hear it first at least, though there was no drowning out Jesus.

Between the battle of the bands he almost didn't hear the phone ringing. No telling how long it had been ringing, so he answered it first, then went to turn down the stereo. It was the captain on the phone.

"Soifua?"

"Yes."

"Soifua, you having a fucking party on Sunday morning? Are you sober?"

"I'm sober, Captain. I just had the music turned up to compete with the Church of the Deaf Jesus."

"What? What are you talking about?"

"Nothing, Captain. What's up?"

"Soifua, I've got to talk to you."

"Now? Can't this wait for tomorrow morning?"

"No, I'm afraid not. Can you meet me here at the country club?"

"Got no way to get there, Captain. Wife took the pickup truck to get the kids to church."

"I'll come and get you. Where are you at?"

"Only about ten minutes away, in Leone, across from CJ's Store. I'll walk up there, meet you in the parking lot."

It was less than a quarter mile from Apelu's house to CJ's Store. He changed out of his lavalava into a pair of jeans, flip-flops, and an aloha shirt and hiked up there. His dogs followed him up to the road, where he shooed them back. The captain pulled into the six-car parking lot in his tan, no-longer-new Lincoln Town Car, and Apelu got in. They turned back toward town.

"This makes the CID look like shit, Soifua. And when the division looks like shit my bosses start to think I smell like shit." The captain wasn't looking at Apelu as he drove. "What the hell are you doing, fooling around with them whores?"

"What whores would that be, Captain?" Apelu asked. Now the captain looked at him. Apelu looked back, met his eyes.

"The whores like the one we fished out of the harbor on Friday."

"I didn't have anything to do with that woman except to see her poor body get hauled up onto the dock," Apelu said, watching the road now because the captain wasn't.

"Don't give me that shit, Soifua. You were her immigration sponsor, along with a couple of other girls suspected of working that same occupation."

Apelu kept looking straight ahead. What had been wrong about the whole scene of the dead girl began to focus a little, but it was still strange and unexplained. "That's impossible, Captain. I've never sponsored anyone to come here, much less women I don't know."

"What?" the Captain said.

"You heard me. I don't know what you are talking about. Watch out for that truck." A pickup filled with churchgoers had pulled casually out in front of them. The captain cursed and swerved around them, on a curve, into a luckily empty oncoming lane.

"No, Soifua. We've got the goods on you—signed immigration forms, your name and info, everything."

They drove along in silence for a bit. Apelu didn't know what to say, what to think. The whole thing was ridiculous. It did cross his mind that when Sina heard these allegations—and she would—there would be no way for him to just dismiss them as absurd. Such stories, even if proven untrue, took on a life of their own in her rumor world, where the *ma*, the shame, would taint her reputation even more than his. The captain turned off the main road onto the golf course road.

"Where are we going?" Apelu asked.

"To see if the attorney general is still at the country club. He wants to talk with you. You've made me look like a fool, Soifua. One of my men involved in a prostitution ring, without my knowing it. You inspecting her dead body when you're supposed to be on suspension. Me okaying your little trip to Apia on the department's dime to recruit new girls from that Ulifanua woman. Fuck shit, Soifua. The commissioner is not going to want to hear any of this."

Neither do I, thought Apelu.

The side road into the country club was a washboard of gulleys and potholes, and the captain hit half of them in his haste, but when they got there the AG had already teed-off. His foursome included the commissioner and the publisher of the *Samoa News*. If the captain had been anxious before, he was now nearly apoplectic. He commandeered a golf cart to catch up with them, flashing his badge and making demands. Apelu refused to get in the cart with him and walked away. The captain, swearing and loudly angry, took off up the first fairway, telling Apelu to wait there for him, that he was under arrest for something.

Apelu didn't wait. He left. He walked back up the gullied side road to the blacktop then stopped, looked right then left. His mind and body were very still, the calmness of a captured mouse staring into a boa constrictor's fascinating eyes. It was a sort of catatonia he'd known before, a familiar numbness. In this state, even though everything was totally fucked up and out of his control, his choices were really quite simple—engage or escape, fight or flight. Nothing normal applied any longer. He looked right then left again. Several miles to his right was his home, where he would be found and arrested, trapped in someone else's lie, where his wife could choose not to believe him and not to forgive him. To his left was the unknown, solitude, time for contemplation, Wild Man freedom.

He turned left toward Piapiatele, cutting off the busy road onto side paths as soon as he could, his mind numb, his limbs feeling an energy, an adrenal urgency they hadn't felt in years. When he hit the jungle paths the world became wonderfully still and a new tune, a melody he had never heard before, began taking shape in his head. Its beat matched the rhythm of his steps; its chorus was the calls of the jungle honeyeaters that announced his solitary passage.

It was around noon when Apelu approached Piapiatele. The sky was mostly clear, and it was hot and still in the tunnel-like track he had found that twisted through the high pandanus toward the sound of the surf on the cliffs. At one turn in the trail he had surprised a *manuali'i*, a big purple swamp hen, who screamed an almost human scream, spread its wide but mostly useless wings, and half flew, half crashed away up and then off the trail into the bushes. The *manuali'i* was an ominous and secretive bird. Older Samoans still believed that the bird's appearance augured the death of a chief, and they would attack them with stones on the rare occasions when one would present itself outside its jungle keep. It had startled Apelu out of his dense trek reverie, the tone poem that had shaped in his mind like an armoring anthem. He stopped for his heart to slow down and to recapture the melody—E minor, D major, C.

He approached Ezra's house from the cliffside, keeping the house between himself and the kennel. He did not want to set off the dogs. What he wanted was silence and solitude. Without going near the house he found the sand-filled cup in the cliff where he had sat before, but his body was still too restless to sit. He took off his flip-flops and his sweat-soaked shirt and stashed them under a rock, then he picked his way down and across the cliff face to a shelf he had seen just above the wave break. This was better, closer to the action. He found a spot to sit at the edge of the spray. Why had the girl been killed? How had she gotten there? How had her face been smashed in? Why was the only thing she was carrying—her passport—the last thing someone like her would be carrying? What had she done to deserve such a fate?

Apelu saw the rogue swell rising a good minute before the wave broke. He pressed himself farther back into the hollow he had chosen to sit in until his back was against the rock cliff face. He was sitting cross-legged and he found two outcrops to hang onto. His injured ribs flamed at the effort. The crest of the wave broke five feet above his tucked-down head. The force of it implanted him against the rock. But its retreat was worse than its attack—its suction trying like a banshee to suck the air from his lungs and him from the rock. He almost lost his grip as it pulled his legs out from under him, twisted him. He grabbed a lungful of air before the second, weaker crest in the rogue set hit and he crouched fetus-like, leveraging himself in as many places as possible within the rock. This time it was more like a Jacuzzi of sea-foam, a game the ocean was playing with him. He stood and faced the third, final, and weakest wave of the set, his feet braced and his arms locked against the rock lip above him. It rose only to his knees.

Apelu picked his wet way up the cliff face in the opposite direction from where he had entered. At the top he stopped and sat again. He thought he had seen it just as the last wave broke, and there it was, the white reef heron, circling, one wing tip down, a hundred yards offshore where the waves were born. It circled slowly again then headed off west along the coastline, away from Ezra's. Apelu rose and followed the white heron around several coves. The white one would always wait for him or circle back. Then it disappeared down into a deep cove that cut farther than the others into the black lava and basalt cliff. From the edge of the cliff Apelu could see the white heron alight on a boulder close to a hardscrabble beach at the end of the cove. Apelu searched and found a way down, almost a trail, from boulder to boulder. He squatted on the final rock at the edge of the broken-shell berm. The bird was still there.

He didn't notice the spot of white until it moved, far out on the facing wall of the cove. It disappeared into the shadow of an outcrop not far above the wave break, then reappeared a little higher, moving slowly. It was a white T-shirt, he realized, a tank top. As it moved toward him he could make out a pair of tan shorts, then tan limbs and a splash of pale hair. Asia, her face to the rock, moved as surely as a crab up away from the wave break, closer to him, back toward the end of the cove. It took her another ten minutes. When she finally jumped from the wall onto the dry berm, the white heron took wing, wheeled, and vanished among the tops of incoming breakers.

Asia stopped when she saw Apelu sitting on his boulder. She paused, then waved and came toward him across the rough tumbled rocks and shells of the beach.

"You look like you've been in for a swim, Apelu. You didn't just wash up here, did you?" she said as she walked up to the base of his rock.

"No, I came the hard way," he said, gesturing with his head up the cliff.

"Oh, the way all us other mere mortals have to get here?"

"The hard way."

"To use an old line, come here often?"

"I always go bird watching on Sundays," he answered.

"Is it Sunday?" Asia asked, truly curious.

"Most places, yes, but not here," Apelu said, indicating with a glance the beach, the cove, and the ocean.

"I always liked Sundays."

"I've always hated them."

"Good thing we don't have them here then," she said, echoing his glance around them.

Asia untied a thin cord around her waist that held a cinched burlap bag full of something hefty and propped it on his rock. On her belt there was a sheath with a short-bladed boat knife snapped in it.

"So, I suppose this is your front yard. Out gardening?" Apelu asked.

"Gathering, actually," Asia said as she opened the burlap bag. "Dinner." And she reached into the bag and pulled out a palmful of glistening black shells the size of large foreign coins.

"*Sisi!*" Apelu said. "Where in the world did you find them? I thought they were all gone, harvested out years ago."

"I have my secret places," Asia said and smiled at him.

"Seafood of the gods. I haven't seen them since I was a kid." Apelu reached out and picked a large shell from her hand, turned it over to see the lucent still-alive muscle of the delicacy inside. He looked up at Asia with a slight raising of his brows. Her eyes smiled and her eyebrows answered his. With a single motion he raised the *sisi* to his mouth and scooped it loose with his teeth. He held the fragrance of its freshness in his mouth for a moment before swallowing.

"They're really good with a cold beer," Asia said.

The route that Apelu had found down to the beach was roughly the same route by which Asia led him out. It was, in fact, her front yard. The weakness in the rock that had allowed the deep cove to form continued inland up a narrow cleft of eroded tree-shrouded valley. Implanted there was a small house raised on concrete piles above the bed of an intermittent stream, its back set into the incline. A veranda fronted it. They ate on the veranda. Asia brought out two bowls—one filled with the *sisi*, the other with fresh *limu* seaweed—and two bottles of cold Steinlager. They didn't speak as they ate and sipped their beers. They chucked the empty *sisi* shells over the railing of the veranda as they emptied them. Beneath the constant pounding of the surf, the place was very still. They emptied both bowls and both bottles, and Asia took them indoors and returned with two new bottles of Stein.

"Have you been here in a storm?" Apelu asked.

"No, not yet."

"I don't know if I would stay here in a hurricane."

"I don't know if I would either. Would you like a shirt?"

"No, I'm fine." Apelu felt his jeans. "I'm getting dry."

"Tell me something about yourself, Apelu, anything."

And for some strange reason Apelu told her everything that had happened in the past few days, starting with his suspension and his visit with the attorney general right through to his walking away from the country club. Asia was a good listener. As he told the story, Apelu found himself questioning things, speculating, saying things like, "Don't you think it strange that...?" and "That doesn't seem right, does it?" Asia would make a small, noncommittal sound in the back of her throat and take another sip of beer. She didn't watch him. She only listened.

At the end of his story—when he had decided to walk to the cliffs to escape and think—Apelu fell silent for a while. Asia said nothing.

"I guess I had to talk that out," he said. "Thanks for listening."

"That poor girl," Asia said. "I can't imagine being caught in such a cruel trap."

"I've wondered if it was a suicide," Apelu said, "if she jumped, and the damage to her face came later, like if she hit something submerged when she jumped. She left all her valuables behind for the other girls, just took her passport so that when her body was found someone would know it was her."

"Maybe, but I don't think so," Asia said to the view off the veranda. "I don't think she would have thought that way. Is it true about the boat girls?"

"I guess so. We never get involved in it. I guess because no one complains. I mean no crime is ever reported."

"Who is 'we'?" Asia asked.

"The police department, the Criminal Investigation Division. I've been on the force ten years now and I can't remember one bust for prostitution or promoting prostitution. Every so often the Immigration guys will make a sweep of the boats and pick up four or five girls as overstayers and deport them back to Western. We never hear about it until after the fact. It always seemed sort of random and haphazard to me."

"But someone must be organizing it, profiting from it. I mean, an eighteen-year-old girl doesn't just one day decide, Gee, maybe I'll be a whore, that would be fun." Asia got up and walked to the railing at the far end of the veranda. "Why would your captain tell you he had all this proof that you were her sponsor when you're not?"

"Don't know. Her name was on a list of names of missing girls that the authorities in Western Samoa were concerned about. I was trying to find out the identities of their sponsors over here."

"What are you going to do now?"

"Collect my shirt, my shoes, and myself and head back into the real world to try to find answers to some of those questions, I guess. What else can I do?"

Asia came back and sat on the railing in front of him. "Will they arrest you?"

"They might. While they're inventing things they might as well invent a crime or two."

"Will you get a lawyer?"

"Do you think I should?"

"I don't know," she said. "Probably."

They stared at each other in silence. They were only about three feet apart.

"Look, I didn't mean to—"

"That's all right," Asia interrupted him. "I'm just sorry that—"

"Don't be," Apelu interrupted her back. "Thanks for the great meal."

"I guess you better be getting back," she said, "to the real world."

"Yeah, I guess I'd better do that," Apelu said, standing up. "Thanks again, for everything."

Asia reached out and put her hand on his arm as she stood up. "You know, I feel like you've made me an accomplice in all this now. You will have to let me know how things turn out. I want to know."

But as Apelu walked back along the coastline he realized he wasn't ready to go back to the real world yet. He had no plan. He had no information. He had no idea what might come down next against him. He retrieved his shirt and flip-flops and went back to Ezra's house. The patio door was still unlocked. From the phone in Ezra's bunker he called his house. Sanele answered and wanted to know where he was. He said working and asked to talk to Mom.

The first thing that Sina asked when she got on the phone was also where he was. Her tone was not good, sort of shrill but controlled at the same time. He didn't answer but asked her if there had been any calls. Yes, the captain had called, looking for him. The captain had told her that if Apelu came home she should keep him there and call the captain immediately. She wanted to know what was going on. He asked her what else the captain had said. Well, she had also asked the captain what was going on, and at least the captain was man enough to answer her question and tell her that Apelu had been suspended and was under investigation for his activities in Apia and for being connected to some dead prostitute. Thanks, Captain, Apelu thought, I'll do the same for your home life someday. Then later a squad car had stopped at the house, two uniformed policemen looking for Apelu, and what about the kids and what the neighbors must think, police cars coming to the house? And had he also caught some sort of venereal disease in Apia that made it too painful to satisfy his own wife? And who was this prostitute he was connected to? Was that why he worked late and on weekends so often? What girlfriend's house was he calling from now? What had he really been doing in Apia? Where was that really nice shirt with the skyline of Manhattan on it that she had given him? Sina's shrillness had lost its earlier control. Apelu hung up, glad he wasn't in the same room with her. This was condition red, high *musu*.

So, there was no going back right now. The catatonic numbness returned. Apelu went and sat in Leilani's chair with the lace throw at the front windows. He sat with his hands clasped between his knees, where his elbows rested, his head bowed. He sat like that, very still, for a long time, his brain a thought-empty, unused bruise. He sat like that until the sun through the windows was low enough over the ocean to soak all of him. He sat like that until he gave up.

Apelu stood up and took off his clothes. He emptied the pockets of his jeans onto the chair, and then, naked, he took his shirt and jeans and briefs to the washing machine in the hallway behind the kitchen and tossed them in with some laundry soap he found there, set the water level to low, and turned it on. He went to Leilani's room and in one of her drawers found a flowered silk lavalava that he folded to loincloth length then cinched around his waist. From Ezra's bunker he took the fire knives and, standing in the middle of the front room in the dying sunlight, he started the twirling and passing patterns that his teacher, Seutia, had taught him twenty-five years before. He did them slowly, super slowly, as if in a trance. The pain in his side didn't matter. He worked through the basic drills, remembering them perfectly. The grips of the knives felt slender in his hands. The knives felt light. His right heel began beating out the drum's rhythm. He felt his back straighten and his shoulders push back. On their own his arms extended away from his body. In slow motion the knives took on a revolving life of their own. He imagined their ends on fire. This was the warrior's dance, the dance of defiance. Now he was stomping with both feet, his knees bent. He began passing the blades between his legs and around his shoulders and neck, still slowly, getting into it, going back.

Then the dogs started barking and he thought he heard a voice. Apelu carried the fire knives with him back to the kitchen. The washing machine had finished its cycle. He went to the storeroom with a window that looked out at the kennel. Asia was there. He ducked back from the window into the darkness of the room, but she hadn't seen him. Her back was to him. She was outside the fence of the kennel, scooping dry dog food from a galvanized garbage can into a plastic bucket, all the while talking to the dogs. When she straightened up and turned, Apelu stepped sideways out of her line of sight. Asia felt along the two-by-four ledge above the gate, and her hand came down with the key to the Yale lock and unlocked it. Nick and Nora were going wild in greeting and anticipation. Then they all moved out of his view deeper into the kennel. When the dogs stopped barking Apelu figured they were eating. Asia was still talking to them. He could hear water running into their tin tub water basin. Then Asia reappeared, carrying the empty plastic bucket, left the kennel, and locked the gate behind her, putting the key back up on the ledge. She placed the bucket upside down on top of the garbage can and left. From a kitchen window Apelu watched Asia's back disappear across the back lawn and into a break in the pandanus he hadn't noticed before.

Apelu found the codeine pills in Ezra's bathroom and took some. He moved his clothes from the washer to the dryer. He returned the knives to Ezra's bunker and took a shower. He found a can of soup and some crackers in a kitchen cabinet, fixed the soup, and ate in the final light of the day. He had decided against turning on the lights inside the house—no need to advertise his presence—but then as dusk settled in a timer somewhere clicked and outside lights went on. Perfect. Enough light came into the house for him to move around in interior darkness. He would spend the night here and let tomorrow take care of itself. Something about the darkness made the surf seem louder. He locked the patio door.

In Leilani's room, with windows that looked out only on to the ocean, he closed the door, drew the drapes, and switched on the bedside lamp. The bedsheets were musty but clean. Along one wall was a low bookcase filled with photo albums labeled by years. The earliest one, Apelu discovered, held yellowed clippings and programs and faded black-and-white photos of Leilani as a young girl dancer in Hawaii more than sixty years before. They were all lovingly, carefully, artistically mounted with little cut-out paper hearts and colored strips and stars, every page its own creation of a girl's musings and dreams—a young male dancer's glossy publicity shot with ancient outline traces of a lipsticked kiss across his bare chest; a Matson Cruise Lines performance flier with a photo of four young beauties in coconut shell bras, one of them Leilani, another with a drawn-in moustache and randomly blacked-out teeth. Storybooks, Apelu thought as he paged through them, watching Leilani grow from a child troupe performer to a strikingly pretty young woman headliner.

Apelu had an idea and did the mental math. He skipped ahead and pulled out the album for the years when he would have been sixteen, seventeen years old, the years when he sometimes danced for Ezra and Leilani's company. And sure enough, in a group photograph of the whole troupe posing in costume at the entrance to the Sands Casino in Las Vegas, he found himself, bare-chested in a grass skirt, shell armlets, and a modest Afro, at the end of the back line, holding a fire knife above his head.

Who was that young, skinny guy? At least he wasn't a fugitive. Well, maybe a fugitive from his youth, but not hiding out like some perp on the run. Apelu put the photo album back in its place on the shelf, opened the drapes, and turned off the lamp. There was a half-moon over the ocean. His mind searched for a thought and found none. He went to bed and almost immediately to sleep.

CHAPTER 10

○

THE MOLD ON WHAT ONCE HAD BEEN COFFEE GROUNDS INSIDE the coffeemaker was so fascinating that Apelu took the whole filter bowl out into the early sunlight to look at it. There was one type of mold growing on another type of mold with a wholly different type of ferny mold growing out of that up the sides of the stained filter bowl. What it most closely suggested was a healthy coral reef of many self-sustaining vivid species and colors—pinks and grays and bold greens with sick yellows. He sniffed it. It smelled alive, not rotten at all. He wondered how long it had been left alone to become so much itself. At least as long as Leilani had been gone. He knocked it out against a tree beside the back patio. It was a lovely morning. A flight of maybe a dozen bright Ruddy Turnstones took off in squadron uniformity from the lip of the surf-sprayed lava cliff, then turned in perfect synchrony, flashing their russet and harlequin plumage as one and vanishing over the edge.

Apelu found the ground coffee but not the coffee filters, so he used a paper towel. His clothes were clean and dry, but he was still wearing Leilani's silk lavalava when he took his mug of coffee out and sat at the patio table. He wasn't yet ready for the real day—the day involving other people—to begin.

"I was wondering if you were still here. You look right at home." It was Asia, coming up behind him from the break in the pandanus.

"I'm hiding out here. It's a secret. You're not supposed to know. Would you like some coffee?"

"Yes, I would. Thanks." Asia took a seat at the patio table as Apelu stood up. "Black?" he asked.

"White," she said, "one sugar."

When Apelu returned with her mug of coffee, Asia handed him the morning's *Samoa News.* "Page three," she said.

"Sorry, no milk," he said and sat down to read page three.

"Foul Play Suspected In Satala Drowning," the headline read. The story was reported straight enough. The victim's name was not given, but she was identified as a nineteen-year-old Western Samoan currently staying in the village of Leloaloa at a house where Immigration officials had previously apprehended young women overstayers to be deported. They didn't say anything about prostitution—no one, including the *News,* wanted to go there—but the neighborhood, her sex, age, and situation implied all that. Then there was a sentence that stood all by itself as a paragraph:

"The *Samoa News* has learned that the young woman's immigration sponsor is a member of the Dept. of Public Safety, Sergeant Apelu Soifua, who is currently under internal investigation."

"Oh my," Apelu said.

"Yes, right," Asia said, taking off her sunglasses. "You've been outed."

"Screwed is more like it."

"You've got yourself some serious enemies, Apelu. Know why?"

"Haven't a clue, not a clue."

"Do you know where that house is?"

"The one she was living in? Yeah, I think I know the house. The captain sent us out there once on a follow-up after an Immigration sweep, trying to look involved. Not a nice place."

"Let's go there," Asia said, looking at him.

"Why?"

"I'm worried about those other girls on your list. Maybe they're there. Maybe we can find them through there."

"That's not exactly your business, is it?" Apelu said, looking back at her.

"I couldn't sleep, thinking about your story and those girls. When I came over here last night to feed the dogs I watched you working out with your dance knives and I knew you were thinking about them too. I saw the look on your face. Those girls are in trouble and scared. One of them is already dead. We've got to find the others and get them back to their families."

"We do?" The fate of those other girls hadn't really been on his mind.

"You've got to do something to defend yourself, find the other girls, and find out who their real sponsors are. It's *we* because I have to do something to help them. So, I'll help you and you'll help me and we'll help them. It's a win-win-win situation." Asia took a sip of her black coffee. "No milk, huh? Tastes like mold."

Apelu got dressed and followed Asia to her house. She had him wait while she changed and reappeared wearing a sleeveless, scooped-neck, dark blue belted dress and sunglasses. She had done something with her hair. It was a different Asia. She was carrying a purse. "Let's go," she said. Her car was parked at the end of a gravel driveway a short hike into the bush behind her house. She had a brand-new Kia sedan, black with dark sun-screened windows. Like so many vehicles on the island it had no license plates. The Office of Motor Vehicles was habitually, almost traditionally out of new license plates. No new cars had had plates in over a year. The air-con made the Kia quickly cool.

"Let's take care of Ezra first," she said. They stopped at one of the bigger bush stores and bought three two-liter bottles of cranberry juice. Then they stopped at a small bush store and bought several small bags of mango *seemoy* candy. They put it in the box with the juice and labeled the box "For Ezra Strand."

"Will he get it?" Asia asked.

"No guarantee," Apelu said. "Just tell the guard at the gate that it's on doctor's orders and with the warden's permission. It's weird enough for the guard to run it by the warden, and he'll get it to him."

At the correctional facility Apelu stayed in the car behind the darkened windows and watched Asia walk with the box through the open gate. She had to wake up the uniformed officer on duty there to give him the box and the instructions.

"Good system they've got there," Asia said when she got back in the car.

"Makes you feel secure, doesn't it?" Apelu said. "Sort of an honor system."

On the way into town Apelu asked Asia how she happened to end up living alone above the cliffs of Piapiatele. She was straightforward about her story, almost as if the quicker she could tell it the better. In Hawaii she had met and married a Samoan Army Officer, Armored Division, Schofield Barracks. He had been killed in action, she said. After his death she came down to Samoa on a visit because this was where Paulo—her husband—had grown up and she had never been here. Paulo used to talk about his golden island childhood. His family was all up in Hawaii or on the mainland now. Well, a couple days' visit turned into a couple of weeks, and she had found the house near the cliffs for rent, and she was still here these few months later. There was something about the island and the people and the pace that reminded her of Paulo, comforted her.

"You know, nobody hassles me, but everybody is friendly," she said. "It's very affordable, and every day is warm and interesting. The solitude out there is very peaceful."

"No wonder," Apelu said. "That piece of coast is well known for its possessions and disappearances. No one is going to hang around there."

"That's why I was surprised to see you in the cove. I thought at first they might be right about the ghosts, all glistening wet in the sunshine."

Apelu decided not to ask any questions about her husband, like in what action he had been killed or his family name. He didn't want to hear her talk about him. "No kids?" he asked instead.

"No. That's a very Samoan question, isn't it?"

"Is it?"

"That's like the second question every Samoan asks me. After 'Are you married?'"

"So, it's important information."

"In the States that would seem such a woman's question, askable about ten minutes into the conversation. You're a guy; you're supposed to ask me what I do for a living."

They were coming into the town area now. Traffic was getting heavier and crazier.

"So, what do y'all do for a livin'?" Apelu asked in as poor of a Southern drawl as he could manage.

"I'm not going to tell you now. You already know the nonsecret about my nonkids. That's enough for one day. How about you?"

"Me?" Apelu said. He was appreciating her fine driving.

"Married? Kids?"

"One wife, four kids," he said.

"Only one?"

"Well, considerably less than one right now, but, yep, only one."

"No wedding ring," Asia observed.

"Kept losing them. Wife finally gave up on buying me new ones."

"Pity."

"Yeah, they always made surefire Christmas presents for me, a no-brainer—another wedding band for hubby. Figured I was doing her a favor."

"And I already know what you do for a living."

"Right, I'm a cop collecting a paycheck for being on the run from the cops."

Leloaloa was the bayshore village just past the village that the cannery and marine railway had taken over, less than a mile hike to the tuna boat docks. Apelu remembered the house referred to in the *News* story because it had been a problem house even before the Immigration raid. One of those places, a run-down rental that belonged to a family whose kids had all left island. God knew who the transient renters of the place paid their rent to, some Korean or Filipino agent probably. There had been fights there, 911 calls, neighbors' complaints. The house was one-story, built on the concrete bank of a deep junk- and litter-filled drainage ditch that periodically became the course of a raging mountain stream on its final furlong race into the sea. You couldn't drive to the place, which was just as well. Apelu had Asia park in front of a sewing shop down on the road.

"No black-and-whites," Apelu said. "No government plates. Let's walk up."

There were two ways to get to the house—a cement step and sidewalk route along the drainage ditch to its front door and a side route through a struggling patch of banana trees. Apelu led Asia the second way. The first thing he noticed was the absence of any yellow-and-black police line tapes around the house, no officers in evidence. As they got closer to the house they could hear a radio playing. It sounded like the Samoan pop music station from Apia. They stopped to listen. They could also hear voices, women's voices speaking in Samoan, an argument or else one person telling someone else off. Apelu went around to the front door, Asia right behind him. The door was open. There was a worn bead curtain. Apelu knocked on the doorjamb and the voices stopped. Asia stepped forward and pushed the bead curtain aside.

"Hello," she said in English. "We're here from Human and Social Services to see if you ladies are all right."

No answer.

In Samoan Apelu said, "Can we come in or will you come out?"

"We don't need your help," was the Samoan answer.

Then the argument continued, in hissing whispers. Someone began to weep, a low, muffled, regular sobbing. Asia went through the bead curtain. She was speaking Samoan now. "We are just here to help, to listen to your story and see if there is anything we can do. It's terrible what's happened to your friend. You must feel awful. It's so sad." Asia's Samoan wasn't that good, but it did the trick. It surprised them into listening.

Apelu just stood at the doorway and watched. There were four young Samoan women in the room, one of whom abruptly left by another door into a rear room when Asia entered. The other three women were all on the floor on mats. There was no furniture in the room. Two were sitting cross-legged; the other was prone, crying into a pillow.

Asia sat down on a mat across from the girls, tucking her legs beneath her, *palangi* style. They began to talk, sometimes in Samoan, sometimes in English. Apelu stayed standing by the door, occasionally smoothing over the language thing with translations, but he let Asia do the talking. After a while the fourth girl rejoined them, slipping into the room, stooping down and finding a mat to sit on along the far wall, removed from the rest but listening in. Asia was good. She soothed the girl who had been crying. She assured them that everything would work out fine. She introduced herself as Sally and got their first names—or at least the names that they gave to her. When it came to getting their story, however, they were more reticent, the three girls looking over at the fourth girl against the far wall, but slowly it came out. In the process, the fourth girl got involved and ended up giving the most precise information.

Neither police nor Immigration officers had been to the house, but the woman had come two days before on Saturday and told them to pack, that they were being deported back to Apia. They called the dead girl Tracey, although Apelu knew that wasn't the name in her passport. At the mention of her name the crying girl started crying again. There was another girl, Tracey's friend, whom they hadn't seen since the night Tracey didn't come home. They were worried about her. Maybe Sally could find her. One of the girls went into a back room and came back with a Western Samoan passport to show them the missing girl's photo. Apelu took a look at the passport and noted the girl's name and particulars. She was one of the other names on Lisa's list. Maybe he had sponsored her too.

"Who is the woman you mentioned," Apelu asked in Samoan, "the one who told you to pack?"

"Mrs. Woo, Atalena," the fourth girl said, angry.

The girls believed that Atalena, who was Samoan from Apia, and her Chinese husband, Mr. Woo, were their sponsors now. They worked for them. This house where they lived belonged to the Woos.

Neither Asia nor Apelu asked them what work they did for Mr. and Mrs. Woo. Apelu asked if they had any idea what had happened to Tracey and the other girl. Silence.

"They just never came home that night," the fourth girl finally said, and the crying girl started crying again.

"She didn't come home from work?" Apelu asked.

The crying girl nodded agreement.

"Where did she work?" Apelu asked.

"At the Captain's Table," the fourth girl said, "as a cocktail waitress."

"Like all of you?" Asia asked.

Their collective silence shaped an affirmative response.

Suddenly from down by the road came a chorus of car doors slamming and the indistinct squawk of a police radio. Asia looked up at Apelu, and he motioned with his eyes toward the back of the house. There was the sound of shoes on the drainage ditch walkway. All the girls' heads turned in that direction as if they could hear with their eyes.

Asia got to her feet. "We'll find your friend," she said, "but only if those people"—she nodded toward the walkway—"don't know we were here." And she followed Apelu through a door to the back of the house. They were out a kitchen door before they heard a man's voice declaring, "Immigration. Everybody stand up and nobody move."

Apelu and Asia found a way down into the ditch along the roots and limbs of an overhanging ficus tree, then retreated up the streambed, picking their way over boulders and box springs, fallen limbs and rusted pieces of appliances, a trashed swing set, a very dead and bloated dog.

Once they got far enough beyond the dog so that they couldn't smell it, Apelu said, "I think this is far enough. No one is following us. They got what they wanted."

They were above the village now and its trash, back in bird-song and spotty sunlight through the jungle canopy. They were both sweating. They sat in silence for a while on adjacent stones at the edge of the stream.

"I get so pissed off when I think about the girls," Asia said, staring down the stream.

"Those girls?" Apelu asked.

"Those girls and all the others here given nothing to choose from. The Filipino girls in the sewing shops, the Vietnamese girls imprisoned in the garment factories, the Tongan house girls making next to nothing. It makes me sick, the female slavery that no one seems to care about."

Apelu didn't know what to say, so he said nothing. Fruit doves cooed in the forest above them.

"I mean, this place is paradise. Why do people have to screw it up?"

"To be rich like other people," Apelu said. "To have what they never had and never needed before. To become someone other than themselves, other than their parents. You can get crazy going there. I know. You don't want to go there. Sometimes it is best to pretend that all of those people like that, the ones who only care about themselves, belong to a different species, a species so low it doesn't deserve to be studied. Good Christians too. Just ask them. True believers in the total truth of the word of the Good Book, and doesn't Deuteronomy tell them that they may beat their slaves because their slaves are their property?"

Asia just looked at him and didn't say anything. The jungle birds entered into a long conversation, and after a while Apelu and Asia moved wordlessly down the streambed, past the silent and empty house, and to her car.

They couldn't see Apelu's house from the road, whether there were any cars there or not, but they drove in anyway, slowly.

"No stakeout, nobody home," Apelu said. "I'll be quick."

He had to get some things. His son's zippered bag from the Apia trip was still slouched empty against the front room wall. He took it into the bedroom and stuffed some clothes into it. He got his keys and cash that he had left behind the day before, his ID and badge case. From the bathroom he got his razor, toothbrush, deodorant, and Tylenol. He was rushing. He wanted to get out of there before he started thinking about the kids. The phone on the kitchen wall started ringing and he almost bolted. But he stopped himself and made himself go into the kitchen as the phone was ringing to look and see if Sina had left him a note anywhere. She hadn't. The phone stopped ringing. He left. Asia had turned the car around. The engine was still running, the windows up, the air-con on.

On the ride back to Piapiatele Apelu asked Asia about her Samoan. It was not a language white strangers often knew. Outside the islands there was no reason to know it, and even in the islands the vast majority of *palangis* never made any effort to learn it beyond hello, good-bye, and thank you.

"It's not bad," he said. "It's not especially good, but it's not bad."

"It's a very different language," she said.

"Oh, how so?"

"Well, it's ergative, for one thing."

"Which means what?"

"Well, there is no passive voice, among other things. And its grammar is very relative. Context supplies a lot of the sense markers."

"I'm glad I don't know any of that or I'm sure I wouldn't be able to speak it. How did you learn?" Apelu asked.

"I studied languages in college. They interest me. Then, when Paulo and I got together, I started teaching myself Samoan—with his help—so that we could have our own private language in public, and so that I could understand his Samoan friends and family when we were with them. They were great about it. First they taught me all the things I shouldn't say. Then we sang Samoan songs, covers of American songs so that I'd know the English lyrics already. They took me to their Samoan Baptist church services in Kalihi so I could listen to their endless Sunday sermons. That didn't help much. And Paulo and I spoke Samoan at home much of the time. Though when we argued I had to argue in English. Samoan is really such a lovely language, so soft, almost swallowed when spoken well, and Samoans are so forgiving. When I make mistakes, they just laugh and make a joke out of it."

"You'll never really get it, you know," Apelu felt impelled to tell her.

"I know. The more I learn the less I realize I know. Did that make sense to you?"

"See if you can say it in Samoan, then I might understand it better."

Asia turned up an unmarked dirt side road into the back of the village of Vaitogi. The road branched and branched again into narrower side roads. There were only occasional bush houses, many of them old Samoan style with no walls, and plantation sheds. There were well-tended plots of banana and coconut and taro, and dotted among them a surprising number of ruins of old hurricane-broken houses.

She finally parked on the leveled gravel space behind her house When they left the car she locked it and beeped on its alarm. Apelu took his son's bag with his stuff, which he dropped inside Asia's back door after she had opened it and turned off the house alarm.

"You want to stay here or what?" Asia asked. "You're welcome to."

"No, I think I'll trek on to Ezra's place, use that as headquarters for the time being. Maybe I'll save you as a fallback position or something. A lot to do."

"Want to take Ezra's shotgun?" Asia asked, not quite seriously.

"I'll leave the ordnance with you," Apelu said. "I've got the dogs."

"I'll be up to feed them later."

Apelu took his bag and left by the porch, taking the steps down toward the cliffs.

CHAPTER 11

———— o ————

A PELU HAD SLIPPED LISA AH CHONG'S BUSINESS CARD INTO the leather space behind his badge in his ID case. From the phone in Ezra's bunker he called her Apia work number. She wasn't in. They asked him for his name and number. He said, no, he'd call back. He called headquarters and asked for the captain, who was in. He had calmed down from the day before. He asked Apelu where he was.

"On leave, remember?"

"Well, there are a couple of people who would like to talk with you."

"Has the commissioner named a board of inquiry for my internal investigation yet? I believe that's the way this is supposed to be done," Apelu said. Such internal investigations at the department were all too frequent. Normally nothing ever came of them. Reports were never finalized. The charges evaporated with time, and the next new scandal would eclipse all interest in the old.

"Nothing official yet, but there are some questions you should answer."

"I don't think so, Captain. I'll be retaining counsel, and he'll like to see something specific from the board of inquiry. I've not been charged with anything, have I?"

"Listen, Soifua, let's not get ahead of ourselves here. Maybe if you came in and answered a few questions, there won't be any need for an internal investigation or charges." The captain was using his flat, unconvincing voice, and he didn't even know it.

"Plenty of time for all that, captain, inside the proper procedures. I've got something a little more pressing for you—another girl who's gone missing since the night our floater took her last swim."

"I heard all those girls were swept up by Immigration," the captain said.

"Well, check and see if this girl is among them," and Apelu gave the captain her name. "If she's not, she's among the missing."

"Hold on," the captain said. "Give me that name again."

Apelu did.

"Yeah, she's another one on your list of sponsorees. No wonder you're worried about her. Your little side industry's gone a bit flat, Soifua? You want the department to go find your missing whores for you?" The captain was getting excited again. "How much do you take in a night from these bitches, eh, Soifua? I am not in the find-your-missing-whore business."

"I just wanted to give you that identification, captain. The girl may be in danger."

"From whom? You?" The captain's voice had risen noticeably. Apelu could almost see the spit hitting the receiver.

"You are a worthless asshole, captain," Apelu said and hung up.

His second call to Lisa got through, and she was there. He gave her the news about the girls—one dead, one missing, the rest unaccounted for, though she might want to check today's and tomorrow's returning flights. Lisa wanted details. Apelu gave her what he knew, along with the names of Mr. and Mrs. Woo.

"Although I doubt their names are on the sponsorship papers," Apelu added.

"Did you find out any of the sponsors' names?" Lisa asked.

"Only one. Mine."

"What?"

"I've been told that I was listed as the immigration sponsor for both the dead girl and the missing one, probably others."

"What's going on?"

"I don't know," Apelu said. "I'm sort of at a loss. I never sponsored anyone. You know these Woo people?"

"No, I don't, Apelu. Why would I? Because they have a Chinese last name like I do?"

"Well, the wife is Samoan, from Apia, first name Atalena. Just wondering," Apelu said. Lisa seemed a bit testy.

"I must say, Apelu, that whatever you've done hasn't been very helpful or constructive."

"I didn't kill the girl, counselor."

"Maybe not, but she was alive before you became involved, and I can't help feeling that there are things you haven't told me about all this."

Maybe I shouldn't be telling you anything at all, Apelu thought. How do I know who you are talking to? What else is going on here? Why did you get me involved in this in the first place?

"Listen, Lisa," he said, "I don't know what else I can do for you on this end. It's getting a little personal."

"Bailing out?"

"Bailing in. I can't do anything official for you now, but I'll stay in touch." Whatever trip Lisa was on now, he didn't need it. The sense of irritation in her tone reminded him of Sina.

"You'll stay in touch?" Sarcasm.

Oh, fuck this, Apelu thought. What is it with women? So quick to take offense, always trying to put him on the defensive. At least he could remain polite, treat her like a fellow professional.

"Yes, I'll stay in touch. You could do me a favor, though. Two names—Willie Schneider and Ulifanua Malolo—whatever you can find out about them."

"So now I'm working for you?"

"It's called cooperation, Lisa. It goes both ways. It's free."

"Uli who?"

"Ulifanua Malolo, early thirties, maybe."

"I'll see if I can cooperate, or reciprocate. I'll see if I can have one of them killed for you."

"Don't be that way, Lisa."

"I don't take orders from you, Apelu."

"Make it a request then."

"All right. Let's back off a little here. Your phone call has not made my day, and your suggestion that I know who these pimps are just because he's Chinese was not appreciated."

"I didn't say that. I just asked—"

"Oh, forget it," Lisa cut him off. "I just got the same ethnic shit from our Immigration inspectors here earlier. Just to get back at me for making them work, they sent over a list of random Chinese names they had found in their entry logs when they were looking for the names on my list of missing girls. They attached a sarcastic note asking how many of them I was related to. I didn't ask for that and I didn't ask for your ethnic innuendo either. There are no Woos in Western Samoa. I know every Chinese family here."

"I don't do innuendo, Lisa. I'm not smart enough. I'm just a dumb cop without answers, remember? And this has not been exactly a stellar day for me either. If I ever do figure anything out I'll give you a call."

There were two khaki-green geckos, each about five inches long, either fighting or having foreplay on the wall beside the bathroom mirror. Apelu wondered if they knew which they were doing. They made saurian barks as they circled each other like predators. He would tell if they were fighting if one of them ended up without a tail.

Apelu was standing in front of the mirror in Ezra's bathroom, shaving off his moustache. This was an unusual thing to be doing. He had had the moustache most of his adult life, ever since he had stopped being a performer—fire knife dancers weren't allowed to have facial hair. He had to shave slowly because he had no scissors to cut it down to stubble length. It felt strange. He finished one side, then flashed his old and new profiles back and forth in the mirror by turning his head. It made a difference. He looked less like an Arab without the moustache. He finished up and splashed cold water on his face, then some of Ezra's Old Spice aftershave. His upper lip was tender and felt naked but it wasn't that much lighter in color than the rest of his face. He had found a pair of Ray-Ban sunglasses on a dresser in Ezra's bedroom. He tried them on. He never wore sunglasses. He almost didn't recognize himself.

In Ezra's closet he found a red-and-white-checkered shirt large enough to fit him—something he would never wear—and a faded San Diego Chargers baseball cap, which he put on backward, the way the kids wore them. A black T-shirt, a pair of jeans, and his Nike cross-trainers completed the outfit. He wore the checkered shirt out and open. There was a full-length mirror in Leilani's room. He had to admit he looked younger. He left by the patio door, leaving it closed and unlocked. As he walked up the driveway toward the slack chain, Nora then Nick started barking.

At the golf course road Apelu caught an *ainga* bus headed toward town. *Ainga* buses were the sole means of public transportation in Samoa aside from taxicabs. They were all privately owned and operated, and all handmade—wooden bodies on truck chassis. They were pretty much the same in construction, if individual in their character and imaginative paint jobs. They had names like Titanic, Light on the Ocean, Spiderman, South of Pago Pago. One thing they all had in common was a sound system. At the driver's left hand was always a pile of cassettes and a tape deck haphazardly wired to invariably giant speakers. The sound systems all had only one volume setting—loud. Teenagers picked their buses by their soundtracks. The benches were unpadded wood. The windows were sheets of Plexiglas that slid up or down in wooden tracks, sometimes. The buses were always packed. After one bus wreck several years before, a *palangi* coroner had listed the fatalities' cause of death as "death by splinters."

While the exteriors of the buses were decorated with their distinctive names and spray-painted scenes related to them—or maybe a portrait of the owner's baby daughter—the interior décor was pretty much the driver's domain—flags, posters, decals, family photos, Christmas lights, bobblehead animals, Last Supper paintings on black velvet, political bumper stickers, beer ads with rugby players, and all variety of holiday trim. Apelu's favorite was still the bus with the triptych of full-color posters above the front window—an effeminate Jesus showing his Sacred Heart flanked by Sylvester Stallone as a battered Rocky and war-blackened Rambo.

The speakers on the bus Apelu boarded had been so blown out by their volume that it took him a while to separate the words from the noise. The lyrics were in English—a rapper song that exhorted its listeners to no end to rape the hos and kill the honky motherfuckers. Seated beside him on the cramped wooden bench was a shriveled gray-haired auntie, who smiled at him when he sat down then looked rather blissfully out the window as they sped and braked down the road, their bodies comfortably leaning into each other as they bounced and lurched along.

She seemed removed from the rap racket, but Apelu, hearing the words, was embarrassed for her. Instinctively, he reached for his badge and ID. He would make the asshole bus driver change the music. Then he realized he couldn't do that, because he was supposed to be incognito. Then he did it anyway.

Apelu walked to the front of the bus, keeping his balance by hanging onto the backs of the wooden benches. He squatted down beside the driver.

"Listen," he said and tapped the driver on the shoulder to get his attention. "Listen, turn off this crap and put on a nice Samoan song."

"Says who?" the driver said, not looking.

"Says my grandmother in the back and says this." Apelu pulled his badge case out of his back pocket and shoved it, open, in front of the driver's face. "And now. And turn it down."

Apelu got up and returned to his seat before the driver could say anything, but the music was changed—a Samoan song—and turned down. The old auntie didn't seem to notice, but a couple of other passengers around him muttered their thanks. A girl across the narrow aisle held out her can of Cheetos to him. He took one. It made him realize how hungry he was. It was well on into the afternoon, and he hadn't eaten yet. He got off the bus in Nu'uuli and ate at a plate lunch place. He ate a big meal since he figured that would be his main feed of the day. Then he caught another bus.

At Seau's Garage in Utulei Apelu walked to the side lot where the Tongan crew fixed and changed tires. It was the main place on the island to get that sort of thing done. Apelu had known the head of the Tongan crew a long time. Nothing special, they'd just been doing the same thing in the same place for years, and the big Tongan was a garrulous type, chummy with everyone. Apelu had to take off his glasses and cap and tell the Tongan who he was.

"Didn't recognize you, Pelu. You undercover now?"

"Sort of. I got a question for you."

"Sure, shoot." The Tongan went back to work on his tire-changing machine, stripping a blowout off its rim.

Apelu asked him about the truck Asia had seen picking up the loot at Ezra's. The Tongan and his crew fixed just about everybody's tires on the island. He had a great memory for vehicles and their owners. Asia hadn't given him much of a description. "Pickup, black, maybe ten years old"—she had said that it "wasn't new"—"Toyota probably"—the beds on Toyota trucks rusted out faster in the tropics than those on American trucks, but otherwise they ran so well it was worth putting a wooden bed on them—"with a homemade wooden slat-sided bed, no plates."

"Samoan owner?" the Tongan asked as he threw the badly worn tire into a pile of other badly worn discarded tires along one wall.

"Yes," Apelu guessed.

"That's not much to go on. I can think of a number. You sure it's Toyota?"

"No, but Japanese probably."

"Yeah, the bed. Regular tires?"

"Don't know. Bum muffler."

One of the Tongan's assistants had been listening in. He now volunteered something in Tongan to his boss, who in turn asked him a couple of questions in Tongan.

"Sione here thinks he knows the truck. He says his cousin just changed the muffler on a truck like that."

Sione laughed and said something else in Tongan. By now the whole Tongan crew was listening. At the end of Sione's story everybody laughed.

"What's the joke?" Apelu asked.

"He said, everybody knew about it because the Samoan guy paid his cousin in frozen meat, but it was all thawing out and going bad and his cousin had to cook it all, so everybody in their little neighborhood got to eat steak that night."

"That would be our man," Apelu said.

"You go undercover to chase meat thieves?" the Tongan asked, then repeated it in Tongan to keep the laughs coming.

"Does Sione's cousin know the guy's name?" Apelu asked when the laughter died down.

Sione answered him directly, in Samoan. "They call him J-Cool. He lives up top Canco Hill."

"Well, thanks, you guys. This is very helpful." Apelu reached out to shake their grime-caked hands, but instead they each made a fist and butted their fists with his.

"No problem, Pelu. Anytime," the big Tongan said. "Hey, you assholes, get back to work."

Apelu put back on his sunglasses and backward baseball cap and walked on into what served the island as downtown. He had to walk past the building where Sina worked above the bank and past headquarters. No one paid him any attention.

The Captain's Table lounge was in a low, patched-together, tin-roofed building near the water's edge beyond the farmers' market. There was a back entry from the dockside, and Apelu used that one. It took his Ray-Ban'd eyes a minute to adjust from the full sun glare of the streets and the bay and focus inside the saloon's gloom. What struck him first was the smell of the place—a beer-soaked waft of cigarette air and the twin aromas of the bathrooms' disinfectant and what it failed to mask. The place was echoingly empty, just a few regulars hunched in drunk meditation at the beer-sign-lit bar. But there was a waitress. She turned around from a conversation with the bartender to glance at Apelu. He sat down at a round Formica-topped table in a booth toward the rear, and the waitress came over. Apelu studied her face until he was fairly certain he didn't know her, and then he took off the sunglasses, smiled, and ordered a beer. He was enjoying this loss of identity. Or was it a new identity—nobody?

When the waitress returned with his Steinlager, Apelu asked her if Atalena was around. She said no as if she were turning down a lewd proposition. Apelu waited. By the time he had finished his second beer and the daylight was quickly fading from the bayside windows, a slightly built Chinese man entered by the front door and quickly disappeared through another door behind the bar. Mr. Woo, Apelu concluded. The bar was beginning to fill up now—after-work drinkers, early starters. More lights had been turned on, including a disco ball revolving and reflecting tiny dim squares of light around the room, but the place was still gloomy. Music was coming from behind the bar now—a tape of dated Samoan rock-and-roll songs. Apelu recognized three cops from headquarters—out of uniform—with their heads together over a table near the front door. He put his sunglasses back on and slouched lower in his booth. He was waiting for Mrs. Woo, because he figured if he was going to pull anything off, get any information, he would have to do it in Samoan with a Samoan, and he wanted to meet this Atalena.

The waitress—a new one, younger and flirtier—had just brought Apelu his third beer when Mati came in the front door. Apelu could tell he was not a regular because he stopped a few steps inside the door to study the room before he went and took a stool at the bar away from everyone else, and it took the bartender a while to come and get his order. Apelu noticed that Mati had on his good loafers and was otherwise overdressed for the place. So this was the FBI in action, Apelu thought. There were five law enforcement officers in the room, but if anybody had called out Pin the Tail on the Pig, everyone in the place would have pointed at Mati.

One of the waitresses, though—Apelu now counted four of them, all dressed for the evening in shorts and halter tops—went over to Mati and leaned against the bar beside his stool, flirting with him. Apelu's waitress returned to ask him if everything was okay and if he wanted to dance. Apelu shook his head in his best gangsta imitation, and she shrugged and walked away. A couple of patrons and girls were already dancing. Apelu watched them in the disco light. His beer was empty. He ordered another, along with a shot of Johnnie Walker on the rocks, a bag of chips, and another pack of cigarettes. The music switched to Motown. His waitress again asked him to dance, and he scowled at her.

Mr. Woo came out of the door behind the bar, said something to the bartender, and headed for the front door. Apelu sat up and swung his legs out of the booth. Might as well follow him out. Then he saw Mati get off his stool and brush past the bar girl now seated beside him, cutting to head Mr. Woo off before he got to the door. Apelu sat back down again. He couldn't hear through the music what was said, but Mr. Woo barely stopped when Mati confronted him. He waved Mati off with a furious shaking of his head, pushed him away, and fled. To his credit, Mati didn't follow him but returned to his barstool. The bar girl had split.

Apelu ordered another Johnnie Walker, and a new waitress brought it to him. She also asked him—almost as if it were a joke—if he wanted to dance, and he said yes. It was a Smokey Robinson song. She wasn't much of a dancer, but she smiled a lot and kept touching him. Apelu asked her about "his friend" and he gave the name from the missing girl's passport.

"Who?" she asked.

Apelu repeated the name and added that she used to work there.

"Oh, you mean Tia. Tia doesn't work here anymore. They fired her."

"For what?"

"Don't know," she said and smiled an end to that conversation.

Apelu was beginning to wonder what he was going to do with the rest of the evening, how he would get home to Ezra's, when Asia walked through the front door. She was dressed in jeans and a dark T-shirt, her hair pulled back. She didn't see Apelu as she slipped into an empty booth. Apelu watched Mati watching Asia as she ordered a drink.

The Smokey song ended and the dancing waitress gave Apelu a little too-lingering peck on the cheek. He went back to his table, picked up his drinks and cigarettes, and went and sat down across from Asia in her booth. He was still wearing his Ray-Bans and backward Chargers cap. Asia was stony and only glanced at him briefly before looking away.

"To use an old line, come here often?" Apelu said. Asia looked at him, and he removed the sunglasses.

"You almost look like someone I know," she said.

"That's good," he said. "I like it like that. Call me A-Cool."

"How did you get here?" she asked.

"The hard way."

She reached out and touched his upper lip with an index finger. "Tender?"

"Ouch," he said.

"Find anything out?"

"Well, I believe our Mr. Woo has come and gone, but no Atalena. I asked about the missing girl, whom they call Tia, and was told she had been fired."

"Who'd you ask?"

"One of the waitresses."

"She called her Tia?"

"Tia."

"Let me try," Asia said, and she got up and went to the bar, where she got the bartender's attention then leaned across the bar to talk with him. She was three or four stools down from Mati, who took a good look at Asia's trim body as she bent forward. Asia didn't notice. When she turned and came back to the booth, Apelu made sure his back was to the bar. He didn't want to talk with Mati in this place, in these circumstances. Mati had ferreted through his things in Apia, looking for secrets. Apelu wanted to keep his new secret, his anonymity.

"Yeah, according to the bartender, Tia got fired the same night Tracey, the dead girl, got fired. Mrs. Woo fired them. There had been some sort of disagreement in the back room. Tia came out crying with blood all over her face. She told the bartender and the other girls that Mr. Woo had thrown a stapler at her. Then Tracey came out of the room and grabbed Tia and took her away. That was the last anyone here saw of them."

"The night Tracey died?"

"Yeah, four nights ago."

"Anything else?"

"Yeah, that Mrs. Woo hasn't been around since," Asia said. "Though I don't necessarily believe him." Then she stopped and looked up over Apelu's shoulder.

"Hi. Can I join you guys? Buy you a drink? It's sort of lonely over at the bar." It was Mati's Kiwi voice from right behind Apelu's baseball cap.

"Sure, why not," Asia said. "I'm Sally."

"And I'm out of here," Apelu said. "Got some shit to do. Be cool, Sal." Because of the Ray-Bans Apelu couldn't send her any eye signals, and he slipped out of the booth. "Later, dude."

Mati hardly noticed Apelu's leaving. He hadn't made him. His eyes were only for Asia.

Apelu walked to the taxi stand beside the deserted market and caught a cab to near the turn-off to Piapiatele then walked from there. It was a peaceful walk. None of the dogs that barked at him got farther than ten yards away from the houses they considered themselves protecting. Why were they barking at nobody? Apelu wondered.

CHAPTER 12

———— o ————

APELU WAS AWAKENED BY THE DOGS. IT WAS DAWN. HE HAD been dreaming about a house he had once lived in as a teenager in San Francisco. It hadn't been much of a house, just one in a row of identical run-down flat-faced two-story wooden houses running up a steep hill street in Hunters Point with a Bay view of docks and cranes and derelict ships. It had been their first house in the States and the one they had lived in the longest. His sister had written him that it was gone now. That street was now lined with new redbrick semiattached condominiums. In his dream he could remember every window, board, doorknob, and creaky stair of the place. In the dark he knew where the light switches were and how to sneak in or out of the pantry window without making a sound. He went back there now, all alone in a home that existed only in his long-term memory, as real as a smell. The dogs barking would be Mrs. Ybarra's paranoid Dobermans two backyards away. The night fog was thick off the Bay. Where was he going? Up the alley between their house and the Simpsons' house, then right up the hill to get out of there the hard way. Then the dogs again, the Dobermans going wild.

Only they weren't Mrs. Ybarra's Dobermans. They were Nick and Nora, and Apelu was now wide awake, his dreamed-up youth slipping away from him. He was in an old lady's bed in a house on the edge of a cliff. Breakers were softly booming below him. At least he was still alone. The dogs were still barking.

Apelu pulled on his jeans and walked to the back of the house. From the window in the kitchen storeroom he could hear Asia's voice as she talked to the dogs. She was apologizing as she fed them. Apelu splashed water on his face at the kitchen sink, then went back to Leilani's room to get a T-shirt. By the time he came out the sliding glass door Asia was sitting at the patio table pouring coffee from a thermos into its plastic screw-off top.

"Get a cup," she said. "This doesn't taste like mold."

He did. As they drank their coffees, Asia talked. The night before she had figured by the way Apelu had instantly split that Mati was some sort of cop. Their conversation hadn't gotten very far because he just wanted to know about her—where she was from, what she was doing—and she just wanted to know why he was there and what he knew. By the time he got around to pitching her his pickup line she was ready to leave. She left him there. Apelu confirmed that Mati was an investigator from the AG's office, but said nothing about FBI, holding onto that card. Asia wanted to go after Mrs. Woo. Someone had to know where they lived. Maybe the missing Tia was being held there. Surely Apelu could find that out.

Apelu made a number of phone calls. He had some contacts and old owed debts uncollected in the Korean community. The Koreans had nothing to lose by ratting on the Chinese. There was no love lost or shared there. He got an address—well, a location, really, because there were no street addresses on Tutuila. The house was at the end of a back road by the airport. Really by the airport—the road to it ran along the main runway's peripheral fence. For years that side of the airport had been just one long forest on both sides of the fence. Then these new fancy houses started going up, and the wild land along the outside of the fence began to disappear. But the mini-mansions were still buffered from the runway proper by the forest inside the fence. Then the whole federal airport security thing became a big deal—even here where the biggest threat to travelers was that their flight might be cancelled—and the jungle inside the fence was cut and bulldozed too, for security reasons. Apelu explained the changes to Asia as they drove down the dirt road.

"Why more secure?" she asked.

"Line of sight, I guess. Maybe something left over from Vietnam—no jungle for the bad guys to hide in."

"By which logic a desert would be the best place to be."

"See 'em coming a mile off."

"It is pretty ugly."

"But the folks in charge of what's inside the fence feel more secure. A trade-off."

At one point along the road a construction company had set up its staging area and equipment yard along the fence side of the road. The six-foot-high chain-link fence was all that separated the big front loaders and dump trucks from a cleared-land rumble to the main runway.

"If you thought like a terrorist, that would look fairly inviting," Apelu said.

"Makes all the check-in security routines at the terminal look pretty meaningless, doesn't it?"

"I'm beginning to like the way you think."

"When I sound like I'm thinking like you," Asia said and laughed.

"Well, it's a perfect example of what happens when the feds come in here with all their off-the-rack mainland rules and regulations. It just fucks up a good thing, a nice place, so that we can adhere to some paranoid *palangi* federal standard that we never agreed to nor wanted and is totally unnecessary. I ran across this term once—'administered world.' Know what that means?"

"I think I know what you mean."

"A world where, like, there's a whole class of people whose job it is just to make up more bullshit rules, like in a church or a cult or something."

"Yes."

"Well, that's what the feds are like. We already have our own set of rules, our own ways of making things come out even. We got to avoid more rules, outsiders' rules. They screw up the balance. We got to avoid being pulled any further into that administered world. Like making us cut down the trees to be more secure, just like them. What bullshit. We live in the jungle, for Pete's sake. Cement is nice and secure, but you can't grow anything to eat in it. Fucking feds."

"I feel your pain, Apelu, but I don't fully understand it."

The Woos' place was one of the newer trophy houses. The landscaped plants around it had not yet begun to grow. There was a collection of newish SUVs and trucks and sedans parked on the cement apron in front of the house when Asia and Apelu drove up the driveway in Asia's Kia. One of the SUVs had its back hatch open. A house girl was loading luggage into it. Apelu told Asia to stay in the car. The house girl looked back over her shoulder at Apelu as she walked back toward the house.

Apelu called out to her in Samoan, "Please, Miss, could you tell me if Mr. and Mrs. Woo are home?"

"*Ioe*," she said. "But they are just leaving."

"Airport?"

"*Ioe*. They are going to Apia."

At that point Mr. Woo came out of the house, carrying a briefcase. "What? What you want? Who you? Go way."

Apelu pulled his badge and ID case out of his jeans pocket and held it up for Mr. Woo to see. "Police. I have a few questions about your missing employee."

"Already talk police. Girl dead, too bad. Not good girl. Too much trouble. No more question. You go." Mr. Woo walked past

Apelu to the SUV and shut the back hatch hard. "No want trouble. You go."

"No, Mr. Woo, I'm not asking about the dead girl, but about the missing girl, Tia."

"We neither employ nor know any girl named Tia. May I see your identification, please?" Mrs. Atalena Woo was coming up behind Apelu from the house. She was one of *those* Samoan women—indefinite age, forty, plus or minus five years, fifty pounds over an ideal weight, no neck to speak of, hair that had been so frequently colored and permed that it looked like orange thatch, fat wrists and fingers heavy with gold. She was wearing a tailored flowered tent. Apelu pulled out his badge case again and handed it to her.

"Oh yes, Sergeant Soifua. I read about you in the paper. You're on suspension or something, aren't you?" She handed his ID case back to him.

Apelu said nothing.

"Well, I guess we'll be going." She pulled out a cute little cell phone and said, "If you don't leave this property immediately, I'll call 911 and report you as trespassing and threatening. Goodbye, Sergeant."

Mr. Woo was already sitting behind the black glass of the SUV's passenger side door. Atalena got in the driver's side and drove away.

Asia got out of her car, which was parked down the driveway. "What was that all about?" she asked as she walked up to Apelu.

"Well, fuck her," Apelu said and he walked up to the front door of the house and knocked. The house girl answered. In Samoan he told her they were looking for a young Western Samoan girl named Tia. Did she know her? Had she seen her? The house girl seemed frightened. She knew nothing. There was no one else in the house, she said. Asia and Apelu left.

"I've got another lead," Apelu said. They were sitting in the car, eating meat pies in the parking lot outside a bakery in Nu'uuli.

The car was still running, the air-con was on, and the windows rolled up. "But this one I got to run alone. Can I borrow your car and drop you some place?"

Asia gave him a long look, then said, "Sure, drop me home."

"The top of Canco Hill" was a pretty nebulous address, so Apelu just kept driving up. There was only the one road up there, which branched near the top. He figured he knew who lived on the right-hand branch—only a couple more high-scale *palangi* houses—so he cut left at the fork. He heard the music first, its bass through the bush. He turned into a crushed-rock driveway toward it. It was midafternoon. No dogs came out to bark. There were a couple of past-their-prime pickup trucks parked in the shade and the weeds at the edge of the driveway, and in a carport was the truck from Ezra's that Asia had described. Apelu pulled up behind it and turned off the engine. He had his Ray-Bans and backward Chargers cap back on. When he got out of the air-con car, he was smacked by how hot the still-air day had become, and the Ray-Bans fogged up. Finally, a dog barked. The music was turned down.

Two young Samoan men came out onto the porch of the house. They were both bare chested and barefoot. One wore a lavalava, the other a pair of cargo shorts. Normal-looking guys in their twenties.

"Yo, I'm looking for J-Cool. Is this the place?" Apelu called to them. He had decided he would be from California, play it that way. He had decided his name would be Dorset.

They didn't say anything. One of them went back inside, and the other one—the one in the lavalava—walked slowly toward the car. "What's up, dude?" he asked.

"Just looking for J-Cool, hoping we could do some business."

"This the place. Who are you?"

"Dorset. Name's Dorset, from San Francisco. Yours?" Apelu stuck out his right hand.

"People call me Torque," the man said and shook his hand. "Come on up."

Thus far they had been speaking in English, but on the porch Torque returned to his natural tongue—the simplified street slang Samoan of Pago kids, peppered with American phrases and terms.

"Get yourself down," he said, gesturing to a wooden bench beside a picnic table on the porch. Then he went to the screen door and called in, "Please, Sister, bring us two beers, thank you." He sat down on the bench across the picnic table from Apelu. "Dorset? What sort of name is Dorset?"

"Made up," Apelu said. "But I made it up so long ago and I've been using it so long that it's become my actual name." His Samoan sounded sort of stiff compared to Torque's—which was just as well. "It was the name of a street in the neighborhood I grew up in."

"Which was where?"

"San Francisco. Ever been there?"

"No, never been mainland."

A young Samoan woman came out of the house, put two cold bottles of Bud Light on the picnic table, and went back into the house.

"What's the business?" Torque clinked bottles with Apelu and said, "*Manuia.*"

"Maybe I should talk to J-Cool about that."

"You are talking to J-Cool. Like you, I got more than one name. J-Cool is my DJ name. What business?"

"I want to take a bunch of Samoan music CDs back to the mainland to sell, looking for wholesale. I heard J-Cool was the man to see."

"Heard where?"

"In Apia."

"Apia's a big town."

"Yeah, it is."

145

"What you looking for?"

Apelu named a bunch of the groups he remembered from the inventory of CDs that they had found in Ezra's bunker and threw in a few others that weren't there but that his kids played. "Big market for them in Culver, Oceanside, San Diego. I could probably move whatever I could get."

"Got family here?" Torque had finished his beer and called for two more.

"Not really. A couple of cousins back in Apia about all that's left in the islands."

"When you goin' back?"

"Soon as I get this and a couple of other things settled."

A group of kids came walking up the rocky driveway—two boys in their late teens, then ten or twelve yards behind them three girls around the same age. The boys were dressed in the baggy clothes and the girls in the skin-tight clothes that sartorially distinguished their genders these days. Both of the boys and two of the girls were carrying school backpacks. They nodded and said hello as they filed into the house. Almost immediately a hit song from Apia by one of the groups Apelu had just mentioned sounded from somewhere inside. Their next two beers arrived.

"Payment?"

"Cash. I'd need a day to get it." Apelu finished his first beer but let the second one sit there sweating. He had forgotten how much he disliked insipid Bud Light.

A phone rang and was answered inside the house, and then the woman who had brought them their beers came to the screen door and said, "Jay, *telefone*. It's Tia."

"*Ioe*," Torque answered. "Excuse me." And he went inside.

Another teenage girl came walking up the driveway to the porch. She was carrying two white plastic bags of groceries. She was sweating. It was a long hike up from the main road. When she saw Apelu sitting alone at the picnic table, she gave him a big smile and said hello as if they were old friends.

"It's a hot one, isn't it?" he said.

"A scorcher," she said, "but it's cool here," and she went inside.

The sun was indeed hot, and the air was as still as a slab of baked cement, but to the east there was a charcoal gray wall of weather that fell from the top of the sky to the earth. Here and there, inside the dense advancing curtain, distant silent lightning flashed both high and low. There was nothing like these tropical summer open-ocean squalls. No one was like any other except in their insistence on getting and keeping your attention. Apelu had been inside one once in which ball lightning had flashed among trees around him thirty feet above the ground, and the wind seemed to come from every direction at once. Cataract rains, sometimes weirdly horizontal, erased all other information from your visual world, and the children were right: the great noises of the squall—if you closed your eyes—could be heard best as huge angry human screams and moans and laments. This one was coming on fast, but the sun was well to the west and still out of its hard-edged upper reach.

Torque came back out onto the porch with two handfuls of CDs and dropped them on the picnic table. "This the stuff we got in stock I can get you fast. Anything else you got to order. We don't ship or deliver. Cash up front."

Apelu went through the CDs, making a stack of them in front of him. They were all samples of the bulk CDs from Ezra's stash. "Cool, dude. I can take eighty at least of each of these, depending on the cost. Quality?"

"Ninety percent." Torque didn't seem at all embarrassed at admitting that they were pirated copies. "But the liner art and print shit is all original. Got a deal with the printer in Apia."

"Could I listen to one?" Apelu pulled a CD from the pile at random.

"Take what you want. Play 'em on your own system. Tell me you hear any difference." Torque sat down to his unfinished Bud Light and finished it. At which point the sun went out like a door being closed. "Your windows up, man?" he asked calmly.

"Yeah, yours?" Apelu said, taking a small sip of his warm, uninviting beer.

"Yo," Torque yelled over his shoulder into the house, "incoming." Then to Apelu, "Dorset baby, we ought to get our asses inside." Between them they collected the CDs from the picnic table.

The house was much roomier, deeper than it looked from the outside. Its ceilings were low, but it was open all the way through to a screened-in kitchen in the back. Hallways and doorways led out of the big central room. It was also hivishly, humanly busy. There were folks in the kitchen preparing food, folks busy shutting louvers on the east and south sides of the main room, folks just moving about in a purposeful way. They were all young. Apelu followed Torque to a table back by the kitchen. He had left his beer outside. The woman Torque had called Sister asked him if he wanted another. When he declined, she offered him a cup of koko Samoa instead and he readily accepted. It was thick and warm and not too sweet. Perfect.

"What is this, some sort of dormitory?" Apelu asked.

"Oh, these are all just Sister's people. She takes them in the way some people take in dogs or cats. If a kid's in trouble and their family don't want 'em, they find their way up here till their shit straightens out."

Then the squall was on them like a Viking raid. In spite of the quickly closed louvers, doors slammed shut and curtains went horizontal. Papers flew around the big room, kids chasing them, laughing. You could feel the mist on your face. The gale hammered down on their hilltop roof and raced up the ridge from below, meeting itself in a swirling scrimmage. Loose things in the yard went crashing. Trees creaked and moaned in confusion.

The power flickered once then went out. There was a sudden chill in the air.

"I hope it don't lightnin'," Torque said. "I hate it when it lightnin's."

Then right on cue the first flash hit, followed five seconds later by an encompassing dynamite crack.

"Oh shit, oh shit!" Torque's eyes were flashing around the room, looking for a place to hide. Sister came running from the kitchen and grabbed Torque just as the second bolt of *uila emo* arced. Together, Torque clinging to Sister, they raced toward a side door and made it just as the second clap of *faititili* slapped the house. The next flash and crash were even closer. The girl who had given Apelu the nice smile on the porch slipped into the chair beside him at the table, grabbed his arm, and pulled her chair up against his.

"Aren't you scared?" she said. "I am." She was trembling.

"Not much we can do about it," Apelu said, and he reached over with his other hand to hold her shoulder.

"It's just that up here it's so much closer, and…"

"And you're not home."

"Uh-huh," she said just as an almost simultaneous explosion took place on top of them, and she pressed herself into his side, her face in his chest, her fingers gripping his shirt.

After a few more near-miss shockers—and body grips—the cataclysmic line passed on as quickly as it had arrived, and Apelu learned that his gripper's name was Lucy and that she was a freshman at the community college, no major yet, mainly just remedial courses plus drama. Then Sister reappeared and shooed Lucy away from him. Although the lightning and thunder had passed, the back squall was blowing hard, and there were wind-driven-rain leaks to deal with, dinner still to be fixed, Lucy's things to pick up. Sister gave Apelu a suspicious look as she rushed on to other duties.

Torque never reappeared, so after a while of being ignored Apelu went up to the counter between the main room and the kitchen, where Sister was overseeing dinner preparation, and told her he'd be going, maybe he could give Torque a call later about the CDs. Sister gave him a look over her shoulder, then wiped her hands on a towel and came over to the counter. She wrote a cell phone number down on a post-it pad, pulled it off and handed it to him without saying a word.

"Thank you," Apelu said in Samoan. "*Tofa*, have a nice evening." He picked up the CDs Torque had given him and left. It had almost stopped raining, but the road down the hill was a rushing stream of tumbling rocks and debris, and he had to take it super slow, worrying all the way about the Kia's low ground clearance, wondering if that was their Tia whom Torque had gotten a call from.

CHAPTER 13

———————o———————

THE NEXT DAY, BENEATH SECURE BLUE SKIES, APELU RETURNED to the place on top of Canco Hill with Asia. Asia would have it no other way. They had talked about his visit when he returned her car. She had to meet Sister. She was sure that it must be the same Tia. Apelu had called Torque first—at the cell phone number Sister had given him—and asked if it was okay for him to come up and close the deal. Torque wasn't at home at the time— he was on the road—but he said he'd be there later, around noon. Asia insisted that they get there earlier, before Torque got home, and Apelu could see her point—if they were already there when Torque returned Apelu might not have to explain why he had brought Asia along. So it was a half hour before noon when they arrived at the house on Canco Hill. It was quiet. Torque's wooden-bed pickup was gone.

Apelu got out of the car and went up to the porch screen door, knocked and called hello. No answer. He knocked again, more softly, and called into the house in Samoan, "Hello. It's me, Dorset. Anybody home? Torque?" Again no answer. He walked back to the car, where Asia was standing outside the driver's side door. "Nobody home, I guess," he told her.

"Yes, what is it?" Sister was standing in the open screen door, holding a sleeping toddler. "Oh, it's you. Torque's not here. He won't be home for a while."

Asia came around the front of the car and walked toward the porch. "Oh, what a beautiful baby," she said and smiled and went up onto the porch to admire the child.

"He's asleep," Sister said, but she didn't protest Asia's approach. "He's had a fever, teething."

The child had long golden brown curly hair of the type highly prized by Samoans. Asia reached out to touch it, and Sister shifted her weight to move his head away.

Asia pulled her hand back. "He is so precious," she said in Samoan.

"He's my darling," Sister answered, and for a series of seconds they both stood there admiring the sleeping child.

"How do you call him?" Asia asked in proper Samoan.

"This is Peni, *lou penina*," Sister said softly, my pearl. "You can wait for Torque if you want."

Apelu remained standing in the dirt of the yard, watching, a wholly unnecessary adjunct to this scene. The child stirred in Sister's arms. She soothed him, and then with a turn of her head and a raising of her eyebrows she invited Asia inside. A tentacle of some sort of bond had been established between them. They disappeared into the house. Apelu went up onto the porch and sat at the picnic table, lit a cigarette, smiled, and shook his head.

The silence of the place pleased him. He felt an unusual peace sitting there at the picnic table on the porch at the top of Canco Hill, the peace of being someone fictional—Dorset—the peace of being disemployed from bosses and routines, the peace of being with a woman who didn't feel duty bound to find his faults and outline them like a body at the murder scene of a relationship. It was a bit like what he imagined being in a movie would be like—everyone playing a part not themselves. He was no longer Detective Sergeant Apelu Soifua. Torque was really neither

Torque nor J-Cool. What was Sister's actual name? Tia wasn't Tia. The kids who lived here—Lucy et al.—were just extras on location, away from home and their own real selves. Was Asia playing Sally the social worker now? What would baby Peni's given name be when the credits rolled? Maybe it all made better sense when you weren't playing that character called yourself, when you got to make it up as you went along. Someone had once told him that few people lived more than twenty-seven thousand days, and that number had stuck in his head, as few numbers ever had—it seemed so small, so few afternoons after all to be pissed away being the same person, perfecting inertia.

Asia came quietly out the screen door onto the porch. She was carrying a mug with a tea bag tag hanging out of it. She sat down beside Apelu. "She's putting the baby to bed," she said.

"Plot line?" he asked.

"I told her I was your girlfriend, that I came here with you from California on holiday, first visit."

"And your command of Samoan?"

"That I worked with young Samoan women, mostly girls in trouble back in South San Francisco, that that was how I met you."

"What? That I was one of the guys that got the girls in trouble?"

"No, that you were one of the local Samoan businessmen who helped support the halfway house I worked in."

"I don't think I can play that role."

"You don't have to. Ignore it. It will seem like humility."

"And are you Sally again?"

"Yes, Sally Matthews, RN."

"And are you?"

"What?"

"Either Matthews or a registered nurse?"

"What a silly question, Dorset. Here she comes. Give me a smooch." And Asia leaned over, put a hand on the nape of

Apelu's neck, and gave him a quick kiss on the lips. It was nice. It felt almost real.

"Did she ask you how many kids you have?" he asked.

"Yes, she did," Asia said, and she kissed him again just as Sister came onto the porch. She too was carrying a mug of tea.

"I don't allow that sort of stuff here," Sister said, "but then you two haven't been teenagers for a while, so I suppose it's all right."

"Dorset told me what you do up here for the kids. I think it's great," Asia said, playfully pushing Apelu away as if their kissing had been his idea. "I want to hear more. Maybe we can work together somehow. I mean if any of your girls need a mainland escape route or connection to family or something we can do."

Asia was writing the script now, and she ran with it. Soon she and Sister were exchanging feminist war stories. Sitting there listening, Apelu felt embarrassed. He had noticed horseshoe pits and stakes in the yard and without excusing himself he got up and walked out to examine them. He found three horseshoes scattered in the weeds nearby. There was probably a fourth somewhere, but he was only going to play against himself. So, as the ladies talked, Apelu clinked horseshoes back and forth between the two stakes. He hadn't thrown horseshoes in years. That too felt good, a nicely mindless, numbing exercise. He raised a sweat.

After a while the baby started crying in the house—maybe the clanging horseshoes had awakened him—and Sister disappeared inside. Apelu walked up to the porch railing.

"You know, that baby's not hers," Asia said. "One of her girls in transit just left it here a year ago."

"Good for Sister," Apelu said. "Any other news?"

"Well, she thinks where Torque is this morning is trying to connect with this girl Tia."

"Just another girl in trouble?"

"Yes and no. Normally the girls find Sister. This time Sister doesn't know anything about her. She's always called for Torque."

"Is Sister jealous?"

"I didn't get that impression. I'm not sure what their relationship is. Maybe they really are brother and sister."

When Sister came back onto the porch she was carrying baby Peni again, who was fussing. He had been sweating in the crib, and his curly locks were now stuck to his head in disarray. "Here comes Torque," Sister said. Apelu could hear a truck struggling up the hill, and in a minute or two the old black pickup turned into the driveway. They could see two people sitting in the front—Torque and a woman. Sister went back into the house with the baby.

As Torque got out of the truck, Asia said, "I recognize him from Ezra's. He was one of the guys smoking the joint."

And as the woman got out, Apelu said, "Yeah, that's our Tia. I recognize her from her passport photo. See the birthmark by her left eye?"

In spite of the almost black birthmark on her left cheekbone, Tia was a handsome young woman, round faced and round bodied. She was as tall as Torque and was wearing a simple sleeveless sundress. She carried herself well—shoulders squared, head back.

When Torque saw them sitting on the porch, he squinted, then nodded, then turned to say something to Tia. When they came up to the porch, Tia gave them just the briefest glance and half smile of greeting before going into the house. Torque was right behind her. He managed a "Yo, Dorset, howzit?" on his way by.

"And we?" Asia asked.

"Wait," Apelu said.

As they waited they watched the chickens, wild Samoan chickens. People liked having chickens around their yards because they kept the insects—especially the centipedes—under control. The chickens weren't cooped. No one searched for or ate their eggs. No one ate the chickens anymore, either. Sometimes you threw scraps or leftover rice out for them to eat so that they would hang around. Apelu had discovered that the chickens in his yard liked the raw chicken fat he trimmed from his frozen store-bought birds. They would fight over it. They were pretty birds—the hens mainly russet and black with rust-colored heads, the cocks black, gold, and scarlet. They spent all day strutting and pecking and they slept in the trees at night. In Torque's yard, a new cock was moving in, staying to the edges. The cock of the yard would charge in the young cock's direction every so often, keeping him marginal. Then one time the new cock didn't turn tail but stood his ground.

"Watch this," Apelu said.

The feathers on both birds fluffed out, and they half arched their wings—like body builders showing off or pro wrestlers entering the ring. The cocks circled each other head to head. The hens ignored them. Then they simultaneously burst into the air about six inches off the ground, wings out, and attacked. The youngster forced the adult backward, and they broke and circled again. In the next burst, the senior used his height to hit over the head of junior, pushing him down, but junior didn't back off. They went at it again, talons out into the opponent's breast.

"They're really quite graceful," Asia said, "in a martial arts sort of way."

"It's like ballet with claws," Apelu said.

"Is it to the death?"

"Never. One of them will always retreat and the winner will quickly mount the nearest hen. To prove something, I guess."

They went at it again, and the bigger, more experienced *toa* began to take over. In Samoan *toa* meant both rooster and warrior. But the younger bird refused to surrender the field easily and pushed Pops to the limit before finally conceding. Pops was bushed. Maybe next time or the time after that the result would be different. Pops was so tired he didn't even claim his prize.

"I thought you said…?"

"Maybe they're more polite about the screwing part when there's a woman present."

Torque came out the screen door alone onto the porch. "So, Sally, right? Dorset's mainland squeeze. Torque," and he went over to shake her hand. "Welcome to our mountain home."

Asia half stood to meet him and shake his hand. "It's a pleasure to be here."

Torque turned to Apelu, "Sorry about yesterday, man. I just had to take a little rest."

"No problem. Hey, I listened to the CDs. They're not bad."

"Good, good," Torque said, sitting down.

"But that's not why we're here, really," Apelu said. "We're here to talk with Tia," and he pulled out his ID case and badge to show Torque. He sort of hated saying good-bye to Dorset.

"Okay," Torque said, "the CD deal is off. I don't do business with cops."

"Good idea. You can't trust them with money," Apelu said. "But you can talk to us. How do you know Tia?"

"Don't really. She called a couple of days ago, needed a place to stay." Torque seemed to have nothing to hide.

"How did she know to call you?"

"Mutual friend in Apia. You guys want some lunch? Sister is fixing some."

"That would be nice," Asia said. "I'll go help."

"No need. Sister and Tia got it covered."

"A mutual friend?" Apelu asked.

"Yeah, a mutual friend."

"Did Tia or your mutual friend tell you that she was in trouble?"

"Figured that out myself."

"So do you usually hide people in trouble with Immigration?"

"I don't think her trouble is with Immigration. Look, Dorset, or whatever your name is, the girl's in a bind. I haven't done anything wrong. She hasn't done anything wrong."

"How do you know that?"

"I just know, okay? Tia's just got to lay low for a while that's all, and then we'll get her back home."

"Smuggle her back?" Apelu asked.

"Are you hungry?" Sister said, coming onto the porch, carrying a big plate of cold pan-fried reef fish and a metal bowl full of breadfruit in coconut cream. Behind her came Tia with a tray holding tall glasses of what looked like Tang. They put their things down on the picnic table, and Tia turned to go back inside.

"Oh, won't you join us?" Asia asked, but the girl just smiled and kept going. "Tia, please eat with us," Asia said in Samoan, and Tia stopped, then turned and looked at Torque, who nodded.

They ate together, the five of them around the table, without talking. When they had finished Tia got up to remove the dishes, but Apelu gestured her back into her seat. She obeyed.

"Tia, I'm Detective Soifua from the Territorial Department of Public Safety. We"—Apelu indicated Asia with a nod of his head—"have been looking for you. We were worried about you, after what happened to your friend and you disappearing."

Tia was not a crier. Her eyes got larger and a little moist but they flashed, and her chin came up and out toward Apelu.

"So, you're a detective," Sister said, giving Torque a hard look. Then to Apelu, "What are you talking about? What happened to her friend?"

"Tia's friend Tracey died last week. I think she was killed," Apelu said, watching Tia's face. At the mention of the dead girl's name Tia's posture became even more military and she caught the tips of her lips between her teeth, but she didn't blink.

Torque twisted nervously, crossing and uncrossing his legs beneath the table. "That's enough, man. We don't know anything about any of that. You're out of here, unwelcome. Good-bye. None of us have got to talk to you."

"I think you all should talk to me, before some goons with a little bit heavier attitude show up here and don't even bother asking questions." Apelu didn't raise his voice, but he made it hard.

"You trying to scare me, man? Because I don't scare easy. You going to tell these goons where Tia is at? Because that's the only way they'd find out. Tia's my guest. You're not. Now get out." The muscles in Torque's face had tightened up. His shoulders went back.

"If I leave now, you'll have to come with me, Torque, downtown to answer some questions about smuggling and burglary and interfering with an investigation by stealing all the evidence from Ezra's house."

Torque was instantly on his feet, pushing himself up and away from the table. "Now you are pissing me off, man, coming in here pretending you're someone you're not, sticking your nose in my business. Now threatening to bust me. I'm gonna take shit like that here, in my own crib?"

Apelu was also on his feet now, and Torque's fist caught him hard but glancingly off his cheek. Something inside Apelu, some inner tether that had been holding him down for all these days, snapped. His calmness exploded like when you throw kerosene onto a hot ember fire. A very small, distant part of him with no control whatsoever over what was happening watched him go over the picnic table and pick Torque up by his shirt and lift him off the floor.

"You stupid pile of pig shit," he heard himself say. "Maybe you'll understand it better unconscious," and he slammed Torque backward against a wall. The small part of him watching was not happy with this, but it was beyond him now. He knew from past experiences—rarer now as he got older—that once that switch had been thrown the ensuing scene could not be stopped. His body, his very angry and tense and unsettled body, was in control now. Everything he had had to pen up, all the frustrations and confusions and insults and accusations, escaped in a fury. Nothing would hurt. Nothing very much mattered beyond the venting, the release, the just punishment about to be delivered. His arms slammed Torque against the wall again, then threw him down onto the porch floor where he could stomp him properly.

The sound of the metal bowl against his temple startled him. He swung in that direction, a little stunned. The second blow was the plate smashing over the back of his head. His sight lost its white balance. He could hear himself cursing loudly in Samoan. Another smash to the side of his head from the bowl put him down.

He wasn't out long—the women were still helping Torque up off the floor—but the red warp spasm of fury was passing. He pushed himself up into a sitting position against a porch pillar and felt his head. It was bleeding. "You shouldn't have hit me," he said to Torque. "Don't ever hit me."

"I won't, man. I won't."

"You Samoan bucks should be kept in cages," Sister said to the porch at large.

Asia came slowly over and squatted in front of Apelu, looking at him curiously. Finally she said, "I thought you were a peace officer."

"I'm a Samoan first," he said. The blood of his subsiding rage was still ringing in his ears, and his voice sounded strange to him.

"So, who won round one, Mr. Toa?" Asia said, reaching out to divert a rivulet of blood falling over one of his eyebrows.

"Whoever won, at least he was Samoan."

The repair work took a while. Torque had a nice wall-inflicted split on the back of his head. Apelu had a few plate-induced slashes on his scalp and a growing purple egg on one temple. There was a fair amount of blood on the deck of the porch, which Tia cleaned up. Sister gave Asia one of Torque's T-shirts to give Apelu to replace his blood-soaked shirt. The women dealt with the aftermath—efficient, rough, acting judgmental. After about forty minutes, bandaged and cleaned up, Apelu and Torque were back sitting across from one another at the picnic table. For both of them the pains had begun, but Sister had denied them any pain killers. "Just suffer," she said. Then Sister, Tia, and Asia had driven off in Asia's Kia on some errand. Torque got up, went into the house, and came back with a bottle of tequila. "All I got in the way of painkiller," he said. They passed the bottle back and forth, still not speaking.

Apelu finally broke the silence. "Is Sister really your sister?"

"Actually she's sort of a cousin. We grew up together, anyway. Her parents did like she does and took in asshole kids like me when my parents gave up on me. Nice people, gentle. I never went back to my family. I'd spent my kidhood getting beaten up by my father. Sister's dad never laid a hand on me. He just talked a lot. How's your head?"

"Hurts."

"Here, have more. Is Sally really your girlfriend, or just another cop?"

"Neither. I'm not sure what she is."

"What do you know about this girl, Tia, and the dead chick, Tracey?" Torque asked, taking the bottle back.

"They were turning tricks on the dark side, something went wrong. Tracey turns up dead. Tia doesn't but she knows enough to vanish. What do you know?"

"I knew that shit was going on over there, but I didn't want to know about it so I ignored it. Then Willie called and told me to try to get together with Tia because he was worried about her. Then she called me. Willie had given her the number, and, yeah, I could smuggle her back to her village in Upolu tomorrow if I wanted to."

"Willie. Would that be Willie Schneider?"

"Yeah, Schneider. How'd you know? Willie and I go back a long way."

"Was it Willie who also told you to clean all the goods out of Ezra's place?"

"You are starting to piss me off again, man. If you're going to arrest me and charge me with something, then do it. Read me my fucking rights like on TV."

"If I wanted to arrest you, I'd have done it already for assaulting a police officer. That's a lot heavier than being a possible flunky in a smuggling operation. I'm just trying to figure out what's going on. I'll tell you what, Torque, I'll make a deal with you. I won't charge you with the assault or anything to do with the smuggled goods and the burglary, if you tell me what's going on."

"I'm no stoolie, man."

"You don't have to name people—I already know about Ezra and Tia and Willie—just what else you know about this whole show."

"Like what?"

"Like about where all that stuff at Ezra's came from. Like about what Willie's connection to Tia is. Shit like that."

"I don't think so, man."

"Then I'll have to make that little 'You are under arrest' speech, and I don't want to do that."

A group of the teenagers came walking up the driveway.

"We can't talk here anymore. Let's take a little hike," Torque said.

After the kids went into the house Torque picked up the bottle of tequila and left the porch. Apelu hesitated for a second then decided Torque wasn't the type to try anything drastic. He followed Torque up a trail behind the house into the bush.

The bunker was only a short hike farther up the ridgeline. It was bare gray concrete with straight walls and a curved roof partly covered by vines and bush. A path led up to a rectangular space where a door once hung, open now into the interior darkness. Apelu recognized it as one of the bunkers the US Marines had constructed on the island at the onset of World War Two when everyone had expected the islands to be attacked by the Imperial Japanese Navy. Thanks to the US Navy's defeat of the

Japanese fleet at the Battle of Midway far to the north the invasion here had never happened, but the bunkers and pillboxes and gun installations still remained, scattered along the shorelines and ridgelines of the island. At one point in the war there had been as many US military personnel on the island as there had been natives, and the term *afamalini*—half marine—had entered the language. Those children were all pushing sixty now.

This bunker was bigger than the others Apelu had seen, and when they entered it he was surprised to find it dry and clean. In the middle of the ceiling was a large circular opening where an air vent once had been. A homemade ladder led up to it. Torque tucked the bottle of tequila into the waist of his shorts and climbed the ladder. When he had cleared the hole in the roof Apelu followed him. The concrete roof was hot in the sun, but a large fau tree shaded one side of the roof, and in its shadow the concrete was cool enough to sit on.

"Antiaircraft command bunker," Torque said. "There are concrete pads for the guns all along here. We still find live ammo all over the place."

From where they were seated they could see what the guns would have been protecting. Below them, along the edge of the ocean, was the airport, which had started its life as a Marine airbase in 1942 when most of the island's defense work had been done. It was a good view of this end of the island.

"Okay," Torque started, "I don't like the Tia and Tracey thing, and I got nothing to do with it, so I'll talk, but I don't think Willie was involved in that either. I think he just knew about it too."

"Why don't we start with what you do know about—the deal with Ezra."

"Sure, that's like no news, old news, and I guess it's over now." Torque took another swallow of tequila, grimaced, and began to talk.

The smuggling operation went back a long way, back to when Ezra's father had run the interisland shipping business. Willie's dad, whom everyone called Billy, had worked for Ezra's old man, and when Ezra was young those two had gotten the smuggling business going. It was like a given. Everyone got paid off. No one complained. Everyone looked the other way. It was just *palangi* regs they were ignoring. There was as much illicit cargo as legal stuff on every boat. It went on for decades. It was still going on when Ezra retired from show biz and came back to the islands, and he got back into it, running the Pago Pago end, Billy Schneider still in Apia. When old man Schneider died, his son Willie took over that end. But then Ezra started acting weird. He wouldn't move stuff, business fell off. He started pissing people off.

"You can't have anybody pissed off in that business, man. Everyone's gotta be happy because it's all built on trust, on knowing the money is regular and nobody is skimming or ratting or cutting you short." Torque shook his head. "There was never any violence, man, threats, shit like that. Everyone was cool. For everybody involved it was just a side business, a way to make a couple of extra bucks above and beyond your shitty paycheck."

"So what was Ezra's problem?"

"Don't know. Maybe he was just losing it."

"So where were you in all this?"

Torque stopped and took another swallow of tequila. "You said you won't use anything I say against me, right?"

"That's right. You can trust me."

"My old man was a Customs agent. He ran the deal on the docks here, had a government truck with special plates. I was his driver, hauling the shit there and away."

"I thought you said you didn't go back to your family."

"I didn't go back to the family, man. I went into the family business." Torque laughed. "My old man is dead now, anyway. Then you guys got onto Ezra, I guess, and I got this call to clean his place out."

"From Willie?"

"No, from someone I didn't know. But they knew what they were talking about and they told me where I should take it and all. So I did. Kept the CDs as my payment. I was the one who ordered them anyway, then Ezra wouldn't give 'em to me. He pointed a shotgun at me, that asshole, when I went to get 'em. That whacko old asshole. But it's over now, I guess. Willie said that it was a shutdown and that I just should cool it."

"When was that?"

"When he called from Apia to ask me to look out for Tia. He said something was shaking up over there and that he would be gone for a while. That probably means out of Apia, back to Auckland for Willie."

"Willie and Tia connection?" Apelu had a bunch of questions.

"Like I said, I don't think he was in on that importing prostitutes deal. He's too classy for that shit, likes the ladies too much. A romantic, know what I mean? All the ladies are delicate saints to Willie."

Then a voice called up from somewhere below them, "Yo, Torque, you up there?"

"Yo, what's up?"

"Sister called. She says she needs your help."

"Where's she at?"

"At the police station. She said to tell you that she's been arrested."

CHAPTER 14

— o —

ON HIS WAY TO TOWN AND THE POLICE STATION TORQUE GAVE Apelu a ride to where he could catch an *ainga* bus back out toward Piapiatele. His head was pounding. Sister had said nothing about Asia or Tia when she'd called. From where the bus dropped him off he walked first to Asia's house. She wasn't there, and he began to worry.

Back at Ezra's, Apelu went to the bottle of codeine pills in Ezra's bathroom medicine cabinet and swallowed several. When the pain pills hit the tequila he almost threw up, and he rummaged around in the kitchen until he found a packet of saimin noodles. He broke them up and ate them raw the way his kids did. They were stale, but he ate them all, as if they were a part of his medicine. He felt woozy, so he went to Leilani's room to lie down. He had trouble finding a nonpainful position for his head on the pillows but must have succeeded because he finally dozed off.

He dreamed there was a bird in his hair, but it was a deadly bird, a bird with a poisonous beak, so he must remain perfectly still lest he startle it into attack, just stay calm and let it fly away.

"Apelu, Apelu." The bird had a voice and it was Asia's. The bird was Asia's hand smoothing his hair away from his wounds. Asia was sitting beside him on the bed in the twilight. Not all the waves pounding were inside his head. He could smell her—musk, sweetness, and sun-dried hair.

"Apelu, you're bleeding again. We'll have to change the bandages. Can you get up?"

"I was worried about you," he said.

Her hand came to rest on the side of his face. "It's almost like you were always here in this house," she said, with that same curious look as before on her face.

"It's been a long day," he said and tried to smile, but it hurt enough to make him stop.

"Nice try," she said, just touching his lips with her finger. "Come on. I've got better bandages and antibiotic cream and some codeine and Steinlager, some Chinese takeout. I even brought your bloody shirt back too. You're not brain-damaged are you?"

"Always have been," he said, sitting up with a pulse of pain. "Why change?"

Asia took one of his arms to help him stand up. He was still shaky, but once on his feet, with his king-size head at a steady altitude, he was all right. "Say, Doc, will I still be able to play the piano?"

"You don't own a piano. You're a cop."

"Oh, right."

As Asia ministered to Apelu's wounds she told him what had happened that afternoon. After the fight, Sister just wanted to get out of the house. Tia didn't have a single change of clothes, so they drove down to get her something else to wear. By the time they got to the Clothes Mart the baby was asleep, so Asia stayed in the car with the sleeping baby and the air-conditioner on while Sister and Tia went in to shop. It seemed to be taking a long time and Asia was thinking about going in to see what the delay was about when a police car came pulling into the parking lot under siren, and two uniformed officers went into the store. Asia pulled out of the parking lot and backed into a spot farther away on the street, where she could see what was happening but could get away quickly. Then Sister and Tia were both brought out of the store with their hands cuffed behind them and put in the back of the squad car, which drove off under siren toward town. The siren woke the baby up, who started crying. Asia followed the squad car all the way to the police station, but by the time she got there they were already inside. She didn't know what to do. Who was she? If she went in, what would she say? The baby, who had gone back to sleep while she was driving, was awake again and screaming. She couldn't leave the baby. She had never been responsible for a baby before. She thought of calling Apelu, but she didn't know the number of the place on Canco Hill. So she drove back out there, but by the time she got there Apelu and Torque had left. All the young people were there. They knew that Sister had been arrested, but they didn't know for what. They were glad to see Peni and immediately took him off to change his diaper and feed him. She had left the baby there with them. Was that the right thing to do? Then she came here to Ezra's house, but Apelu wasn't here, so she went looking for him.

"Why in the world would they be arrested?" she asked as she opened the Styrofoam plates of Chinese takeout on the coffee table in the front room. "I can't see them shoplifting."

"When they came out of the store were there just the uniformed officers with them?" Apelu asked.

"No, actually, there was a man in regular clothes who put them in the squad car then drove off after them in his own car."

"Immigration guy maybe. Made Tia in the store. That birthmark is hard to miss if you're looking for it."

"Then why arrest Sister?" Asia was spooning shrimp fried rice and beef with broccoli onto plates.

"Maybe she tried to interfere, got in the guy's face or something, caused a scene." Apelu ate gratefully. The cold Steinlager tasted especially good. "Get anything from Tia?"

"I was saving that. It's interesting. The poor girl."

As they ate, Asia told Apelu Tia's story. "You don't mind if I get a little graphic, do you? We girls can talk pretty dirty when we're by ourselves and angry about something."

"I'd consider it a privilege to be privy to as much unedited reporting as you care to give. I am familiar with most of the common bad words that guys use."

"Okay. Well, our girl Tia has got quite a mouth on her and she wasn't shy about dishing to Sister and me. I think she needed a sympathetic ear, and Sister definitely has one. They really got into it. Sometimes they'd forget I was there and speak Samoan when they got excited, but I got most of it. Tia's not shy about what she did for a living over there. Most of her johns were Korean fishermen, although a few of your fellow law enforcement officers were regulars. There are a couple of back rooms at Woo's place where the lie-down part of the business took place. There was a set fee—forty-five dollars—that they had to give to Mrs. Woo or the bartender, but whatever tips they could boost on top of that were theirs."

"In-house then?" Apelu helped himself to more food.

"In-house mostly, and what Tia referred to as their regular boyfriends on the boats. But recently Mr. Woo has had some special clients that they took care of outside, in hotel rooms and a couple of times at Woo's house."

"Special clients?"

"Yeah, always Chinese men. That's how Tracey and Tia got in trouble. I gather they were the senior girls there, the ones that got the outside assignments, the bigger rollers. Sometimes they would spend days with these men, get clothes and big tips on the side."

"The dark-side big leagues."

"A little sympathy is in order here, Apelu. The girls were slaves. They didn't have any say in the matter."

"They could have walked away, gone home."

"The Woos held their passports."

"They could have come to the police."

"Cops were their clients. Maybe even their sponsors."

"Don't go there."

"They didn't think they had a choice. Their chance at a life as a potentially respectable wife back in their village was already ruined. No one wants to marry a whore, someone Asian men have been paying to have sex with."

"Getting graphic." Apelu was getting a little embarrassed. He wasn't used to talking with a woman about stuff like this.

"Tracey had been there longest. She was like all the other girls' older sister or auntie. She would stand up to Mrs. Woo for them, get them things they needed, take them to the health clinic when they needed that."

There was a pause, but Apelu didn't fill it.

"You can't know, can you, what their lives were like? When all you are is just a sum of some of your external parts—your tits, your ass, your mouth, your cunt—nothing more. When even your real name is meaningless. Just a thing to get ejaculated into."

"No, of course I can't know that," Apelu said. No man wants to know that.

He looked up at Asia, whose head was bent down now as she ate—the delicate features of her suntanned face, the fine bones of her brow and nose and cheekbones. It struck him that she hadn't asked that question to attack him, as he had taken it. It was just a question. A question that not even she could answer. She had never been a prostitute either, but there was empathy there for Tia and Tracey and the other girls that Apelu had never felt, maybe never allowed himself to feel. Which made sense. He had been a cop long enough to know to leave such tender emotions behind when he hit the beat, where they were worse than dysfunctional; they were dangerous.

"Can we get back to Tia's story?" he asked. "So what happened?"

"So, one night last week Mr. Woo drove Tia out to one of his special jobs, in a motel near the airport. 'Very important man,' he told her. 'You treat him good.' Tracey wanted the job, but Woo chose Tia because she was younger. So she goes there, and the guy is a fat pig. He makes her undress while he eats a room service meal. He talks dirty, calls her bad names. He has her play with herself. Then he does all the usual stuff, but he's cruel and abusive about it. After he's done and he tells her to leave, Tia asks him for her money and he just laughs at her, tells her he won't pay for such poor service. He calls her an overweight, unscented, unskilled amateur. He said he had demeaned himself by being with her and that she should pay him for being serviced by the famous Dr. Win Chung. He bragged to her that back home in China he had had the freshest and the best thirteen-year-old girls who were pros compared to her and that soon in Las Vegas he would be enjoying the best professional erotic service available from young blonde American girls. Then he threw her out of his room without paying her."

"What was the dude's name again?"

"Win Chung, I think she said, Dr. Win Chung."

"So what happened next?"

"Well, that night she had to get back to Leloaloa without any money, which is another story, but the next day she and Tracey went to talk to the Woos about her treatment and her not getting paid by Mr. Woo's special friend."

"Which is when the fight broke out?" Apelu pushed his plate away and snapped shut the Styrofoam tops of the take-out containers. Asia had eaten very little.

"No, I gathered that the fight was a day or two later. The first time Mr. Woo just brushed them off, said Tia had obviously done a bad job. Then Tracey convinced Tia that they should go back and push it again, that Tia deserved something for her evening's work. Tracey thought the fact that this Dr. Chung had told Tia he had just come from China and was headed for Las Vegas might be something Mr. Woo would pay to keep secret. This Tracey was something else. According to Tia she wasn't afraid of everything like the other girls." Asia picked up their plates and the Styrofoam containers and walked off to the kitchen. Apelu appreciated the peace of the few minutes she was gone.

"It was at that second meeting," Asia said as she came back, "that all hell broke loose, with Mrs. Woo screaming at them and Mr. Woo throwing a stapler at Tracey, which hit Tia instead, in the forehead. Then Tracey got Tia out of there and stashed her temporarily with some friends in Fagatogo, then she took off 'like on some sort of mission,' Tia said."

"Then dead Tracey?"

"Right. No one heard from her or saw her again until you found her," Asia said as with her right hand she flicked errant leftover pieces of rice from the top of the coffee table into her left hand. If she had ever worn a wedding ring, it hadn't been for long or recently, Apelu surmised, watching her hands. There was something about her hands that didn't match the rest of her. They were older, more used, not as forgiving to look at as the rest of her. They were almost a man's hands, so strong.

"And the blackmail would be?" Apelu asked.

"Maybe Tracey figured out that a self-important Chinese doctor wouldn't be legally entering the US through the back door of Pago Pago."

"Would that be worth killing her for?"

"Can't let your whores get too uppity. These aren't nice people."

As they were talking the wind had picked up, and rain now lashed at the windows with an uneven but increasing frequency. Another seasonal squall was moving in off the ocean. They stopped to listen. The angry urgency of an open-ocean squall line hitting the island's permanence—like two contrary elemental forces vying to occupy the same space—was always arresting. Here on the exposed, lava-bound coast it was even harder to ignore.

"Nasty out."

"No thunder and lightning anyway."

"That usually means it will last longer."

"Apelu, can I stay here tonight? I'm not ready to be alone in that house after everything that happened today."

"Okay, sure. We got lots of room here at the inn. Thanks for dinner, by the way, and the beer."

"Thanks for the company. What are we going to do, Apelu?"

"About Tia and Sister? I'm not sure. Circle our wagons, rally the troops, cash in our chips, pray for rain, round up all the usual clichés."

"You can skip the prayer for rain. No, really. What can we do to get Sister and Tia out?"

"Don't know, can't say. Let me sleep on it. Maybe I'll think of something tomorrow, make some calls. Right now my head wants to lie down."

"You can think for both of us."

"I recognize that line, but you're not Ingrid Bergman."

"Can I call you Rick? Can I call this Rick's Place?"

"Whatever it takes to confuse people." Apelu got up and headed toward the door to Ezra's bunker and bedroom. His arms and legs were heavy. "You can have Leilani's room. If there's blood on the pillows, I'm afraid all you can do is turn them over."

"No, I wouldn't think of throwing you out of your bed. Come on," and Asia took him by the arm and led him back to Leilani's room and to the rumpled bed. She turned the blood-stained pillows over and straightened out the sheets. "Rest is what you need," she said. "I'm going to go feed Nick and Nora. Don't worry about me."

Apelu got into the bed and Asia pulled the sheet up over him. She brought him two codeine and a glass of water then turned out the light. She sat beside him on the empty side of the bed. He could still see her face in the light from the other room. With one of her strong hands she smoothed the sheet then softly touched the purple egg on his brow. She had that curious look on her face again. He closed his eyes. She left. The rain scratched and streamed down Leilani's ocean-side windows. He slept.

He awoke to the momentary chill of the sheet being lifted. Asia's aroma then her body came softly against him. A hand on his shoulder. It was perfectly dark except for the sound of the rain that defined the boundaries of their safe space inside it.

"Hold me, Apelu," Asia said. "I want you to hold me."

Apelu held her, and after a while their muscles relaxed as they felt each other's warmth, and after a longer while their faces touched, then their lips, their tongues—the taste of comfort—and then deep inside the darkness and the deeper rain their bodies did what bodies do when laid side by side at night. They let their lonelinesses mingle and cancel one another.

In the morning they both were shy. The rain had stopped. At first light Asia left for her house. Apelu went back to sleep. When he finally did get up, he got the cold leftover Chinese food from the refrigerator and sat eating it where he and Asia had eaten the night before. He sort of wished she was still there. The morning light felt incomplete without her. He wondered what she was doing, what she might be thinking. Their lovemaking had been gentle, wordless, lingering, the act melting into the memory. In spite of his aching ribs and head, he was smiling.

Apelu took two more codeine and thought of calling his house, but it was late. The kids would be at school. He did not want to speak with Sina. He did not want to think of Sina. He called Mati at the attorney general's office. He was in.

"You still on-island?" Mati asked. "The smart money all had you gone."

"Listen, Mati, what's going on?"

"After the news of your sponsoring that dead prostitute came out there was talk about how there should be some sort of investigation, but when you vanished the AG let the talk slide by. He even seemed a little relieved that you weren't around. Where you been?"

"No, Mati, I mean what's going on about your boss pretending he didn't know what you were doing with me in Apia?"

"Yeah, he asked me about that. Listen, I can't talk about this on the phone. Let's meet somewhere so that I can get you up to speed."

"All right. You know where Vailoatai is?"

"Yes."

"Just east of the village along the coast road there's a bunch of graves, Korean fishermen, right by the road, on top of the cliff. You can't miss them. I'll meet you there. When's good for you?"

"Vailoatai? I'll be there in an hour."

"Good. I'll meet you there. Come alone."

Apelu got dressed and quickly set out. The sleep had helped his head, though there was no hiding the purple lump on his temple. He was lucky with the buses and got to Vailoatai in enough time to find a comfortable hiding place in the high bunch grass on the incline across the road from the Korean fishermen's graveyard. Mati arrived about ten minutes later, alone, in a government car with bright yellow LA—Legal Affairs—plates. He parked on the shoulder, got out of the car, walked down to the graves, and looked around. Apelu gave him a couple of minutes to make sure he was alone. This was a pretty deserted stretch of village road. No more cars passed. Mati sat down on a gravestone with his back to the ocean, which Apelu thought strange because the seascape was especially spectacular here. So Mati spotted

Apelu right away when he stood up and came down to the road. Mati waited for him on his grave.

"That looks like you, Apelu, only a younger you who has been mugged."

"Tough life living in the bush."

"I thought that was you with that Sally woman in the Captain's Table. It was you, wasn't it?"

"Yeah."

"You look good without the moustache, but purple is not your color."

"Cute. Come on. There's a spot where we can't be seen from the road, though I must say that your plates are a bit conspicuous."

Mati followed Apelu down a crude path to a wide lower shelf in the cliff face where they sat down facing the sea.

"So talk to me, Mati. Tell me things I don't know."

"Well, I'll tell you I think you're a good cop, an honest cop who's been set up."

"I said tell me things I don't know."

"I know you weren't involved with that woman, that you weren't her sponsor."

"How do you know that and everyone else knows something different?"

"Because I know who her real sponsor was. I think even you might be surprised at the name."

"A secret?"

"For the time being. I have to confirm it."

"So who switched the mystery person's name to mine?"

"Who is in charge of the Office of Immigration?"

"Sometimes it seems like nobody is in charge over there. What do you mean?"

"What government department is the Office of Immigration a part of?"

"Why, your office, the Attorney General's Office."

Mati didn't say anything.

"You mean the attorney general changed the sponsorship names?"

"I think my boss the attorney general has it in for you."

"I'm flattered, of course, but why do you suppose that is?"

"I think he thought you were sniffing around his house of cards too close for comfort, and he wanted to discredit you, scare you off the case. Which is why he was relieved when you disappeared."

"What case?" Apelu lit a cigarette.

"You know, I picked up an interesting piece of information in Apia. I wasn't just there checking numbers. Know who the AG is related to? Mrs. Strand."

"Leilani?"

"Yep, his auntie. That piece of the puzzle fell nicely into place. I was looking for that one extra connection, and there it was, the family thing. I think I can make a case now, at least enough of a case to get some subpoenas brought down."

"Look, Mati, I already know you're FBI."

Mati looked at Apelu. For the first time they looked at each other sort of as equals.

"I knew you were a good cop," Mati said, "but I didn't know you were that good a detective. Anyone else know?"

"I didn't tell anyone, if that's what you mean."

"That as general knowledge would not be helpful at this juncture."

"Why all the secrecy? You feds don't trust us?"

"Do you trust us?"

"Not especially, unless you are collaring some international fugitive here."

"Well, we trust you guys even less, and it is the top law enforcement official in the territory we are going after. When I was implanted here I was told to keep my cover."

"Then you shouldn't have gone through my things in Apia."

Mati snorted, nodded, and looked out to sea. "Say, isn't that your bird?" he said.

And sure enough, circling slowly a hundred yards or so offshore was the white heron.

"*Talofa, lo'u susuga. Afio mai,*" Apelu said to the bird. "He's here to help me handle this well," he said to Mati. "So, why FBI? What's the big deal? A little interisland smuggling in the middle of watery nowhere."

"That's the way it looked to us too, at first. Your assistant commissioner made an unofficial back-channel request for an investigation through the Department of the Interior. Interior to Justice, then the State Department got involved too because the case crossed international borders. Everybody wanted to look good for the other agencies. So what started out as—I gather—just a play in a little old political battle between the assistant commissioner's family and the AG's family—grinding an ax that went back a bunch of generations—turned into full federal involvement. It's on the docket of a federal grand jury in San Francisco, and they're ready to bust the AG—if I can come up with enough to present to them."

"Ezra's old smuggling ring before a federal grand jury? That's hilarious."

"Well, it's not just Ezra's old smuggling ring. The AG has been involved—through his family connection and for a cut of the profits—in protecting it since he came into office. That's what the assistant commissioner had on him. That's what Interior didn't like, the official corruption angle. But now, thanks to you, I think we may be able to connect him to the sex trafficking trade as well."

"Thanks to me?"

"Yeah. You know the AG called me into his office and questioned me about your claim that I was in Apia working with you on the smuggling case, and I denied it, said sure, I was over there on vacation, chasing a little pussy, and we ran into each other and talked about what you were doing, but that I had nothing to do with it. How could I? I had never been assigned that job, and I don't do anything I'm not assigned."

"So nobody in your office knew you were working on that?"

"No, when I wasn't in the office, they just thought I was goofing off. I told the AG that you must have just made up the bit about working with me in a desperate shot at giving yourself some sort of plausible excuse. I think he bought it, because he has a rather low opinion of my...um...my work ethic. Anyway, he seemed sort of obsessed with getting you suspended. Then when your name was in the paper as that girl's sponsor, that seemed really strange to me, so I did some checking around. You gave Immigration a list of names of overstayers you were wondering about, right?"

"Yeah, a list of Western Samoan women's names."

"Well, I found that list and followed up on it, and for every one of those women the name of their sponsor had been changed to one of two people—to either you or the assistant commissioner. Then I uncovered who their previous sponsors had been—they forgot to deep-six records of who paid their original immigration bonds—and another cover-up looked pretty obvious."

"Your mystery name?"

"Names. Let's just say they were already familiar to me."

"From your smuggling investigation?"

"From the smuggling investigation. Well, when I reported that to my home office all sorts of lights went on, because a new directive had just come down about prioritizing cases of human trafficking, and here we had a possible case of sex slaves being imported from a foreign country into a US territory for criminal purposes. In addition to which one of the sex slaves had just died in mysterious circumstances, and one or more high-ranking local political figures were possibly involved. Well, piranhas could learn from the feeding frenzy that set off."

"And no one else here knows about any of this?" Apelu flicked the butt of his finished cigarette over the lip of the cliff.

"Nope. Just the assistant commissioner, not his boss nor his boss's boss. Just him, me, and now you."

"And why me?"

"Partly it's that enemy-of-my-enemy thing. My job is to get enough on the AG to indict him, and he thinks that you are his biggest threat. The mere fact that he set you up twice—having you suspended for your Apia trip and then hanging the dead whore around your neck—proves that you're not one of his guys. And I need a little backup here. The assistant commissioner is off in San Francisco talking to the grand jury. My office is trying to get a couple more agents down here, but that won't happen before this weekend's flight from Honolulu at the earliest. And I need this girl Tia. I need her testimony. I could use your help with finding her. I figured that she was what you were looking for at the Captain's Table that night, not picking up white chicks but looking for Tia. Any luck?"

"You mean you don't know?"

"Know what?"

"Well, yeah, I found her. Then I lost her. She was picked up by the police yesterday afternoon. They took her downtown."

"Immigration?"

"Gotta be. Plainclothes bust."

"Shit. Shit." Mati got up and started pacing. There wasn't much room on the ledge to pace, so it was more like turning around in one place.

"But I got her story," Apelu said.

A car horn started honking up by the road.

"Sparks, Sparks," someone was yelling.

"Who the fuck is that?" Mati said. He was irritated. He darted up the trail to the graveyard, out of sight. "Yeah, what?" he yelled.

There were four rapid shots, the solid pops of a high-powered weapon with a muzzle silencer. The first one missed. Apelu heard it ricochet off the stony ground. The other three didn't miss. Apelu could hear those too, stopped with a squishy thud. Mati uttered a sound when the first slug hit him—a two-note combined complaint and plea. The second slug elicited only a surrendering groan. The third slug was met by silence. Apelu heard the body hit the hard earth. He was quickly on his hands and knees, looking over the edge of the cliff for a way out of there when he heard the screech of departing tires. By the time he got to Mati the fleeing black sedan had almost reached the first curve in the road leading away from them. Apelu caught the flash of a bright yellow government plate above the rear bumper, just like the plates on Mati's car.

CHAPTER 15

——— ○ ———

I T WAS A FOUR–TO FIVE–MILE HIKE BACK ALONG THE COAST
from Vailoatai to Piapiatele, and stretches of it were not easy
walking. Beyond Sliding Rock Apelu had to find bush trails
because the cliffs were too treacherous. He didn't hear any distant sirens and he wondered how long Mati's body would lie
there before it was found. The last shot had been to the head, and
there wasn't much left of it. On the edge of Vaitogi he stopped at
a bush store and bought a liter of water and a couple of apples.
Food didn't interest him, but he knew he should eat something.
He stopped at Asia's house, but she wasn't there. Apelu was sort
of glad for that.

Back at Ezra's he stood under the shower for a long time, but
when he got out he still didn't feel clean. He washed and dried
all his clothes in the machines, throwing his blood-stained shirt
from the day before into the trash. He wanted a song in his head,
but there was none. He wanted to hear music, but there was nothing there to play it on.

Apelu called Lisa Ah Chong's office number in Apia and got
her. Before he placed the call he had decided not to tell Lisa anything about the FBI, Mati, and the case he had been trying to

make against the AG, any of it, especially not about the day's events, which he still had not fully absorbed.

"Lisa? *Talofa*, Apelu here, checking in for a little information exchange. How you doing?"

"Apelu? Where are you calling from?"

"Why does that seem to be the first thing everyone wants to know about me?"

"You sound like you're still in Tutuila from the connection."

"Yes, I'm still in Tutuila. Why?"

"Because yesterday we got a request to keep an eye out for you over here."

"A request from whom?"

"Your Attorney General's Office, I believe. It didn't say you were wanted for anything, just that they wanted information about your whereabouts."

"Is that usual?"

"No, it's highly irregular, which is why it was brought to my attention, for a legal opinion."

"Which was?"

"That, seeing as we get so little cooperation from them on similar requests, screw them, show them the mirror. There are no legal grounds for us to do anything. What have you done?"

"Pissed off a few people, I guess. No big problem. They just couldn't find me for a couple of days. Like you said, I'm not wanted for anything. It's being straightened out." About as straight as a pig's intestines, Apelu thought. "Listen, I wanted to let you know that the missing girl turned up alive, okay, and she got picked up by our Immigration. I guess they'll send her back."

"All the others are back. I've got tabs on it."

"Talked to any of them yet?"

"No. I've been told that I can't, have no reason to, that they didn't break any of our laws."

"Come on, Lisa."

"I'll be seeing two of them this weekend, on my own time."

"That's more like it. Got anything for me?"

"I looked into your Mr. Schneider and Ms. Malolo. Turns out I've met Mr. Schneider, though I didn't know the name. Everybody I know calls him Uila, not Willy, and he moves in a crowd that goes by just nicknames. A bit of a playboy. In fact, he made a play for me in a bar once. Good dancer, I must say. He's got two priors, both for grand theft. One he got dropped on a procedural technicality—all of the physical evidence against him went missing. The other he got plea bargained down to a fine and parole-level violation. No time. Current whereabouts strangely unknown. I even hit the places that would be regular for someone like him the other night and didn't find him. No one has seen him around in a week or two."

Apelu grunted.

"Your Miss Ulifanua Malolo I could find nothing on."

"Figures," Apelu said. "I've got another name for you to look into, if you don't mind. It happens to be Chinese. No offense, no innuendo. Doctor Win Chung."

"No offense taken. Wait. That sounds familiar. Win Chung? Hold on. Yes. Remember that joke list our Immigration goons here gave me, of recent arrivals of people with Chinese surnames? Win Chung was one of those names. Only there's no Doctor in front of it, just Win Chung."

"I think there's a connection between him and our dead girl."

"What sort of connection?"

"Circumstantial. Let's call it circumstantial. How many Chinese names you got on your list?"

"Eight, nine counting your Dr. Chung. Why?"

"What's your policy on Chinese nationals as visitors?"

"Pretty loose. Though we don't get many. They're treated like any other tourists, automatic thirty-day visas. Come on, they've got an embassy here. They're very generous with aid."

"Built you a new sports stadium, I believe."

"And a very nice one too, much nicer than anything you've got over there in American Samoa. Listen, Apelu, what's going on over there? Your authorities have ignored these girls as over-stayers for months, years in some cases, now suddenly there's a dragnet out for them? Some sort of turf war going on or what?"

"No, not a turf war, I don't think. There's no evidence of that. Something else is going on. Something's falling apart." Apelu thought of a bright yellow license plate on a black sedan disappearing around a curve on a seaside road. "I don't know what exactly. I'll get back to you."

Apelu fixed himself a bowl of saimin, fixing it properly this time, pouring hot water over the noodles and letting them soften in their sauce before eating. Then he took two more of Ezra's codeine and went out to feed Nick and Nora. They were happy to see him. He did what he had seen Asia do. He scooped dog food from the galvanized garbage can into the plastic bucket, and then he found the key to the lock on the ledge above the gate, unlocked the lock, and went into the kennel. He dumped the dry dog food into one trough and filled the other with water from the hose. Nick watched him carefully as Nora ate.

"Kind of boring in here in the cage, big guy? It would be more fun out there running around in the jungle, wouldn't it?"

Nick's eyes were a yellow gold.

"Well, at least you got your buddy here with you."

Nick finally nodded and bent his head down to eat.

Apelu left them eating, locked them in. The song that finally arrived in his head was not a very cheerful one, and he tried to push it away, but couldn't, something by Simon and Garfunkel, but he couldn't remember the words just the melody, slow and sad, then the bridge bringing it back.

The road out from Piapiatele, after you got to the macadam, took a curving detour around the landing end of the airport's main runway. From the slight rise of the road you could look over the barbed-wire-topped security fence at the *palangi*-precise lines of landing lights—amber and red then green and white—stretching out toward a mutual vanishing point a mile away.

Apelu stopped there, off the downside of the road, as he often did when passing this spot, especially at night like this, the runway lights making all that surrounded them darker. Their bold insistence upon how correct they must be was like a jeweled gauntlet thrown down across the natural chaos through which they sliced. What at his birth had been jungle and reef was now an electrified statement visible to satellites. Not that he yearned for those old days back—he didn't—but surely all this was too quick, too much a challenge for a people who welcomed change, but only in the time frame of a grandchild or two. It was still a shock to him—an alien landing strip, an enemy installation.

No planes landed while Apelu sat there. At one point the lights at the distant end of the runway disappeared in rain then reappeared. He hiked on in the dark, shoulders slumped, baseball cap down over his eyes. When headlights came from behind him he walked as far off the roadway as he could. When they came toward him he ducked his face away from them until they swept past, leaving a darker blackness behind them. It was only another two miles or less to the VA Hall in Tafuna. There were no other pedestrians.

The bingo game at the VA was the biggest one on-island on Thursday nights, and the parked cars and pickups overflowed the hall's parking lot along the road and into an adjacent field. From the outer edge of the parked vehicles Apelu could hear the announcer calling out the numbers in Samoan over the PA system, "*B-sefulu*." It took him about fifteen minutes to find his wife's pickup near the far edge of the unlit field. He stretched out in the bed of the truck on his back, looking up at the stars. There was an old Samoan superstition that if you lie on your back beneath the open sky it would bring rain, but there was hardly a cloud in the sky now. The moon wasn't up yet. The stars were bright, the Milky Way, `*avina*, like a brush slap of whitewash across the sky, swooping, irregularly graceful—the opposite of the runway lights. After a while, listening to the repetitive drone of the bingo numbers being called out, he drifted off to an uneasy sleep, dreams of cars speeding away.

The sound of the truck door opening woke him up. He laid still and listened. There was just the one door, no voices, so Sina was alone.

"Sina," he said without sitting up. "Sina, it's me, Apelu."

"Pelu? That is you. Why are you hiding? Where have you been?"

Apelu sat up. "I wasn't hiding. I was resting. How are you, Sina? How are the kids?"

"We're all fine, if feeling a bit deserted. Your captain brought your paycheck to my office on Tuesday after you didn't pick it up. He asked about you again. Are you okay? Why haven't you been home? Where are you staying?"

"I'm all right, and I have as many questions as you do about what's going on, but not many answers yet."

"Well, come home and we'll talk about it there instead of out here in the dark."

Apelu liked it there in the dark, where he didn't have to see her. "You won tonight, didn't you?"

"Yes. How did you know?"

"You always leave early when you win. Why is that? Are you worried about winning twice in one night?"

"You wouldn't understand, and besides it's not important. Why don't you come home?"

"I don't think it's safe to come home right now. In fact, I was thinking it might be best for you and the kids to go visit your mom in Apia for a while."

"What have you done?"

"I haven't done anything. I was just going along, doing my job, when, like, everything went negative."

"If you haven't done anything wrong, then why are you acting so guilty?"

"I'm not acting guilty."

"You disappear. Nobody knows where you are. That's the sort of thing guilty people do."

"Did you put my paycheck into our joint account?"

"Yes."

"Good. Use it. Kids' tuition's due next week. You don't want to go see your mom then?"

"You want the whole family on the run?"

"Okay, don't then. But if anybody asks about me just say that I haven't been around, that you haven't seen me."

"That wouldn't be a lie," Sina said. In the dark they were just two shapes with voices. While Apelu had dozed, rain clouds had gathered. The stars were gone. "People are talking, Pelu. Why are you doing this to me?"

"I'm not doing anything to you. I'm just doing what I have to do."

"It's like I don't know you anymore. I'm not even sure I want to know you." That familiar scolding tone had returned to her voice. "Why did you come here?"

"I'm not sure now. I don't trust the phones. Look, just tell the kids I'll be home soon, that I love them and think about them every day. And think again about taking them all over to visit your mom."

"You don't care at all about me, do you? Or what you are putting me through?"

The last bingo game had ended, and people—mainly women—were pouring out of the VA Hall.

"Give me a ride as far as the country club?" Apelu asked.

"You can go to hell, Pelu," Sina said, but she got in the truck and started it up and beat most of the traffic onto the road toward the country club. Apelu scooted down in the bed of the truck so that no one would wonder who was riding in the back of Sina's pickup. When they got to the country club road Apelu beat on the side of the truck with his hand, and Sina pulled onto the shoulder. Apelu climbed out over the tailgate. He was about to go up to the driver's side window to say something—he wasn't sure what, just something, anything so that it didn't end this way—but Sina pulled away with a screech of tires, spraying him with dirt and gravel.

It started to rain on his hike back to Piapiatele.

When Apelu woke up in the morning he found a note from Asia and a small ring of keys on the bedside table in Leilani's sun-flooded bedroom. They had not been there when he went to bed.

"Dear Apelu, Gotta go. Explain later. Here are keys to house and car for your use. Be careful. Don't forget to feed Nick & Nora. XO Asia."

Within two hours Apelu had transferred himself entirely to Asia's house, leaving Ezra and Leilani's as much as he had found it as he could remember, except for one thing—he took the fire knives from Ezra's bunker with him, knowing no one would miss them. He left Nick and Nora in their kennel with full troughs of water and food.

He caught the ten o'clock local news on the radio in Asia's car leaving her house. There was nothing on the news about Mati or a shooting. That seemed strange, very strange. There wasn't much the local news liked better than a bullet-riddled corpse. He stopped at a bush store and bought that morning's *News*. Nothing. For a minute or two he toyed with the idea of driving by the Korean graveyard to see what was happening, and then he rejected it. That old saw about returning to the scene of the crime. Instead he drove up to the house on Canco Hill, looking for Torque, who was there, sitting on the porch with Baby Peni crooked asleep in one arm and a Bud Light in his other hand.

"How's your head?" Torque asked as Apelu came up the porch steps.

"Head? What head? How's yours?"

"Sister's still in jail," Torque said. "Do you know how much trouble these things are?" he said, jerking his chin toward the sleeping baby. "I think she got her ass arrested just to teach me a lesson."

"Which one?"

"That if you spread the seed, you got to tend the weed."

"You mean that baby is yours?" Apelu asked. The only similarity he had noticed was a certain testiness.

"Yeah. Peni was my dad's name."

"The guy you hated?"

"You can't really hate your parents, man. You're just embarrassed by them."

"What did they bust Sister for?"

"Interfering with an officer of the law, resisting arrest, disorderly conduct, biting."

"Biting?"

"Sister's got a mean set of fangs on her, man."

"It can be a criminal act."

"Looks like she'll spend the weekend in jail. Her lawyer, a little public defender bitch—"

"*Palangi*?"

"Yeah, ratty little thing. She couldn't get Sister's hearing scheduled for today. So, first court appearance Monday, I hope."

"Where's the baby's mother?" Apelu resisted an impulse to take the child from its bent-neck discomfort inside Torque's elbow.

"Long gone, maybe back in Apia, Auckland. Who knows? Sister is his only mom now. Where's Sally at today?"

"Busy. Listen, Torque, you said when you and your guys cleaned out Ezra's you took the stuff somewhere. Could you tell me or show me where you took it?"

"It's sort of hard to describe, but I could show you. Why?"

"Nothing to do with you, just following the track."

"You cops lead really boring lives, don't you?"

"Yeah." Apelu watched as the baby stretched and twisted trying to get comfortable, and Torque almost dropped him. "What do you say?"

Torque was struggling with the baby, who was now awake and complaining. "You mean now?"

"Yeah, soon. Here, give me that child." Apelu stood up and took Peni out of Torque's hands. Its disposable diaper was full and dripping. "Shit, Torque," Apelu said.

Half an hour later Apelu had cleaned the baby and changed his diaper, found a jar of baby food and fed him, and had given him a nipple bottle of formula to suck on. He didn't search for baby clothes. "Here," he said, handing the peaceful child to Torque, "let's go." They went in Asia's car, with the darkened windows rolled up and the air-con on low. "Just tell me where."

"A container in Tafuna," Torque said. "Don't you have a kid's car seat?"

Shipping containers had become a fact of life and a curse on the landscape of Tutuila. Sometimes the big orange or red steel boxes seemed to be everywhere you looked—taking up space in parking lots, dumped beside stores, piled four high along the once scenic road by the dock downtown, filling Pago Park, forgotten in the weed trees of vacant lots, even parked in people's front yards. If you lived here, you ignored them. If you noticed them, you wondered how long it would take for them to just rust away.

The dirt road that Torque directed Apelu to was the same road that the Woos lived on. The container in question, in which Torque had deposited the goods—minus the steaks and CDs—that he had taken from Ezra's house, was one of about a dozen strewn randomly in an overgrown field a couple of lots before you got to the Woos' place. Apelu parked the car in ruts leading into the field when the median grass between the ruts got too high for Asia's low Kia. He and Torque, carrying the baby, walked the rest of the way. The grass in front of one of the containers had been recently beaten down. There were tire tracks in the mud.

"This it?" Apelu asked.

"That's it. Number 12483, like they told me."

"It's locked."

"No, it ain't. It just looks locked. If you lift up the door handle there you'll see that the bolt wasn't thrown before the latch was padlocked."

Apelu lifted the door bolt handle and turned the bolt ends at the top and bottom of the door clear of their brackets. "You're right." The door opened surprisingly easily. "That's Ezra's stuff all right," he said, as sunlight lit up the interior.

"Hey, man, let's go. This place gives me the creeps. You want some of that stuff or what?"

"No, just checking," Apelu said, closing the door and turning the door bolts back into place. "Know who the container belongs to?"

"Haven't a clue. Come on, man, let's go. It's hot out here. The baby doesn't like it."

On the road back out Apelu had to pull off onto the shoulder at one point to let a big black SUV coming at them pass. Apelu looked through the windshield to see if it was the Woos returning, but it wasn't them. There was a male Samoan driver he didn't recognize and a young woman in the front seat. They were talking. They never looked down at them in the short Kia. Apelu had driven on another hundred yards before it struck him where he had seen that woman's face before. There was a gravel driveway into another container field. He pulled in there.

"What?" Torque asked. Peni was almost back to sleep in his lap.

"Wait," Apelu said. "Listen to the radio, put the seat back, and take a nap with your kid. I won't be long."

Apelu left the car running with the air-con on and walked back up the dirt road the way they'd just come. There was a dog-leg to the left where the road ran up against the airport fence. Apelu stopped there and checked around the corner before walking on more slowly. There was the sound of a larger vehicle coming up the road behind him, and he sidestepped out of sight into the tall *manioka* and wild papaya brush before it turned the corner. It was a large flatbed truck and it proceeded slowly past him up the road and then turned into the ruts that Apelu and Torque had just come out of.

Apelu worked his way up slowly through the brush to where he could see them without being seen. Both doors to the container they had visited were open, as were the doors of two nearby containers. The black SUV was there as well. A discussion was in progress—four Samoan men and the woman, who was wearing sunglasses now, her hair covered with a bright patterned scarf. She was just as striking as the first time Apelu had seen her, serving iced tea to Leilani and him in the luxury of Werner's house above Apia. She was giving the orders. The men all nodded and began to unload the containers onto the flatbed. Apelu slipped back through the brush to the road and the car. When he got there, Torque and the baby were both sound asleep. The radio had been changed to a Christian rock station. Asleep together, Apelu could finally see their genetic connection. It was in the nose and the eyes. He tried not to wake them as he drove them home.

CHAPTER 16

———— o ————

THE NEXT DAYS WERE NERVE-RACKING FOR APELU. NOTHING
happened, and he didn't know how to make anything happen.
It was the weekend. There was no news on the weekends. No newspaper, and the radio station reporters always took the weekend off.
Even if Asia had had a TV there would be no news broadcasts on
the only channel, which, being government owned and run, was
staffed by government employees who also got the weekends off.
Broadcast news was sort of a western thing anyway, a very minor
type of infotainment compared to what was out there on the coconut wireless, and Apelu had no access to that either. The rest of the
world could annihilate itself, but they wouldn't hear about it until
Monday morning. At least there was a CD player at Asia's place
and a slim but interesting selection of disks to play. She favored
female country-and-western and ballad singers, Nashville. Apelu
listened to the backup slide guitars and fiddles, not the lyrics.

The days were long and empty, filled with too many thoughts,
all of them uncertain. At least he felt comfortable, at home in
Asia's house and sleeping in her bed, which still held her aroma.
He practiced with the fire knives, muscle memory returning. Late
afternoons he walked down to the cove and then over to Ezra's

to feed Nick and Nora. Saturday he went shopping for groceries in Asia's car and brought home a six-pack of Steinlager and a bottle of Stolichnaya. Saturday night he got solo drunk listening to Emmylou Harris. He had a lot of time to think, but he didn't reach any conclusions.

Monday morning there was still no word of the shooting on the radio news, and he drove over to Vailoatai and past the graveyard. No car, no body, no yellow crime scene tape. He called Lisa's Apia office. No answer. He called the home number she had given him and got an answering machine but didn't leave a message. He called Torque and found out that Sister was still in jail. They were still waiting for charges to be formally filed. Monday night, at a loss for what to do, he drove downtown and went to the Captain's Table. The place was almost empty, and the only waitress there was an older woman who definitely was not there to dance with the customers.

Late Tuesday morning Apelu was practicing with the fire knives in front of Asia's house when he heard Nick and Nora off in the distance start barking, really excited. They didn't stop. Apelu put down the knives and went to check. He loaded Ezra's shotgun and took it with him, along with his badge and ID case. He had discovered Asia's back trail through the pandanus to Ezra's and he took that way, which brought him up behind the house. Two rental cars were parked above where the driveway got funky. As he watched, two *palangi* men came around from the kennel side of the house. Nick and Nora were still barking at their meanest. One of the two men went into the house while the other looked around outside. He opened the garbage can and rummaged around. Then he stopped and called out to the man inside, who reappeared along with two other almost cloned-looking *palangis*. The guy at the garbage can was poking around with a pen he had pulled from his shirt pocket. On the end of the pen he pulled something out of the garbage can—Apelu's bloody shirt.

In the five days since Mati's murder Apelu hadn't been sure what to do, so he had done nothing. For whatever reasons, Mati's demise had not been made public. And Lisa Ah Chong could still not be reached. He had tried again that morning. All he knew to do was wait for the next development. Well, maybe this was the next development he had been waiting for. The FBI. They had to be the FBI, the additional agents Mati had said were coming. They were all youngish *palangi* males he had never seen before. They all appeared sort of proud of the fact that they didn't fit in to their surroundings. They seemed to be competing in the looking grim and businesslike category. They must have come in on the previous night's flight from Honolulu. Apelu hid the shotgun in a clump of pandanus and walked to the end of the path where it came out across the driveway from the house, maybe fifteen yards away from the four men now all grouped around the garbage can and the bloody shirt.

"It looks too big to be Sparks'," one of the men said.

"Head wound," another said. "Most of the blood around the collar and shoulders. Days old."

"Hello, can I help you?" Apelu said.

Four right hands went for the back of four belts.

"Step forward. Hands away from the body," the tallest of the four said.

Apelu did as he was told.

"Stop there. Who are you?"

"Neighbor. Live up the coast. Heard the dogs. I look after them when these folks aren't here. That's all. Thought some kids might be bothering them. Who are you?"

"FBI," the tall one said, walking toward him. "Turn around." He gave Apelu a quick frisk, found the ID case but left it in his back pocket, probably thinking it was a wallet.

"Something wrong?" Apelu said, his hands up by his ears.

"So, you take care of those dogs?"

"That's right."

"Have there been any other visitors lately?"

"No. No one here I know of since Mr. Strand went to jail."

"Which was when?"

"Couple weeks ago now."

One of the other agents had walked over to one of the rental cars and came back with a file folder. He opened it and showed Apelu a sheet of paper with six photographs on it. "We'd like to know if you have seen any of these people around here."

Apelu took a moment to scan the photos and think. "That's Ezra Strand, his wife Leilani, Mr. Woo—I don't know his first name—and his wife Atalena. That's Special Agent Matthew Sparks, and that's me, Detective Sergeant Apelu Soifua, with a moustache and about ten years younger."

"Put your hands behind your back, please." The tall guy put the cuffs on gently. Two of the agents drew their weapons and conducted a quick tour of the perimeter, while the other two took Apelu inside. Nick and Nora were barking again.

The agents turned Leilani's chair around so that it was facing the room not the windows and sat Apelu in it. As he sat him down the tall guy slipped Apelu's ID case out of his back pocket, flipped it open, nodded, and handed it to the other agent.

The other agent started. "Know why your photo is in that file? Because you are a prime suspect."

"A suspect in what?" Apelu shifted around in the chair, trying to get his hands behind his back comfortable so that he could sit back.

"In the disappearance of Special Agent Sparks. When was the last time you saw Agent Sparks?"

"Thursday, early afternoon."

"Where was that?"

"In Vailoatai."

"Where's that?"

"West of here."

"Why did you see him?"

"He wanted to meet with me."

"Why?"

"To ask my help in locating a witness."

"What witness?"

"A girl they call Tia."

"Okay," the tall agent cut in. "Detective, you look uncomfortable, and you are being quite cooperative. Rick, take those cuffs off him. I think we can treat the detective as if we are on the same side."

Apelu had to stand for Agent Rick to unshackle him. "Thanks," he said.

"Okay, Detective, tell us what happened."

Apelu described the events in the Korean graveyard at Vailoatai.

"Take us there," the tall agent said.

They took both rental cars. At the graveyard, Apelu walked them through what had happened. After a short search, one of the agents turned up four rifle shell casings in the rocks on the ocean side of the road. Apelu took the tall agent to where Mati's body had been. The spot had been covered with fresh dirt and torn-up weeds, but the earth beneath was still dark with blood.

"I'll tell you why you were a prime suspect, Detective," the agent said. "Because your attorney general fingered you, said you and Agent Sparks had something going on and that you were already under a cloud of suspicion."

"Did the attorney general know Sparks was one of you guys?" Apelu asked.

"Not before I told him so."

"If they had known Mati was FBI, he'd still be alive. Too much heat to come down," Apelu said.

"Wait. You think the attorney general had something to do with Sparks being murdered?"

"You mean Sparks never told you he had put all the pieces together and that the AG was the linchpin not just in the smuggling but in the human trafficking too?"

"The last he reported was that he had some new information he had to confirm, That's when he asked for back-up."

"Look, I don't know who pulled the trigger, but the AG had the most to gain from Mati's silence. The plates on the car were from his office."

The tall agent turned and looked out to sea. He was silent for a while. "Nice spot here," he said and then was silent for a bit longer. "Okay, Detective, we'll go with your theory, with your word right now the only thing to back it up. We don't even have a body and nothing to materially connect this attorney general to much of anything. But we'll go with it. Sparks had told us all about you and this girl called Tia. We still have to find her. She's the prime remaining witness in our sex trafficking case."

Apelu told them what he had told Sparks about the girl called Tia being apprehended the week before. "Her real name's not Tia but Sila Fa'afima. I saw her passport. What did the attorney general have to say about Sparks?" Apelu turned away from the bloody uncovered stones and looked out to sea.

"That he just hadn't come into work Friday and Monday, took a long weekend, probably shacked up someplace. Agent Sparks was under special orders to check in with the Honolulu office every day at nineteen hundred hours Honolulu time. When he failed to do so three days in a row, we scrambled. Even if Sparks was shacked up someplace, he'd still have reported in."

"Family?" Apelu asked, still looking out to sea.

"Nothing close. A loner. Okay guy, though."

"That bloody shirt you found. It was mine. My blood too, not Sparks'. An accident."

A car drove by slowly up on the road. The other agents were busy taking photographs and making diagrams on clipboards. The car, a black sedan, drove on.

"What next?" Apelu asked.

"Well, I'm sure your attorney general would like us to bring you in."

"Well, you can't do that. There are still pieces that you guys ain't got and that I can't give you while in custody."

"Like what pieces?"

"Like the girl Tia. Like who shot Sparks."

The name of the tall agent interviewing him was Dwayne. Apelu wondered if there was some reason why he was learning only their first names. Dwayne seemed to be in charge. He told the other agents to finish up their initial investigation of the crime scene, and then they all returned to Ezra's house, where they held a meeting. Dwayne ran the meeting. They would report back their findings that Special Agent Sparks was missing and presumed dead and that they would continue their investigation into his disappearance. They would tell their bosses but not the local authorities that they had connected up with Detective Soifua, who would be working with them on the case. They would continue their search for the Tia woman. The problems were that they had no body and they had no legal powers to pick up anyone for questioning or detain anyone. For the time being they would not mention the suspicion thrown on the attorney general and his office by Detective Soifua's uncorroborated story.

"The AG has got to at least appear cooperative," Apelu said.

"Right," Dwayne said. "We can put pressure on him by forcing him to cooperate."

"Like in finding Sparks' body," another agent said.

"Forget about Sparks' body," Apelu told them. "It's a big ocean, a lot of coastline, a deep jungle. If they wanted him disappeared, you'll never find him. No, follow up on Tia. The police took her in six days ago. Either they handed her over to Immigration for deportation, or she's still in custody. I think all they had her for was overstaying her visa. If the AG is involved in the trafficking for prostitution, as Sparks thought, she is the trump card he'll want to hide. All the other girls—except the dead one—have been deported, I think."

"We can't just let a special agent's murder slide," the same guy protested.

"We won't," Dwayne said.

"No," Apelu said. "Follow up on the cars—Sparks' car and the black sedan, both with government plates. Somebody drove both of them away. Some car or van hauled his body away. There were drivers involved who didn't want to be involved. This thing is getting out of their control. It's ballooning."

"So, what are you going to be doing, Detective?" It was the same agent again, a round blond guy.

"What's your name?" Apelu asked.

"Ethan," he said.

"Anybody got last names?" Apelu looked around.

"Not yet," Dwayne said.

"Well, Ethan, I thought I might help you strangers out by keeping an eye on the only other suspects you've got around right now, the Woos, seeing as I know where they're at and you guys would be about as obvious as a black helicopter. And I thought I might follow up on the murder weapon for you. What were those shell casings you picked up?"

The fourth agent, the quietest one, the one still without a name and obviously the techie, spoke up. "They're thirty caliber, but short rounds, not normal assault rifle ammo."

"Could you give me one so I can check on them?" Finally with something to do, Apelu was getting impatient. The techie looked at Dwayne, who nodded. "How are we going to communicate? Where are you guys staying?"

"The Rainmaker," Dwayne said. "I tried this morning to get cell phones from your Office of Communications, but they didn't have anything available, they said."

"Oh shit," Apelu said. "The Rainmaker is the government-owned hotel. The lines aren't secure. I know that. We've got one happy crew that just spends all its time listening to calls in and out of there. And now that the AG knows you're feds, you'll never

201

get cell phones, which wouldn't be secure anyway. Look, here's a number." Apelu gave them Asia's number. "It's safe. There's an answering machine if I'm not there. Use public phones or private lines—but not the public phone at the hotel."

They set a time when they would talk on the phone the next day—two p.m. As the agents drove away, Apelu went to visit with Nick and Nora. They were excited and upset. Apelu fed them and sat with them a while until they calmed down. Then, as he got the shovel and hose to clean out the kennel, he did something he had never done before—feeling sorry for them being caged up for so many days, he let them go. He held open the kennel gate and told them to go play, but come back when he called them. Nick gave him a questioning look.

"Go on, but come right back," Apelu said and nodded toward the open gate.

Nick barked once, okay, and he and Nora walked sedately through the gate onto free concrete. Then they took one look at each other and tore off into the bush, leaping cleanly over the bordering lava stone wall.

Apelu was sitting at the edge of the cliff, looking out to sea, trying to get straight in his head who knew what and decide what he would do next, when he heard a movement behind him. He froze, then turned slowly in the direction of the sound. Nick was just sitting down behind him, his big mouth open and breathing heavily. Nora was coming up behind him, sniffing at things. When Apelu looked at Nick, he barked once and looked out to sea. Nora flopped down and began her tongue bath. They had been gone maybe half an hour. Apelu reached back and scratched Nick between his ears. They followed Apelu back to the kennel and through the gate, where Apelu filled their food and water troughs again and locked them in. They seemed content.

Back at Asia's house Apelu propped the shotgun, which he had retrieved from the bush, beside the back door. A light was blinking on the answering machine. Dwayne checking out the number already? Apelu pushed the new message button.

"Apelu? Apelu, if you're there please pick up. This is Asia. Apelu? Okay, you're not there. It's about ten thirty Tuesday morning. Would you please give me a call as soon as you get this message. I'm at...," and she left an Apia phone number and a room number.

Apelu called the number—it was the Tusitala Hotel—and got her room. Asia answered on the third European *bring bring* of the phone.

"Taking a little vacation?" Apelu asked after she said hello.

"Out of Dodge anyway," she said. "How are you doing? I thought you might take up my invitation."

"Good good, just kicking back, relaxing. A little zen here, a little zen there."

"How's your head?"

"Relatively clear. What's up?"

"Apelu, you said that you got the list of missing girls' names from someone over here in Apia. I was wondering if you could tell me who your contact was. I'm over here. I may as well follow up on the girls, see what I can find out about how they're doing."

"As Sally the social worker?"

"Something like that."

Apelu's initial reaction was not to give Asia Lisa's number. He liked keeping these things separate in his mind. He wondered if he wanted Asia involved more than she already was, on her amateur citizen's campaign to help victimized women. Then he thought, what the hell, we're on a new roll here, maybe Asia can find Lisa. Asia was a big girl. So he gave her Lisa's telephone numbers and told her Lisa's official position and where her office was.

"But, if you do get in touch with her, have her contact me here at your place."

"Okay, got that." Asia read back to Apelu the numbers she had written down. "And, Apelu, about the other night, I just wanted to say I wouldn't mind repeating it sometime."

Apelu caught his breath. Someone was reading his mind again, sharing the same thought. "I'd like that too," he said, "but you've got to come home first."

Apelu's next call was to a cement company

"RT here, Quality Erections, that's our motto, if you're into that sort of thing." It was a familiar Aussie drawl.

"RT, Apelu."

"Ah, me favorite copper. I saw in the paper where you've started your retirement program. Be careful with them young sheilas, Pelu. They're a perishable commodity."

"I know you're an expert in such matters, RT, which is why I called you. What are you doing for lunch?"

"I was eatin' it before I answered the bloody phone."

"After work?"

"I'll let you buy me a beer."

"Where are they the coldest?"

"The Juke Box."

"Five?"

"Shit, I work for a fuckin' livin', mate, unlike you government types. Make it six."

Apelu had noticed an unfinished house in a lot next door to the Woos' house—two-story unpainted cement block with no roof, windows, doors. The jungle had begun to reclaim it. Such half-finished houses were not uncommon on Tutuila. The family had run out of money, someone had died, fortunes had taken a bad turn, grandiose dreams had been dreamed on financial quicksand. He parked Asia's Kia in the lot of a Laundromat up on the road about a quarter of a mile away and hiked into the house, carrying a white plastic shopping bag containing two tuna fish sandwiches and three bottles of water. The sun was out, and it was hot. Sweat rolled down his forehead from beneath his Chargers cap. At the abandoned house he found some shade in the corner of a wall on the second floor from which he could watch the Woos' front door and driveway. He made himself as comfortable as he could. The bottled water got quickly warm. He ate the sandwiches and sipped the water, smoked cigarettes, and watched the birds—swiftlets and honeyeaters mostly. Every so often a small interisland plane would land or take off from the airport runway on the other side of the perimeter fence. Off in some direction a Weed eater whined its uneven song. Why did the sound of the Weed eater make him think of Merle Haggard? Why did the individual army ants on the opposite wall never wander from their prescribed if undulating trail? How come no one tended to or harvested the banana trees in this yard? They were just going to waste. What would the kids be doing now, just getting out of school? Would Sanele be headed for football practice? Would already-too-chubby Sarah—without Daddy around to scold her—be eating Bongos and drinking a soda? Why didn't he quit smoking? If he had gone to church and pretended to believe in all that shit, would he and Sina still be together? What was it people lacked that made them open to religion? What would Asia's small firm breasts look like, taste like, naked in the sunlight? Why was he a cop? By virtue of what physical forces did that khaki-colored gecko sniping army ants out of their column cling so freely to the vertical wall? Why did he smoke? Maybe he should just quit.

It wasn't a black SUV but a taxicab that finally pulled into the Woos' driveway. Apelu crawled over to the window opening from which he had the best view of the driveway. Two men, both Asian, one skinny, one fat, got out of the rear seat of the cab and looked around. Then the two front doors of the cab opened. Mr. Woo got out of the passenger side and a male Samoan driver got out of the other. The driver opened the trunk and pulled four black suitcases out of it. The Asian strangers—both in black suits—took the luggage, two each, and followed Mr. Woo into the house. The cab turned around and left.

Apelu waited another half an hour, until five thirty, then walked back to the car and drove to the Juke Box, which was only about ten minutes away. On the way he stopped at a bush store and bought a fresh pack of cigarettes.

The Juke Box was more a memory than a bar. Its best virtue was probably its location—if you had never been there before it was almost impossible to find and virtually impossible to give directions to, lost in the maze of unnamed, almost accidental lanes of the Tafuna Plain. Once, years before, it had briefly been a hot spot for a certain social set, with always at least a passable local band playing to dance to and the cachet of being almost a private club where no one you didn't know went. But those years had passed—a couple of fights, a drug bust, several changes of owners—and now it stayed open almost by habit. Its only real business was the dart league that met there once a week—not on Tuesdays like today—and a few Aussie expats who had made it their after-work hangout. It stocked their Foster's Lager. There never had been a juke box in the place.

At six p.m. RT was the only other patron. He was seated at the small bar, talking with the bartender.

"What'll it be, Apelu? Already started a tab for ya."

Apelu got a Steinlager and they moved to a table away from the bar. RT had been in the islands a long time. He was onto his second or third Samoan wife, depending on how you counted such things, but what he was best known for was his arsenal of weapons. Of course, most of them were illegal. Shotguns and .22 rifles for hunting were all you could legally register, although there really wasn't much you could legally hunt anymore after the government had banned the shooting of fruit bats and doves. Apelu thought of RT's collection as more of a private museum than an illicit arsenal.

"You know, you look better without that walrus." RT pointed at Apelu's upper lip. "So good I almost didn't recognize you."

"Maybe you should grow one now."

"Nah, mate. It's bloody red and makes me face look even more like a train wreck. Missus wouldn't stand for it."

Apelu put the shell casing that the FBI techie had given him on the table.

"Thirty short," RT said, just glancing at it. "Not much call for those around here."

"Could this be fired from a weapon with a silencer?"

"Probably was," RT said, "probably was."

"Why do you say that?"

"Because the only firearm on this island that I know of that takes a load like that is fitted with a perfectly lovely Belgian muzzle suppressor."

"Does this firearm have a name?" Apelu liked playing twenty questions with someone who knew all the answers.

"Carmen."

"Carmen?"

"Carmen the carbine. She's an M1 carbine, US Army issue. Though not many around. Little sister to the M1 rifle. Got a special sight on her too."

"Is Carmen dating anyone special these days? Like going steady?"

"I sold her to a bloke called himself Ioane Viliami, couple of years ago. Said he wanted it for shooting sharks from his fishing boat. Be good for that."

"Know where I could find this Viliami?"

"Piece of cake. He's in your bloody lockup, has been for more than a year. Busted for assaulting his wife's boyfriend, shot up his fuckin' truck real good. You remember that one?" RT motioned to the barman to bring them more beers.

"I remember that, but it wasn't a Viliami."

"Some other bloody name then. He had a bunch. Carmen was the gun he used. Never got the boyfriend, just his truck. I was a bit chagrined 'bout that—good weapon and all, wrong use. Glad you coppers never connected me to the fuckin' piece."

"If Viliami is in the slammer, where's Carmen?"

"Seized as evidence, locked up somewhere downtown in the prosecutor's office, I guess. Bloody waste."

CHAPTER 17

———— o ————

EARLY THE NEXT MORNING APELU WAS BACK AT HIS STAKE-out of the Woos. Seven hours of nothing surprising. He limited himself to one cigarette an hour, but in the abandoned house's wild yard he had spotted some sugar cane growing and he cut himself a small stalk to chew on. That helped. It made him feel like a kid playing hooky from school, hiding out with a secret pleasure. Before two p.m. he was back at Asia's house for the call from the FBI, which came precisely on the hour, Dwayne speaking.

"Detective, you're not taping this call, are you?"

"No, Dwayne, I'm on your side, remember? Here, I'll even turn the answering machine off, okay?"

"Are you alone, Detective?"

"Yes, Dwayne, shit, I'm alone. What's the news?"

"Well, we've got a cold trail on this Tia/Sila woman. According to the police, they haven't picked up anyone for over-staying in weeks. No record on her."

"Did you check with Immigration?"

"Zero there too. I even checked with the attorney general, and all he could give me was that you were her sponsor, as well as the sponsor for the dead girl. But Sparks had already told us that. We need that girl as a witness, and after what happened to Sparks, I wonder if we're going to find her."

"The AG is in a bind there. She can't turn up dead, because at least two honest, uninvolved police officers know she was turned over to Immigration, no matter what Immigration told you. Despite what your agency might think about us savages here, almost all Samoan cops are good, honest guys who draw the line at murdering young women. She might disappear for good, but more probably over in Western Samoa or on her way there than here, like lost overboard. Did the AG seem surprised when you asked him about her?"

"Not especially, but he did have that information about you and her at his fingertips."

"What did you tell him about Agent Sparks?"

"Just that he was missing, and we suspected foul play."

"Things aren't going well for the AG just now. Let's put a little more heat on him. Tell him you'd like to run a ballistics test on any M1 carbines that may be on-island."

"That's what fired those shells?"

"A very good chance, and the only M1 carbine I know of was seized as evidence more than a year ago."

"Got you. And don't tell him why we want a ballistics test."

"Yeah, let's see what he does."

"Say, Detective, what do you know about Ezra Strand? One of my agents went to talk with him this morning at the prison, and he wouldn't talk, pretended he didn't know English."

"Ezra's out there somewhere. Maybe not enough cranberry juice."

"What? Well anyway, he spoke English well enough with Agent Sparks."

"Sparks spoke with Ezra?"

"Sure, more than a month ago. Sparks tried to turn him, let him plea to something insignificant if he'd testify to the grand jury about the AG's involvement in the smuggling operation. Sparks was trying to put a quick wrap on it and get out of here, but Strand wouldn't cooperate. Sparks said he went sort of loony."

Apelu was smiling into the phone. So, maybe crazy old Ezra wasn't that crazy after all and might be able to return to the world of the sane if all this gets resolved. In too deep? Act crazy and see if you can get excused from the room.

"Don't worry about Ezra," Apelu said. "If he's of any use at all it will be after the case is made, not in making it. Any luck finding the cars and drivers?"

"Negative. No one wants to talk to us."

"Anything else?" Apelu was still smiling, thinking about Ezra's crazy comfort zone. I guess he knew I'd be smart enough to duck, Apelu thought, just like when fire knife dancing with a partner you had to trust that when you swung the flaming blade at his head he would know enough to duck and that when he swung his knife at your shins in return the timing was right for you to leap.

"We'll hit the AG with the ballistics test request this afternoon. By the way, they've put an all-points bulletin out for you. These guys really don't like you."

"Thanks for telling me. Tomorrow same time?"

"You got it," Dwayne said. "Be careful out there."

Fifty minutes later, after feeding Nick and Nora, Apelu was back on his stakeout at the Woos' house. He could feel things falling apart on the other side. Stuff had to start happening. Apelu hadn't mentioned Dr. Win Chung to Dwayne. The FBI seemed to know nothing about any of that, and Apelu wasn't about to try to explain it to them. Win Chung didn't fit into their case and would just confuse them.

This time Apelu didn't bring three bottles of water and some tuna fish sandwiches to his stakeout. He brought a bucket of KFC takeout and two big bottles of Steinlager. He was determined to stay late. He didn't have to. The sun was still up when the Woos' black SUV pulled up and Atalena Woo and Werner's Fijian girl took Tia from the vehicle into the house.

Apelu instantly realized his dilemma. He now had most of the herd he wanted—Tia, the Woos, the Chinese men, even the Fijian girl—inside a corral, but he had no way of closing the gate. There were no outstanding warrants on any of them—as if he were in a position to ask for or enforce them. He had no backup to maintain surveillance. He wouldn't be in contact with Dwayne until the next afternoon, and even Dwayne had nothing on any of them.

It started to rain, hard, just as darkness descended. He was soaked by the time he got to Asia's car up at the Laundromat. He got even wetter on the twenty-yard dash from Asia's parking space to her back door. He stripped off his wet clothes and toweled off. There was something close to a chill in the air. He called the Rainmaker.

"Dwayne's room, please."

"Who?"

"Dwayne."

"We have no Mr. Dwayne registered here, sir."

"That's his first name. You know, one of the four *palangi* guys who checked in Monday night—Dwayne, Ethan, Rick, and another guy."

"The rooms are not registered by first names, sir."

"The FBI guys. Connect me to one of their rooms." Apelu held the phone to his ear with his shoulder as he cinched the towel around his waist.

"I'm sorry, sir, I don't know who you are talking about. Do you have a last name?"

Apelu hung up. He would have to drive in to the Rainmaker. He rummaged through his bag, looking for something to wear. Even through the rain he heard the car door close up at the end of the lane where Asia's car was parked. He was sure he had locked the car's doors. He switched out the light and got Ezra's shotgun from beside the back door. He was still dressed just in the towel as he slipped through the sliding door onto the deck and then down the steps. He could hear a car's engine departing and someone approaching on the path. He cocked the shotgun, and it made a sound louder than he had expected. The steps on the path stopped. He raised the shotgun in that dark direction.

"Apelu, is that you? Don't shoot. It's me, Asia."

Apelu lowered and uncocked the shotgun. "Wait," he said. "I'll get the lights." And he went back up the steps and inside.

There are about as many different ways of knowing people as there are people to know. Oh sure, we put them in classes—friend, enemy, lapsed friend, acquaintance, someone else's friend—to make it easier for other people to understand affectional distances, but really you don't know any two people in the same way. There are different things to understand for one thing, a different mix. A fact of life that for one person is a badge of pride may very well be a deep secret for someone else. People lie and tell the truth in idiosyncratic ways. You never know. The face they wear for you may be a face they've never worn before. So, is that really them? You know, the girl at work you think is cute, but everybody else seems to hate her guts. If anyone could be just the same self all the time with everyone, we'd consider them handicapped— Down syndrome or something. Apelu had noticed that about himself on the most basic level—language. He recognized the fact that the Apelu who spoke English was not the same as the Apelu who spoke Samoan. One of the dangerous things about being a cop was that far too often you saw only the mask and heard only the ventriloquist voice that people produced when facing the law. That wasn't really them, not the them their kids knew or anybody else knew. If you're a cop too long you begin to suspect that everyone's a liar, when actually they may only be lying to you because you are a cop. Two-faced was much too small a number.

Asia was soaked to the skin by the rain. She dropped her bag at the door and went to the bathroom for a hot shower and change of clothes. Apelu found something to wear besides the towel. He fixed a pot of coffee.

"Now we're even." Asia, dressed in a terrycloth bathrobe, was toweling her hair at the bathroom door.

"Even what?"

"On pointing the shotgun at each other."

"Is this one of them shotgun relationships?" Apelu asked, pouring coffee.

"I'm glad you're all right," Asia said, wrapping her hair in the towel.

"Okay so far." Apelu put the two mugs of coffee on the counter, and Asia came over to take one.

"Apelu, we have got to talk."

"I'd like someone to talk to."

"It's business, Apelu, serious business. Could I have some milk and sugar, please?"

As he went to get the milk and sugar Asia said to his back, "This Ms. Ah Chong, whose name you gave me, are you friends?"

"That would take more time being acquainted to see if it was possible. Why?" Apelu put the sugar jar on the counter and went to get the milk from the fridge.

"I was just wondering how close you were."

"Tell me this isn't jealousy," Apelu said as he stooped down to search for the milk carton in the fridge.

"No, it isn't jealousy. Just sympathy. I didn't know how much it would hurt you when I told you she was dead."

Apelu had found the carton of milk and was standing back up. "You know that?"

"Yes."

"For a fact?"

"A fact."

Apelu put the milk carton down on the counter and went to the telephone. He dialed his home number. It rang and rang and nobody answered.

It was simple the way Asia told it. Crime scenes are usually simple to describe, because it's always after the fact. The action has passed. Crime scenes were static, frozen in those few important minutes of their special history. Lisa's car had been found at the bottom of a ravine off the twisty road back from Aliepata on the eastern end of Upolu. She was found in it, crushed. Two sets of skid marks up on the road and yellow paint impact scrapes along the driver's side of the car indicated her car had been forced off the road, probably by a yellow bus or large truck. No witnesses. Villagers had gotten down to the car fairly quickly—it was obvious from the road that someone had gone over—but she was already dead.

"How do you know all this?" Apelu didn't want to see Lisa in the mangled car. His mind was going there. Where were her glasses? Had someone pushed them back up her cute little nose one last time?

"I was looking for her, remember?"

"And you just happened to find her at the bottom of a cliff?"

"I had help, Apelu, investigative help."

They were standing on opposite sides of the blue Formica-covered kitchen counter, staring at one another, neither one blinking, neither one moving.

"Your name really is Sally something, isn't it?"

"No. At least my name really is Asia. That much is true."

"And the rest of it…?"

"That's why we have to talk, Apelu, to get things straight between us."

This part wasn't so simple. They both pulled up stools, still on opposite sides of the counter, and sat down. Asia fixed her coffee, took a sip, and began to talk.

"I wanted to explain all this to you before, but my superiors wouldn't let me. They didn't trust you. You were just another probably corrupt Samoan cop to them. They didn't know you like I know you. That was one of the reasons I went to Apia, to talk with them about you, that you had uncovered the prostitution trafficking that we hadn't known about, that we had to cut you in on what was going on. Ms. Ah Chong's death convinced them. I'm sorry it took that."

"Your superiors?"

"At the US Consulate there, State Department nerds, desk defenders."

"You work for them?"

"I've been an investigator for the State Department for seven years."

"And your Samoan husband?"

"Oh, Paulo is real enough, but I'm not a grieving widow. We met in college. He was on the football team. But he's not dead, like I told you. He's just ex. He's a high school football coach in Atlanta now. No, I didn't come here to get over his death. I was sent here to keep an eye on Ezra and Leilani's place, to be a spook, because I knew how to speak some Samoan. I thought it would be cool to pull a gig in the tropics with no bosses around. It was nice for several months. Until now." Asia unwrapped her hair from the towel and shook it out, running her fingers through it and back. Those strong hands again.

"How did you get such strong hands?"

Asia looked at her hands. "Ceramics, I guess. I throw a lot of clay when I'm home."

"Which is where?"

"Seattle. You are a detective, aren't you?"

"Why were you watching Leilani and Ezra?"

"We'd picked up a couple of illegals on the West Coast, mainland Chinese. Their paper trail took them back through here to Western Samoa. They were carrying letters of identity from American Samoa, which made them American Nationals. Their papers all had your AG's signature on them. We figured there were more such backdoor immigrants and wanted to staunch it. When the smuggling thing involving your attorney general came up, there seemed to be a connection. I was sent to see if there was one. I lucked into this place. As you pointed out, no one else would live here because of the ghost thing."

Apelu got up and went over to the telephone and dialed his home phone number again. No answer. "Calling home," he said as he hung up. "No answer. A week ago I told her to take the kids and go visit her mom in Apia. She wouldn't."

"Have you spoken with her since?"

"No. I was afraid if I called they would trace the call back here."

"Is that the only reason? It's not a very good one."

"No. I didn't want to talk to her. I didn't want to hear her voice. I didn't know what to say."

They didn't say anything for a long moment, just looked at each other.

Apelu looked away first. "When was Lisa killed?"

"Two days ago, Monday."

"Listen, I've got to get over to the house. I'll take your car. Is that okay?"

"Of course, Apelu, but don't you have stuff to tell me too? To bring me up to date?"

"Yeah. I know where our girl Tia is and where two of your possible potential Chinese illegals are, if they're still there, but that can wait. There's nothing we can do about it tonight, in the rain, and I'm not sure what we could do about it anyway." For some reason Apelu didn't want to tell Asia about Mati's murder or the FBI or the fact that they already had the AG on the ropes. After all her subterfuges he wasn't into full-disclosure mode. It was like all of a sudden he wasn't sure he knew her, wasn't sure how much to trust her. How much else did he not know about her and what she was up to?

"You'll come back?" she asked without any inflection.

"I plan to," he said.

"Nasty night. Be careful." Asia was looking into her coffee cup. "I'm sorry I had to lie to you, Apelu."

Apelu was putting into his dry pockets what he had taken out of the pockets of his soaked pants. "If the phone rings, let the answering machine take it before you pick up. If it's for me, don't pick up."

Asia didn't say anything.

"By the way, welcome home."

"It's not home," she said. "It's just slightly less than being lost."

There was nervous music in Apelu's head, a bad acid rock movie soundtrack. Other drivers irritated him. The rain had flooded the road in places, slowing down traffic to a prow-wave crawl. Killer potholes were hidden. When he came to his driveway in the dark and the rain he drove on by, down to the center of the village on its embayment, turned around and came back up the hill. He hadn't seen it on his first drive-by, but nested in the downhill shadow of a container beside CJ's store across the road from his driveway was a black and white. Inside he saw the glow of a cigarette being inhaled. He drove on by.

He drove up to Torque's place on Canco Hill. The stream was in the road again, only this time he was driving against it. He never got out of first gear. Dinner was just ending when he got there. The kids were cleaning up. They fixed Apelu a plate of *sapasui*—rice noodles in a soup of corned beef, cabbage, and onions—with a chunk of *umu*-baked breadfruit. Torque brought him a Bud Light.

Sister was still in jail. The AG's Office was delaying her preliminary hearing by repeatedly altering the charges against her. Torque had gotten to see her that afternoon, though. She was pissed but holding up well enough. The latest news was that they had taken Tia away. She had been held with Sister until today. The word was that she was being deported.

Apelu pushed his emptied plate away. He was suddenly very tired. It was still raining. It had settled into a regular soak. He asked Torque if he could stay there for the night. He didn't feature taking the Kia down that sluice. Torque called out to the kids finishing up in the kitchen, and the girl Lucy went and got a pillow and sheet and made up a bed for Apelu on a foam pad couch cushion in the front room. The kids disappeared into their rooms, and Torque said good night.

Before he laid down, Apelu called his house one last time. Still no answer. He went to bed and listened to the rain. He had forgotten his pain pills and his sore ribs kept him awake. He got up again and called Asia's house. He told the answering machine that the roads were flooded and that he would be staying up at Torque's. Asia didn't pick up.

Apelu didn't remember the plot of the dream. All he remembered was that it ended in a big explosion that woke him up in pain. The sky out strange windows was just lighting up with dawn. The rain had stopped. No one was up yet, but he could hear Baby Peni fussing. Apelu folded his sheet on top of his pillow and let himself out. It was a beautiful morning with a dry after-storm breeze. The road down the hill was fairly dry but scattered with debris. At the main road he turned left, toward town.

It was after seven by the time Apelu parked at the Rainmaker. He didn't see the FBI's rental cars parked anywhere, and at the front desk the clerk told him that the four strange *palangi* men had already left, complaining as usual about their rooms. The Samoan word the clerk used to describe them was not a polite one.

Apelu stopped at the pay phone outside the entrance of the hotel—the one he had warned Dwayne about using—and called the shipping office where Sina worked. She was normally at work by then. Only she wasn't. The woman who answered the phone— Apelu knew it was Sina's bingo buddy, Tise—said Sina wasn't in. She was on leave.

"Tise, do you know where she is?"

"Apelu? Where are you?" That question again—always where are you? Never how are you? "The police are looking for you."

"Where is Sina?"

"I don't know. She left yesterday after the police stopped here. She said she would be taking leave for a couple of days."

Apelu hung up. He doubted their crack crew of eavesdroppers would be on duty so early, so he made one more call, this one to Asia's house. Again, she didn't pick up after the answering machine came on and he had asked her to pick up. He left another message, telling her he would like to keep the car for the morning, but would be back at her place by two. He hung up the phone, wondering now where the fuck Asia was. What was she up to?

Half an hour later Apelu was at the airport. At that point in time there was only one airline flying between the two Samoas, the Western Samoa national carrier, Polynesian. The American Samoa version, Samoa Air, had gone belly-up the year before. Apelu had to flash his badge to work his way up to the local Polynesian manager to make it happen, but within another half an hour he was sitting behind the airline's ticket counter, checking their bookings to Apia for that day, the next day, and the day before. On the last flight out the day before he found Mrs. S. Soifua and three of his kids. Sina must have left the eldest, Sanele, with his cousins in Aua and taken Sarah and Isabel and Toby with her to her mother's. He found no Woos or Tia by her real name. All that day's flights were fully booked with waiting lists right up to the last flight at four. There were no Chinese names. He thought of Lisa's list then remembered that he wasn't thinking about Lisa. The next day, Friday, there was a Hawaiian Airlines flight arriving from and then returning to Honolulu. For more than an hour Apelu tried to get them to show him the manifest, but it didn't happen—company policy, need approval from home office, home office wants court order or something, FAA regs, someone out to lunch, et cetera. Apelu wasn't sure exactly what he was looking for on that flight anyway, so he gave up on it.

He was standing in the building's shadow outside the Hawaiian Airlines ticket office, having a smoke and wondering what to do next, when he saw her again. A black SUV pulled up to the curb and parked in the no-parking zone, and Werner's Fijian girl, looking brilliant in a green silk sari sort of thing, got out of the passenger side door. She walked briskly—vents in the sari showing lots of leg—toward the arrival gate. Apelu followed her with his eyes, then wandered after her. He saw an airport cop gesture to the driver of the SUV to move on, and it did, slowly. Apelu took a seat in the departure area where he could watch both the Fijian girl and the arrival gate from the customs area. A Polynesian flight from Apia had just landed.

The fifth passenger through the arrivals gate was Werner, dressed both conservatively and conspicuously in a blue business suit, carrying just a black leather briefcase. The black SUV had had to make the complete circuit of the airport's access road before picking up Werner and friend, and Apelu was almost to Asia's car in the parking lot by then. He only had to pass two cars to catch up to them on their way west out of the airport. Apelu knew where they were going. He didn't follow them when they turned up the dirt road to the Woos'.

CHAPTER 18

———— ○ ————

A CCORDING TO THE CLOCK ON THE MICROWAVE IN ASIA'S kitchen Dwayne was four minutes late—it said 2:04 when the phone rang. Maybe the FBI was acquiescing a bit to island time. Asia wasn't home, which was probably good, although Apelu noticed that his messages from the morning and the night before had been erased from the answering machine.

"Okay, Dwayne, I'm all alone here and I'm not taping anything. Progress report?"

"Well, your request for that ballistics test worked in a way, I guess. The attorney general has bolted."

"Bolted?"

"He left island this morning, for Fiji via Apia, to attend a charity golf tournament his office said."

"Are you sure?" Apelu hadn't seen the AG's name on the manifest of any Apia flights.

"No confirmation, but he has disappeared."

"Anything else?"

"Well, we found one of the drivers from Legal Affairs, and I think he'll turn. He said he had to talk to his family and his *fy-fay-ow* first. Who's that? What's that mean?"

"That's his church minister. It means he probably will talk. He had to confess it to his family and minister first—get their support—before talking to you guys, the authorities. You don't take things like that to outsiders lightly."

"Whatever. So, you think this guy will come over?"

"Keep on him, don't give him too much time away."

"What's new on your end?" Dwayne sounded rehearsed. Apelu wondered if Dwayne was alone and/or taping the call.

"I found our girl Tia, late yesterday. I tried to catch you guys this morning at the hotel, but you were gone already."

"You know where she is?"

"I know where they took her yesterday. My bet is she's still there. The police misled you, by the way. They had her in lockup."

"Misled? They flat-out lied!" This part Dwayne had not rehearsed.

"Well, who are you guys to them, anyway? They don't know you. You're not their boss. Why do you want to know? What's the big deal about this girl? You may be the feds, but what are you doing here? Trying to get one of their brothers—or even worse, one of their chiefs—in trouble? I can see grounds for a what-you-don't-know-I-ain't-going-to-tell-you attitude."

"I don't care what you people think. We're the FBI. You've got to cooperate. We have jurisdiction here."

How big is your war club? Apelu thought, but what he said was, "What you haven't got is a warrant, either federal or local."

"We're dealing with that; we're dealing with that. The grand jury warrants for the attorney general and for this Tia woman as a material witness will be here on tomorrow night's flight from Honolulu with the special agent in charge and some backup."

"If they're still here. Once they're in Apia—or in Fiji—they're out of your net. There is no extradition."

Dwayne grunted.

"I checked the flights to Apia for yesterday, today, and tomorrow. No one on our list was booked, and the flights are all full."

"So, where is this Tia woman being held?"

"At the Woos' home, near the airport. If one or more of your guys could take over the stakeout there, we might be able to find out if she's still there or if she leaves. I can't cover it alone. Maybe she'll still be there when your warrant arrives."

"How do we find this place?"

"I've got to take you there, show you the layout. Say in about an hour. I'll meet you." Apelu named the Laundromat near the Woos' where he had parked. "You can't miss it," he said. "It's on the road between the airport and the golf course, on your right as you're heading west."

Apelu had just hung up the phone and was looking for something quick to eat when Asia came in the back door. She didn't close it. Behind her was the assistant commissioner.

"You are such a man of your word," Asia said. "You said you would be here by two, and here you are."

"And here you are too" Apelu said, "and you've brought a friend to arrest me."

"We're just here to finish the job, Apelu. You can't do it yourself." Asia pulled the assistant commissioner into the house with a nod of her head.

"When you vanish, you vanish into comfort, Sergeant," the assistant commissioner said as he walked past Apelu into the living room.

"I should have figured you guys were old friends," Apelu said, looking at Asia.

"Actually, we just met," she said.

"I got in on Monday night's flight," the assistant commissioner said. "I didn't get a chance to be briefed by Agent Bowman here until this morning."

"Agent Bowman," Apelu said, as if remembering a character's name from an old movie.

"And it is true that there is an internal directive out to have you picked up—not arrested, just brought in for questioning. I issued it." The assistant commissioner turned to face Apelu when he said this.

It was funny, Apelu thought, how you could be around people for years and never really look at them, especially someone as plain as the assistant commissioner. In most ways he was typical of a Samoan male of his age, late forties, but in every way he was somehow smaller. His height, his weight, his frame, his head and features, even his arms and hands were all slightly minimized from the norm—80 percent original size—but it was reduced enough for most men—at least for Apelu—to not fully notice him, not really look at him, out of a sort of male embarrassment. Not that he was effeminate. There was nothing effeminate about him. There was nothing memorable about him either. He was neither handsome nor ugly. He wore unremarkable clothes. He was like a servant, a nameless extra, and in spite of his position he was largely ignored by everyone.

"I wanted you brought in because I think this whole thing is getting a bit out of hand, with all due respect to you, Agent Bowman." Even the assistant commissioner's voice was small, like listening to just one stereo track through a cheap speaker.

"We've agreed to what has to be done," Asia cut in. "Let's take that step and see if your skepticism shrinks or grows."

"You see, Sergeant, Agent Bowman here—and her superiors—have imposed upon me to assist them in apprehending a young woman they have reason to suspect is involved in some sort of illegal activity."

He was clean, though, Apelu had to admit as he watched the assistant commissioner speak, always had been—short hair not yet turning gray, clean-shaven. Apelu noticed that when he spoke no part of his body except his lips moved, no gestures, no animation around the eyes.

Asia was impatient. "FBI Agent Sparks found altered immigration records in the Attorney General's Office connecting this girl to individuals involved in the smuggling and official corruption cases, and Sergeant Soifua has identified her as a prostitute connected to possible illegal aliens." Asia, on the other hand, really used her body when she spoke. When she finished, she crossed her arms below her breasts. "In any event, she is an illegal overstayer under your laws, and you can—we will—bring her in today. We have already determined all this."

"We have no record, no report, no knowledge about the girl's occupation. Nothing to prove it aside from the Sergeant's assertion. And the Sergeant, I might point out, is currently under suspicion, suspended, and considered a fugitive at large."

Strange phrase to use, Apelu thought, *at large*. "Actually, I'm right here," he said.

"The attorney general does not involve himself in the record-keeping of the Immigration Office. If there were some irregularities there..." The assistant commissioner felt their eyes on him. He did not like being looked at; he probably wasn't used to it. "Could I have a glass of water, please?" He turned and walked to the windows looking out at the broken black lava fields. Neither of them moved to get his water. "And this thing with the phantom Chinese men. Really. Less than gossip. No proof of illegal activity. If there is anything to it, why wasn't it brought before the grand jury along with the other points?"

"Because the State Department's case hasn't been filed yet, and it will go before a separate grand jury anyway. What's your problem?" Asia's arms were still crossed.

"Evidence, that's my concern. Evidence about these additional accusations against the attorney general. The grand jury had just the matter of the smuggling ring charges before them, not all this...all this grand conspiracy."

"That's what we're going to get today, Assistant Commissioner"— Asia finally called him by name—"evidence, testimony."

"It's all just out of control," the assistant commissioner said. "Too big, too out of control. We don't even have a warrant to enter wherever this woman supposedly is."

"We don't need one in pursuit of an alien fugitive, and we have reason to believe she's also being held without her consent, kidnapped."

"And why do the feds have to get involved? We can handle our own criminal affairs. All these things you're talking about are against local laws as well, and we have jurisdiction. We don't need the feds."

Apelu spoke up. "Might I remind you, sir, that you were the one who first went to the feds, to the Department of the Interior, with your evidence, your little vendetta against the AG?" The assistant commissioner still hadn't turned to them. He looked even smaller standing in front of the windows and their open vista.

Apelu knew what the assistant commissioner's problem was and why he wouldn't give it up. He had just said it—it had all gotten too big. One of his many inherited obligations was to test and torment the attorney general's family. Why? The original conflict—more than likely over a property boundary or claims to a chiefly title—had probably been lost in the retelling generations ago, but the clan opposition endured. It was his chiefly duty to stick it to the AG's clan whenever and wherever he could. He had gotten some goods on the guy and had done so. He took what he had to Interior, hoping probably just to get the guy fired, but now this, this pit of charges opening up, the control of events slipping to outsiders with no loyalty to anyone, and he somehow would be blamed in local eyes for every Samoan, including the AG, who fell into the federal pit. Then what if the feds started snooping into other local affairs? Everyone would think that he was the one who had opened the door to them in the first place, see him as being on their side, outside the *malo*, a traitor to the *fa'asamoa*. Apelu was already thinking those thoughts. Everyone else would too. No one, including Apelu, wanted the feds around. It would be just one more landslide on their once firm mountain of independence, one more American homogenization of their separate Samoan identity.

The assistant commissioner was still standing at the window. The next thing he said was not audible enough for Apelu or Asia to make out its meaning.

"Excuse me?" Asia said.

The assistant commissioner turned around. "I said, Agent Sparks told you that, didn't he, Sergeant? Where is Agent Sparks, by the way?"

"Agent Sparks is dead, assassinated," Apelu said.

"Oh my god, there will be no getting rid of them now," the assistant commissioner said.

"When?" Asia asked.

"A week ago today," Apelu said, watching the assistant commissioner's unexpressive face.

"Who?" he said.

"Someone in a car with Legal Affairs plates and a gun borrowed from their evidence locker. I was there."

"Let's go," Asia said.

"All right, all right," the Assistant Commissioner said. "We'll do this, but if the woman's not there, we stop and take a big step back. There's too much we don't know."

It was Apelu's idea to go in through the back of the house—easy access, less conspicuous, and the back of the house was where most of the people in the Woos' household usually hung out. Apelu knew that from watching the place. He had no choice about being there, seeing as he had to take them there. He realized he would miss his appointment with Dwayne and the boys at the Laundromat. Tough. He liked leaving them out of it, and they had enough manpower. The assistant commissioner had brought three plainclothes CID guys with him, who were pleased to see Apelu.

No one was armed. No one, it turned out, except Asia, who, as they were about to go in, pulled a very professional-looking forty-five automatic out of her purse and clicked off the safety.

"We got three corpses on our side already," she said by way of explanation.

The assistant commissioner sent one of the men around the side of the house to watch the front. The rest of them went in the open back kitchen door—Apelu first, then Asia, then the CID guys. The assistant commissioner stayed at the door. The kitchen was empty, but Apelu could hear a TV set in a side room. He motioned Asia and the others to go on through the house, and without knocking or announcing himself he opened the door to the room where the TV set was on. On a bed facing the TV set at the far wall was the body of a Samoan woman rolled over onto her side, her face away from him. She didn't stir when he came in the door. He walked up to her back and put a hand on her bare shoulder. It was warm. Then it went tense, and the woman pushed herself up and away from him, letting out a sound that a startled wild bird might make. It was the house girl he'd talked to on their first visit there.

"Police," Apelu said. Then in Samoan he told her that no one would hurt her, but that she must be silent.

The assistant commissioner came into the room. "What was that?" he asked.

"House girl," Apelu said. "Watch her." And he brushed past the assistant commissioner to follow the others. He could hear footsteps on the floor above, the sound of doors opening and closing. When Apelu reached the hallway inside the front door, the two CID guys were coming out of separate downstairs rooms.

"*Leai*," they said. Nothing.

Asia appeared at the top of the curving stairs to the second floor and said, "No one up here either."

"Damn," Apelu said as Asia came back down the stairs, still holding her forty-five up and away from her body. "You can stash your federal artillery," he told her.

"You found someone," Asia said.

"Just the house girl. I'll go question her." Apelu turned to the CID guys. "Go check what vehicles are still out front." Asia went out the front door with them.

Apelu had just turned to go back to the kitchen when he heard from outside a loud, if squeaky, command to freeze and the sound of multiple weapons being cocked.

"Freeze" was a really dumb command to give to a Samoan, Apelu thought as he turned back toward the front door. What he found outside was like one of those diorama things—a freeze frame, after all. In front of him on the porch was Asia, arrested in her forward motion, her automatic still in her hand, but pointed skyward. In front of her, already standing down on the driveway, the two CID guys were similarly halted and motionless. Beyond them, half obscured by bushes and walls, were Dwayne and all of his boys scattered along the front of the property, each with his own federal handgun, identical to Asia's, leveled and held in the same two-handed, hunch-shouldered pose.

Apelu put his hands way above his head, palms out and stepped forward. "Yo, Dwayne," he called, and just as he did the third CID guy popped up out of a hedge to the right of the house, and all the FBI guys swiveled on him. Asia dropped to one knee and took aim on Dwayne.

"No!" Apelu bellowed. "You federal fuckheads!" And everybody froze again, in a fresh diorama.

After all the good American hardware had been uncocked and put away, Apelu made the introductions. It would seem interdepartmental communication was not a federal priority. Asia hadn't known that Dwayne and his crew were on-island, and vice versa. The assistant commissioner had been kept in the dark completely until Asia had been told to enlist his help in finding Tia.

Dwayne explained that after Apelu hadn't shown up at the Laundromat, they had gotten direction to the Woos' house from the Korean guy who ran the place, and they were just scoping out the house when the two Samoan males and a woman brandishing a handgun came bursting out the front door at them, and they reacted the way they had been trained to react.

The house girl wasn't much help. She only knew that everyone had left about an hour before, after she had made them all lunch. There were "many" people. Yes, two Chinese men. Yes, a young Samoan woman. When they left, all Mrs. Woo had told her was to take care of the house and not answer the phone. No, she had no idea where they were going, but they took luggage like they would be gone for a while. Yes, there was a man named Werner with them. He liked giving orders, the house girl said.

"Who's this Werner guy?" Dwayne asked, after Apelu had translated for him what the house girl had said.

"Western Samoan, businessman. I happened to see him arrive at the airport this morning and followed him back here. He must be involved somehow, on the other end."

They could hear a small airplane taking off on the runway on the other side of the fence out front. They all turned and looked, with the same thought.

Apelu looked at his watch—4:05. "That would be the last Polynesian flight to Apia. I don't think they're on it."

"Why do you think that?" Asia asked.

"Because I checked the manifests. The flights were all over-booked, and none of our group had reservations."

"Different names?" Dwayne asked.

"No. International flight, got to have passport or photo letter of identity to match your ticket. No, they're on the run, no time for anything that fancy, and Werner's too smart to risk trying to get all of his eggs through two customs in one basket."

"Options?" Dwayne again.

"Boat. We're dealing with smugglers, remember? They'd probably leave from somewhere in the harbor where there are a lot of docks to load from, but there is also the harbor patrol. Maybe some place more out of notice like Auasi, Leone, or Fagasa. Assistant Commissioner, would you mind calling harbor patrol and asking them to stay on duty tonight—like on the water—and stop all boats leaving?"

"It's after four," the assistant commissioner said. "The harbor patrol is off duty."

"Then get them back on duty," Dwayne barked.

"I don't take my orders from you," the assistant commissioner said, again only moving his lips, but he did take a cell phone out of the pocket of his lavalava and call downtown. He walked away from the rest of them and spoke softly into the phone in Samoan. When he came back, he said, "That's done. The harbor is closed for the night. Nobody leaves."

"The other places you mentioned?" Dwayne asked.

"Best split up," Apelu said. "Three teams, CID and FBI on each team. So you can find the places, Dwayne. The assistant commissioner has a cell phone, so we can all get back to him to report in. What's the number, chief?"

"I'm not giving out my private cell phone number."

"It's 358-2840," Asia said, "and mine is 352-1117."

"How did you…?" The assistant commissioner asked.

"You called me back from your cell phone this morning. I saved your number. And what is your problem? Lack of communication just almost got all of us shot."

One of the CID officers volunteered that he also had his cell phone with him, so they'd put one of the people with cell phones on each team.

"So, chief, do we take Sergeant Soifua in according to your directive, or what?" one of the CID guys asked.

"No. You did not see Sergeant Soifua today. Sergeant Soifua is still a fugitive," the assistant commissioner said in a voice even smaller than usual. "In fact, Sergeant, I am cutting you out of the rest of the operation. We will drop you back at Agent Bowman's house on our way to Leone, where you can man her phone and remain hidden for the time being."

"But I—" Apelu began to protest.

"You will do what I say," the short guy said.

Well, either they catch them tonight or they don't, Apelu thought as he walked up the gravel path from Asia's driveway to her back door. He had argued a bit but had lost. The plan now was that the separate teams would report back to him at Asia's. It was getting on dusk, abetted by a low and heavy sky. He was angry and tense, once again forced into inactivity. He walked through Asia's house to the porch, where he had stashed the fire knives, and took them out to the edge of the cliff. He could at least practice at being a warrior if he couldn't be one. As if either shaming or affirming his resolve, the white heron was circling above the surf at the end of the cove, its left wing tucked down into the thermal, holding it there in a ghostly orbit. Then across the lava he heard Nick and Nora tag-team barking.

Back in the house he exchanged the fire knives for the shotgun, then headed up the pandanus trail to Ezra's house. From the end of the trail he could see two vehicles parked on the lawn, the Woos' black SUV and the white van that the Fijian girl had used when she emptied the containers. The house was all lit up. Voices came from inside. Apelu paused, debating whether to return to Asia's and try to call back the teams headed out to their different destinations—assuming their quarry were here to stay in the house for the night—or to wait to see what transpired. Maybe he could get close enough to eavesdrop. The last daylight was fading, Nick and Nora were barking. They were hungry. He started to move forward toward the kitchen window when the front door opened, and he darted back into the shadows.

CHAPTER 19

———————— o ————————

WHEN THEY CAME OUT OF THE HOUSE, THEY CAME ALL AT once—first the two Chinese men with their two pieces of luggage each, then Atalena Woo, holding Tia by the arm, and Mr. Woo, who had to make two trips with their luggage, then Werner and the Fijian girl, and finally the AG, pulling a suitcase on wheels and talking into a cell phone. They all got into the white van, and it pulled away cautiously into the rocky lane. Nick and Nora barked them good-bye. They had left a back-door light and a kitchen light on.

If ever there was a scramble time this was it. The tail lights of the van disappeared, bouncing away up the driveway. Instead of spending the five to ten minutes it would take him in the accelerating darkness to get back to Asia's, Apelu decided to see if he could get into the house and use Ezra's phone to call Asia and the assistant commissioner. The kitchen door was locked, but the first sliding glass door on the patio was unlocked as before. Apelu leaned the shotgun against the doorjamb of Ezra's bunker and went in there to use the phone. He was dialing Asia's number when Leilani came into the room with the shotgun pointed at him.

"No, Apelu. Hang up the phone," Leilani said. "I really wouldn't want to have to shoot you, but I will."

Apelu hung up the phone. "Auntie Leilani, I didn't know you were home."

"I just came in on the last flight. Werner has told me what a bad boy you have been—not just putting poor Ezra in jail, but sticking your nose into a lot of things that really weren't any of your business. Now, I guess you've been spying on us too."

"Auntie Leilani, I don't think you know about what's really been going on. It's not just about Ezra's little smuggling game. There's more. There are people dead."

"Bad things happen when people don't mind their own business, but we don't have anything to do with dead people. We were just running a little business, a little service, not hurting anyone, until you butted in."

"It wasn't just me butting in."

"Now Werner is going to have to shut down our businesses here, and my stupid nephew has got himself caught up in some sort of FBI investigation, Werner says, and has to move back to Apia to avoid something, and now you're spying on us here, which means I should probably go back to Apia too now to get you out of my hair, and poor Ezra in jail, and you probably haven't been getting his cranberry juice to him, have you, and someone has been sleeping in, bleeding in my bed—screwing in my bed—strangers screwing in my bed. And now you. What to do with you?"

"I'm just going to make one phone call, Auntie, and then I'll leave. Or, if you like, I'll leave without making the phone call."

"No, you won't do either," she said and emptied one barrel of the shotgun into the ceiling. "You ungrateful boy, causing all this trouble. Why, I gave you a job when you were just a kid and couldn't speak proper English, and your family was hungry, and you never were that great a fire knife dancer. You didn't have the body for it. You didn't turn on the girls, or the guys either, for that matter. You wouldn't learn new routines. All you knew how to do was that traditional shit you picked up from that crippled faggot teacher of yours, and you were always hurting yourself, and I would have to send you home to that bush-stupid mother of yours with burns or cuts or whatever, and then I'd have to listen to her bitch at me in Samoan over the phone. Oh, I remember you well—Apelu, the purist prick. You were always more trouble than you were worth. You knocked up one of my best dancers in Tahoe one winter. I lost her. You and your family's self-righteous *fa`asamoa* shit. You were a real pill, Apelu. You still are. Now march." Leilani stepped aside and motioned with the shotgun for Apelu to leave the room. He did.

"I think I'll just lock you up with the dogs and take Mrs. Woo's car to the airport, get on Werner's plane with everyone else, and go back to Apia—thank god I haven't unpacked, and I couldn't sleep in that bed—where I'll be safely away from you and your infernal meddling. I don't know why I agreed to come back in the first place, just to get out of Werner's way." She stopped in the kitchen to take a ring of keys from a hook by the door and marched him back out to the patio and toward the back of the house.

Apelu stopped. He thought about doing something, anything besides obey her—try to get the gun away from her, make a dash for it.

"I know what you're thinking, Apelu, but I will shoot you, if only in the legs. One thing I have to say for you as a dancer, you did have nice legs."

"Auntie Leilani," Apelu said as he continued walking toward the kennel, "there are no more planes to Apia tonight."

"Oh, Werner had them add a special flight, just for us. He's on the airline's board of directors, you know. Werner runs a lot of things in Apia."

Like young lawyers who ask too many questions off cliffs, Apelu thought.

"Werner had to cancel a couple of important meetings today just to come over here and sort things out after my stupid nephew screwed things up, and after Werner got him that job as attorney general and everything. I don't know about you young people. You can't seem to get things right."

They had reached the kennel, and Nick and Nora were going wild. Just like the first time Apelu had met them, they were foaming at the mouth.

"Now, I don't know about these dogs, Apelu. They're Ezra's. I don't think they've ever killed anybody, but they scare the bejezus out of me. You're a man, though, so maybe you can deal with them. In any case, it's the only place I have to lock you up, and I'd rather lock you up than shoot you. Now, don't do anything stupid," she said as she held the shotgun on him with one hand and searched through the ring of keys for the right key with the other.

"Auntie Leilani, you are making a big mistake going with Werner. For the time being you may be safe, but too many people have died, both here and over there. It will catch up with you."

"Have you ever noticed what beautiful clothes Werner wears? How he carries himself? Things don't catch up with Werner. Werner catches up with them. He owns Apia, you know, just about. He practically runs that country, from behind the scenes. He gave me this outfit, in fact—Dior, from New York, pure silk, wonderfully lined. It's perfect, isn't it? Everything he does is perfect. No, I have nothing to worry about if I'm with Werner and Gigi, and I much prefer it over there, actually, away from poor Ezra, and I'm not going to kill you or maim you, Apelu. I'm just putting you in with the dogs."

Leilani had found the right key and unlocked the Yale lock. Nick and Nora stopped barking and backed off a ways from the gate, as they did when they thought they were about to be fed. With the shotgun still aimed at Apelu, she opened the gate a crack and said, "Get in there."

Apelu went into the cage, and Leilani quickly latched it behind him and snapped the Yale into place. Nick barked three times. Nora growled. Leilani quickly split.

"So, this is what it feels like to be locked up, hey guys?" Apelu said. Nick came over and nudged Apelu in the thigh with his huge forehead.

"Watch the legs, guy. They're my sole asset as a dancer, and besides, the food's out there. Let's make some noise for the lady's benefit." Apelu made a low growling sound in his throat, then a louder growl.

"Come on, you guys, bark," he whispered, then gave his best imitation of Nick's angry bark. Nora just looked at him with a sort of pitying look, but Nick caught on and answered him. Apelu growled back, and then Nora decided to join in and growled too. Soon all three of them were barking and growling, having a good time.

There was a three-inch gap between the top of the gate and its frame that Apelu got his hand through. He could just feel along the two-by-four ledge on the outside. Apelu figured that if Leilani had known the other key was there she would have used it or taken it. His fingers found it and very carefully pushed it back into his palm. He heard the SUV leaving.

Nick had stopped barking and was now watching Apelu intently. Nora was still barking, but at something or nothing at the other end of the kennel. It was tricky through the chain-link fencing on the gate, but Apelu eventually managed to get the key properly inserted into the lock and turn it. Then the three of them were free. Nick went over and head-butted the dry dog food garbage can, which went down with a crash and a spill. As Apelu headed toward the house, Nora joined Nick for a free meal.

All the doors, including the patio door, were now locked. Apelu picked up one of the cast-iron patio chairs and threw it through the glass door, then knocked out the jagged pieces before entering. From the phone in Ezra's room he reached Asia's number.

"Where are you?" he asked without even saying hello.

"Leone, watching nothing. What's up?"

"Airport," he said. "They're all leaving tonight on a special flight. Contact the others. Get there as fast as you can."

Asia had her car, so Apelu had no transportation. He let himself out the back kitchen door and started to run.

The weather had changed again, the moon breaking through the thinning clouds. Under the three-quarters-full moon the clouds were like an extension of the island, pulling it skyward from its ridgelines, and the silhouettes of the ghostly tallest palm trees somehow anchored, owned all the moonlit cumulus even as they moved, eclipsing stars.

There was no way Apelu could run the several miles around the fenced perimeter of the airport and get to the terminal at the end of the opposite side in any sort of good time. He was way too out of shape for that, but he had to go for it, hoping the others would get there first. He wondered how late Werner's special flight would be. Apelu knew the routines at the airport—the customs officers would all have gone home after the last scheduled flight departed. The terminal would be shut down. Even the tower would be unmanned. The pilots on the Polynesian flights could turn on the runway landing lights automatically by radio from the cockpit—an emergency measure that had become public knowledge one night when it failed to work.

On this side of the airport there was a rudimentary gravel road that ran along the outside of the perimeter fence. Apelu cut to that, off the paved road. As he ran, Apelu thought about Tracey with her smashed-in drowned face, Mati with his face blown off, Lisa with no one to push her glasses back up her corpse's nose—cold, callous murders, not acts of passion or defense or happenstance, acts for which he could sometimes find sympathy, even forgiveness, if that wasn't too loaded a word for a cop to use. He didn't know Werner, but he despised his smugness, his assumed distance above what he had wrought.

He was already winded and slowed his pace. In the old days, his second wind would have kicked in about now, but those were the old days. The gravel road rose and fell much too often, and there were occasional washout trenches that were hard to judge in moonlight shadows, but it was the shorter route. At the end of the runway, he had to go back to the paved road and, gasping, he walked it. There was no traffic. He stopped at his spot where he could look down the darkened runway to catch his breath. As he stood there, leaning with his hands on his knees, the runway lights came on, and behind him he could hear the distant drone of an incoming plane.

He started running again with something like a second wind. At least he found his gait. He cut away from the pavement and back to the fence, where the gravel road had become just a trail. Suddenly, running alongside him was Nora, and then, crashing through the low brush, Nick appeared and barked once. They ran together, the dogs in front, slowing their pace to his. Apelu watched their graceful jumps over hidden low spots and copied them. They hit a pace together, just Nick and Nora and Apelu, out for a little moonlit jog. They covered ground.

The plane, a Polynesian Twin Otter, had landed. Apelu had to stop again, slowing to a walk, which bored the dogs, and they disappeared. Apelu's legs hurt. His lungs hurt. His feet hurt. His head pounded and his ribs where Siaosi had punched him weeks before throbbed.

He started jogging again, and Nick and Nora rejoined him. They were getting close to where the road to the Woos' house cut in when Apelu heard the plane's engine again. It was already heading back out the taxiway toward him and the end of the runway to take off. Apelu and his running mates got to the construction yard along the runway fence before the Woos' place just as the plane taxied by. Three or four guard dogs from around the yard's shack came out to challenge them, but Nick and Nora went after them, and they fled. A man, the night watchman probably, came out of the shack to see what the ruckus was about and to chase and yell at Nick and Nora. They went after him too, and he fled into the bush across the road.

Apelu stopped to hold his knees and grab his breath. He was too late. No one had gotten there in time to stop them. Werner and his crew, including Tia and the Chinese men, were out of here.

He was sweating now. Sweat dripped off his nose and stung his eyes. It dripped from his elbows and his ears. At least he could stop running now. Nick and Nora came back, their giant tongues hanging sideways out of their mouths to cool them off.

"We blew it, guys," he told them. "The outlaws are getting away, crossing the border." The least he could do was tell Asia, he thought, find out where she was, and tell her to stop driving like a madwoman to get there. There was probably a phone in the construction yard shack. He went there and Nick and Nora came to stand guard as they sniffed around. There was a phone on the desk inside the shack, but there was also a board on the wall behind the desk with labeled hooks holding keys to the machines parked outside. The idea took only a second to form a hand and grab him, and he in turn grabbed the half-dozen truck keys off the board.

Apelu ran back out into the construction yard. There was one long earthmoving truck parked with its nose almost against the airport fence. He ran to it. Nick and Nora followed him, barking. The fourth key he tried fit, and the truck started up. He put it in gear where he thought first should be and revved up the big diesel engine. He tried different dashboard switches until he found the one that turned on the lights, then eased back on the clutch. The rig jumped forward, ramming through the fence. The pipe from the top of the fence smashed into the windshield, shattering it into a spiderweb of refracted light lines. He found second gear.

There was a tune going through his head, a ridiculous tune. Nick and Nora ran barking along beside the big truck as it trundled forward across the uneven earth toward the runway. The tune in his head was the theme song from *The Bridge Over the River Kwai*—"doo-doot, da da doo doot doot doo." He shifted up into another gear. Off to his left he could see the headlights of the Twin Otter turning at the end of the runway. He put the pedal to the floor. He had figured that he would just park the truck across the middle of the runway so that the plane couldn't take off, then play it by ear from there. But his timing was slightly off—the plane had already begun to accelerate by the time he bounced the big truck up onto the tarmac. The plane was now speeding toward him, the wing lights of the plane and the headlights of the truck crossing in the middle of the runway.

As Apelu stared at the plane's approaching lights from the truck's driver's seat, he realized how dumb he really was. Why hadn't he just let them leave? Who was this fool with some heroic song from an old movie soundtrack running through his head instead of rational thoughts about survival? He always told himself that he didn't want to be a cop, was a cop only by accident and misdirection. Then why had he just put his life on the line to do a stupid cop thing like this?

He couldn't judge the plane's closing speed, didn't know if he should slam on the brakes or speed up. He was already near the middle of the runway. He hit the brakes. He could hear the plane's brakes screeching too, hear the twin props braking. A frozen moment. Then the plane swerved to its left. Its left wing went down and its right wheels lifted off the ground. The right wing clipped the roof of the truck's cab as it went over him with a tremendous roar.

Farther up the runway there was a small lagoon between the runway and the taxiway. The Twin Otter came to a stop there, its nose in the water, the rest of it on dry land, tilted forward. Apelu got out of the truck and walked toward the plane. Nick and Nora were already there, barking. Apelu felt numb. Two vehicles were speeding up the runway from the direction of the terminal. The plane's door flopped open and down, and people started coming down the steps on the inside of the door. The cars reached the plane before Apelu did and more people—Dwayne, Asia, the assistant commissioner, two more FBIers, and one of the CID guys—jumped out of them. Nick and Nora didn't know whom to bark at, so they stopped.

By the time Apelu reached the group, Werner was talking loudly, jabbing his finger in the direction of the truck. "The repercussions of this...this outrage are going to be stupendous, international, career-shattering. You have no idea who I am. No idea who these dignitaries are. We are on a diplomatic mission for the independent state of Western Samoa."

"I don't care who the fuck they say they are, take them all in," Apelu said. "At the very least, they were all attempting to leave the territory illegally."

More car headlights were headed down the runway toward them.

"Nick, Nora," Apelu said, "let's go." And he turned and walked back toward the truck in the middle of the runway, the dogs walking on either side of him.

"Apelu, wait, wait." It was Asia running after them down the runway. "You're headed...where?" she said as she caught up to them.

"I'm taking the dogs back."

"And after that?"

"I'll make sure they're cared for, don't worry."

"That's not what I meant. You going home, or...?"

"I don't think so. I don't know."

She smiled. "Then I'm coming with you. I'll walk back with you."

The runway lights went out, and after their brightness the darkness around them seemed impenetrable. Nick, or maybe

Nora, nudged up against his leg. "I don't think so," he said, and then he and the dogs were moving.

They fell into step on either side of him, and within a dozen yards or so, he knew Nora was on his right and Nick his left— Nora kept to herself a bit, and Nick stayed tight against him so Apelu's hand would rest on his broad back every so often. Even in the dark, he knew who they were. No question. They were themselves.

"Good dogs," he said, and they walked on.

ACKNOWLEDGMENTS

───────── o ─────────

I WOULD LIKE TO ACKNOWLEDGE THE DEBT I OWE TO PHILIP Patrick and Andrew Bartlett of Amazon Publishing and especially to my agent, Peter Riva, for the faith and confidence they have shown in me and my work.

ABOUT THE AUTHOR

—————— o ——————

JOHN ENRIGHT WAS BORN in Buffalo, New York, in 1945. After serving stints in semi-pro baseball and the Lackawanna steel mills, he earned his degree from City College while working full-time at *Fortune*, *Time*, and *Newsweek* magazines. He later completed a master's degree in folklore at UC-Berkeley, before devoting the 1970s to the publishing industry in New York, San Francisco, and Hong Kong. In 1981, he left the United States to teach at the American Samoa Community College and spent the next twenty-six years living on the islands of the South Pacific. Over the past four decades, his essays, articles, short stories, and poems have appeared in more than seventy books, anthologies, journals, periodicals, and online magazines. His collection of poems from Samoa, *14 Degrees South*, won the University of the South Pacific Press's inaugural International Literature Competition. Today, he and his wife, ceramicist Connie Payne, live in Jamestown, Rhode Island.